MOTHER OF THE CHOSEN

JANEAL FALOR

To learn more about this author, please visit: www.janealfalor.com
Print ISBN:978-1946860057

Cover by Fleur Camacho – Cover Me Designs

Bound to Endure (Elven Princess #2)

Bound by Love (Elven Princess #3)

Standalone

Goddess Ascending

A Genie's Heart

For Mom
The best mother a girl could have.

MAP OF ERTA

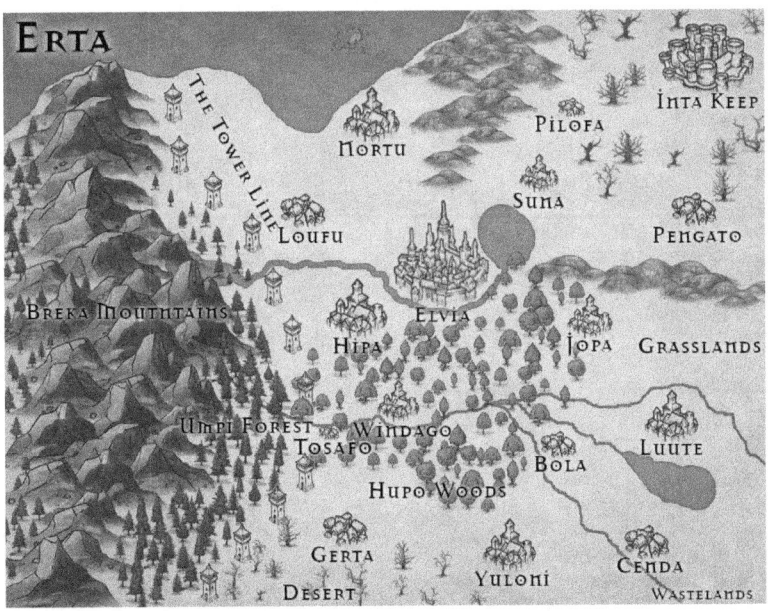

CHAPTER ONE

A fter months and months of waiting, I was finally pregnant. I'd suspected for a while, but now it seemed certain. I was going to have a baby.

I walked with a bounce in my step despite the slight nausea I felt. The woods were silent as I carried my basket of laundry to wash in the nearby stream, my breath visible in the crisp air. Soon, this task would be a lot harder, despite the growing warmth of spring. I grinned at the thought. I couldn't wait to tell Richart, my husband. He wanted children as much as I did, and getting such news would put a smile on his face. And maybe it would give us a chance to get to know one another better. Between our jobs, there wasn't a lot of time to talk, or quite frankly, much of anything else.

The stream came into view, and with it, Candui, bent over and scrubbing laundry of her own. The elven woman had been my only friend since I got married and moved to this bitty town.

I continued forward and crunched on a stick, which caused her to turn around. I expected to see her usual bright smile gracing her soft features. Instead, the expression came out forced, tight and unhappy.

"Morning, Adriella," she said.

"Morning." I placed my basket next to hers, tied my waist-length, wavy brown hair back, and grabbed a cake of soap. I plunged my hands and a tunic into the icy water and hissed. I'd get used to it, but the cold always shocked me. Usually, Candui would tease me. That morning, she remained silent as we scrubbed.

I studied her, hoping to find the cause. Her tall height was bent over the river, blonde hair almost reaching the water but didn't quite make it. She had long fingers working on getting the clothes clean, blue eyes focused on the task instead of twinkling at me as she teased.

Her brooding didn't stop the bubbles of excitement flittering through my chest. Nothing could dampen those. Perhaps I should mention to her what had me so happy. The idea crossed my mind, but no. My husband should know first.

I focused in on Candui. "Are you well?"

She wrung out the tunic she worked on with such force, I was surprised it didn't rip. "It's nothing."

She stood and placed the tunic on a nearby branch to hang until her basket was empty and she could take the clothes home to dry, like we always did. She grabbed another item of clothing but didn't bend down to wash it. Instead, she twisted the garment in her hands before snapping it straight. With a soft groan, she put the back of her hand to her forehead.

I twisted out my skirt, hung it to dry, and moved closer to her. "Are you certain you're well? You're not yourself."

She looked at me, her gaze full of torment.

I placed a hand on her arm. "Tell me what's upset you."

She threw the clothing she held back into the basket and

turned to face me again. "I know you've been trying to get pregnant for a long time, but you've got to stop."

I took a step back. "What do you mean?"

Her lips tightened. "The high king has issued a new decree."

My heart felt as if it stopped beating. A chill that had nothing to do with the temperature crawled up my arms and down my back. "What decree?"

Candui glanced down. "I didn't want to tell you because I understand how desperately you want a child. But there's been a new profecta found."

A rock of prophecy. I clasped my hands together so tightly they turned white. A few weeks ago, a streak of white had blasted through the night sky. Most would say it was from the sun or moon gods, bringing prophecies from their chosen religion, but I believed it to be a falling star, come to guide people along their path. "What did it say?"

Her voice came out a whisper. "A child born with the mark of the star will kill the ruler of all."

"And the high king doesn't like that." Of course he didn't. No person would. How did I feel about it? It confirmed my belief that the profecta came from the glittering night sky, and not one of the moons or the sun.

"He's having the leader of the Sunsit gather all children two and under, as well as any child born within the next two years."

Dread filled me. Why was the Sunsit religion involved? "What is he doing with them?"

She was so somber, I knew the next words out of her mouth would forever change me. "The Sunsire is to murder them all, whether they have the mark of the star or not, to ensure the high king's rule."

The sick churning in my stomach overwhelmed me. I put a hand to my mouth and swayed.

Candui put out a hand to steady me. "Sorry to bear such bad news."

Bad? This was worse than terrible. Nothing could have prepared me for such a disgusting, horrid order. Sun blast it all—I was pregnant.

I sank to the ground.

I pressed my eyes closed and willed everything to go away. How could I finally be with child when something as torturous as this was taking place? How could anyone go through with murdering innocent children? How could the high king not only support such an action, but also call for it? Even if it was to save his own life, why kill so many? I thought he was a good, just man, bringing peace to all of Erta.

I couldn't have been more wrong.

"Adriella?" Candui's voice was faint, but I had to respond. Had to pull myself from this horror before she guessed the truth.

"Sorry." My voice cracked. I glanced up and realized she was crouched before me. "It's a shock. Killing babies isn't right," I said.

To go against the high king was treason. Just for uttering those words, I could be hanged. I should never have said them in front of her. What if she turned me in? My baby's life would be forfeit if they killed me. Would they force a miscarriage on me first or simply slaughter me?

I had to do something.

Candui glanced around before she leaned close and whispered, "You're pregnant, aren't you?"

The blood rushed from my head.

"You're so pale," she said. "It's true, isn't it? You're going to have a baby. You and Richart have been trying for so long..."

"N—no. It's such shocking news. That's all." She couldn't know, not if I was to protect the life of my child.

Then another thought hit me. Richart, my husband, worked

4

for the zasin. The high king's army. He was well-ranked, and even better regarded, especially for someone only twenty-eight years old. Our town was mostly controlled by him. He would be the first person to turn me in. My baby would die.

I leaned to the side and retched, then retched some more until my stomach was empty and my sides hurt. There wasn't any love between me and my husband. Nothing to stop him from turning me in. Sure, we shared a bed and a house, but that was all. Not even the same religion.

"You're pregnant." Before I could protest, Candui continued. "We have to do something about this. We can't let them take your baby." She handed me a clean linen.

For the first time since she started speaking, hope sparked in me. I wiped my mouth with the cold, wet cloth, grateful to have it. "Do you mean that?"

Her fair features took on a look of determination. "We won't let anyone hurt your child."

"Why would you risk yourself?" Because it was a risky suggestion that could be the death of us both.

"I have my reasons."

I wanted to push her, to find out more, but didn't dare chance upsetting her when the situation was so delicate. "How can I save my baby?"

"I don't know yet. But we have to act like everything is the same. Nothing has changed." She handed me a dirty item of clothing before grabbing one of her own. "Do the rest of your laundry. We'll figure this out."

The scrubbing came naturally, since I've been cleaning longer than I can remember. The ideas about what to do didn't come at all. The entire time, my hands were freezing as I scoured the clothes to the point of wearing out the cloth. It wouldn't make a difference. Being the town weaver had some perks.

Would I still have my hands—or even my life—if I messed this up?

Didn't matter. The only thing that mattered was figuring out a way to keep my baby safe, away from the high king and the Sunsire, the leader of the Sunsit religion. Away from the zasin and my own husband.

Candui helped me with what I had left of my laundry when she finished. No plans formed in my mind. If she hadn't thought of something either by the time the laundry was done, my baby's life would be forfeit. Entirely unacceptable.

"What am I going to do?" I asked.

She hesitated. "I have a thought, but I don't know how much you'll like it."

"If it saves my child, I will do anything."

She studied me. "We will run away. It's the thing to do."

I wrung my hands, shifting my weight from side to side. "It's treason to run away from my husband and my job."

"But also the best way to give the baby a chance to live." When I hesitated, she added, "You will be able to hide your pregnancy for a short time, but not from your husband. Richart might suspect something if you're certain you are."

I bit my lower lip. "Wait. You said *we.*"

She nodded.

"You can't come with me. You have a husband and a job of your own. You would be committing treason right along with me. And when they catch us, you'll be sentenced to die right alongside me."

"If."

"If what?"

"You said *when they catch us.* It's not *when,* it's *if.*"

With all the resources the zasin had, they'd certainly be able to find us. Then again, what would be the point of chasing after a couple of barely-known women? "That doesn't negate the fact that you said *we*. Do you want to come with me, knowing it might mean your death?"

"I do."

"What about your commitments?"

"I never cared for thatching roofs. As for my husband... let's say we don't get along too well."

In all the time I knew her, I'd never heard such a thing. She didn't talk about her husband much, but neither did I. They were the husbands the combinare assigned us to, like he did all other women. Someone to have a family with and support the high king with, not that I got to know mine well. But for Candui to be willing to leave hers? To betray the high king and our country? That was more than I expected from a friend of a couple of years. More than I expected of anyone.

"Are you certain?" I asked.

"Positive." She straightened, as if better posture would prove how serious she was. "Act like everything is normal. In three days, after the sun is down and your husband has fallen asleep, meet me behind the bakery. If I'm not there, wait for me. But no matter what, you can't give us away during the next week. Promise me."

There was a way to bind me to that promise, but I wasn't ready to reveal another of my secrets. "I promise."

"Good. Everything will be fine. You'll see." She wrapped me in a hug, startling me. She'd never done anything like that before. It was like getting a hug from one of my sisters, who I hadn't seen in too long.

My throat tightened, but I hugged her back.

"It's going to be all right," she said.

As long as we saved my baby's life. That was all that mattered.

CHAPTER TWO

Three anxious days passed. Luckily, I saw little of my husband. He was so busy leading the zasin, probably dealing with the babies in our small town of Bola. Not that he would tell me if he was. He never talked about work.

There weren't many children in Bola. Just enough to keep the population of humans growing. The elves had a longer life span, but had fewer children and seemed not to have any little ones in town. Though it seemed like there were overall fewer elves around than there used to be.

Dinner was over, and I cleaned up, but Richart stood there in the large room that functioned as our house, staring at me. Hoping he didn't know something about my pregnancy, I ignored his stare and glanced around. We would have gotten a bigger home as children came, but now that had changed.

In the room there was the bed, a small table with two chairs, my loom, a spinning wheel, and a stove for cooking. The bathroom was out back. The excuse I'd give Richart if he caught me sneaking out tonight would be that I needed to use it.

Richart. That brought my gaze back to him. He was all

muscle without his armor on. His wide shoulders tapered down to a narrow waist, but it was his face that captivated me since I first met him. Chiseled features with hidden dimples that appeared when he smiled. Really smiled. It wasn't something that he did very often, though. His blue eyes were alluring, so pale and beckoning. He was nice, but distant.

But I wouldn't think about that now, when I'd be leaving him in a few short hours.

"We haven't talked about this yet, but we should." He rubbed the back of his neck with his hand.

Did he know what I was thinking? Did he guess I was leaving him? I put on my most gracious expression, hoping that would be enough to allay his fears. But what if he knew I was pregnant? I had been sick, but not so much he should have noticed—I didn't think. But what if I was wrong?

"I know how much you want to have a baby, but we can't. Not right now. And it's a good thing we didn't have a child before, either. Maybe the Sun and Moons gods are looking out for us, and that's why it's been so hard for us to conceive," he said.

Not what I expected, but not what I wanted to hear either. Though it was better than being found out. I didn't believe a word of what he said of the gods for a moment, even if he did. But then, I never believed in the gods of the Sun or Moons. It wasn't something that he knew. I stayed silent, willing myself to remain still.

"You've probably heard by now, but in case you haven't, there's a new law, because of a prophecy about a child being born that will kill the high king. The high king issued a decree that all children two and under and all children born for the next two years are to go to the Sunsire with their mothers."

That right there was reason enough to hate the ruler of the Sunsit religion. As if I didn't dislike him enough already. But wait —Richart didn't say anything about the children being murdered.

Perhaps they were taken to the Sunsire for safekeeping. Either way, I refused to hand my baby over, and I refused to go myself.

"I know you'll be disappointed, but it's for the best. And we shouldn't try until this is long gone."

I told myself not to react. Not to do anything to show my true feelings.

"Are you fine with that?" His voice was hesitant.

How would I react if I wasn't pregnant and planning to run away? I didn't know exactly, but I had a faint idea. "I'm disappointed. Of course I am. You know I want a baby."

He stepped closer, raised a hand, and let it fall back to his side. "And we will have one. Just in a few years."

A crazy urge to tell him pushed at me, begged me to tell him. He was the father of my child. Didn't he deserve to know? I scanned the area, and my gaze landed on his sword in its sheath. Right. He was a zasin. There was no telling what he'd do if he found out I was pregnant with a baby the high king didn't want around. I sighed, trying to put yearning into it. "I do want a child, but we've waited this long. A while more won't hurt."

Richart was silent. Did I say the wrong thing? Was that how I would have reacted? Maybe he was getting ready to call the rest of the zasin in here. Or worse, haul me off to them. I gave him a watery smile, hoping it was enough to convince him I was upset but not overly so.

When he gave a faint smile back, it didn't reach his eyes. Didn't show his dimples. I wished I knew what he was thinking, so I'd know whether he was upset about this change or if he was getting ready to take me into custody.

"I'm sorry," he said. "I promise I'll make it up to you. After this is over, we'll have as many children as you want."

I nodded, unwilling to speak.

"All right, then." He folded his arms, unfolded them, and

then folded them again. "I'm going to turn in. I've got an early start tomorrow."

Perfect. Hopefully that meant he'd be asleep sooner rather than later. "I think I'll go to bed too."

Because that was what was expected. Ever since we were married, we'd gone to bed at the same time. Couldn't risk changing that now.

I switched into my nightgown as he put on a nightshirt. I crawled into bed next to him, wondering why I had to be next to a stranger every night. Mother said it would be this way, but it was still odd. I wanted to one day get to know him. To at least be able to talk to him, without feeling awkward.

Now that would never happen.

My baby would never know his or her father. Would never get the joy of quality male bonding. Never know their heritage. I didn't know enough about Richart and his family to give my child that.

I stopped myself before I got teary-eyed, and rolled onto my side, facing Richart so I'd know when he fell asleep.

The time passed slowly. The moons moved across the sky in a slow path, sometimes peeking in my single small window, but mostly hiding their light behind Richart. He tossed and turned, as if he couldn't get comfortable. I kept my eyes closed most of the time, not watching him, in case he opened his own. I couldn't let him know what I planned with Candui.

I kept my breathing even, steady, as if I was asleep. The bed shifted yet again as he turned. A moment later, there was a light caress against my cheek. I barely stopped myself from jumping and remembered to keep my breathing even.

His touch was warm. Familiar. It made me want to open up to him. To tell him everything. But maybe that was what he wanted. Perhaps he was trying to get me to tell him my secrets. He had to know I had them.

His fingers left my face. Maybe he didn't. Perhaps he thought I was the boring wife I always pretended I was. I needed to believe that if I was going to leave him. Needed to think we weren't meant to be together, even if the combinare declared us to be matched.

He shifted around a few more times before his breathing steadied out. Still, I waited. I didn't move. After waiting even longer, I dared to roll onto my back. He didn't move, so I moved to my side, facing away from him. Nothing.

I steeled myself and got up, then turned and glanced back. There was enough faint light that I saw him sleeping. My misgivings grew. He was the father of my child. Didn't he deserve to know?

It wasn't like I could read or write, so I couldn't leave a note. It was probably for the best, anyway. Anything I said would clue him into what was going on, which was what I didn't need. It wasn't like I knew what was going on either, but the high king's men wouldn't like it. Richart wouldn't like it.

I tiptoed away from the bed, not letting myself look. I skirted around the table, only to bump into one of the chairs. It screeched across the wooden floor. Clenching my teeth, I waited for him to say something, but still I didn't sneak a peek.

When nothing happened, I turned to see his form still on the bed, under the covers. That was too close.

My muscles bunched together as I continued my trek across the house. It never felt so large before. So crammed with things. The board squeaked beneath my bare foot. I cringed but kept going. I was going to the bathroom out back if he woke up. Not something to get in trouble for.

When I got to the stove, I reached around to the side, where Richart never looked, and grabbed the bag I packed earlier in the day. Once it was securely on my shoulders, I picked up my shoes by the back door and was out the door. I made certain it closed quietly behind me before stooping down to put on my shoes. Shod, I snuck toward the outhouse, not because I needed to use it, but to retrieve something.

I entered the small room, grateful it was cold outside and masked the smell, but wishing there was somewhere better to keep my secret. I turned to face the door and lifted the loose wooden floor board to the side.

The sight of my star stone gleaming up at me made me smile despite my circumstances. I reached down, picked it up, and placed it around my neck, tucking it into my night gown. I hurried to change, putting my day clothes on as best I could in the cramped space.

I opened the door, half-expecting Richart to be there, but there was no one. I exited the outhouse, closed the door, and hurried away from the small place that had been my home the past several years. Would I ever see it again? My head said *no*, but my heart said it hoped so.

I crept around the back of the houses on our street, careful where I stepped but still making rustling noises. I'd gone down three streets, not seeing anyone, when I reached the bakery.

Hurrying around back, I expected to see Candui. I needed to see her to know our plan was in effect. But there was no one.

Where was she? I took so long that I was certain she was going to beat me here. I paced in the back space until I realized that it made too much noise.

I sat on the ground, forcing myself to hold still. I couldn't do anything until she got here. But what if she never came? I'd have to do this alone. I needed to do it without her. Needed to do whatever it took to save my baby.

I bit my lower lip and watched the moons move slowly across the sky. She was never going to come. I stood, readying myself to leave.

"Adriella," a voice hissed.

I glanced to my left. "Candui." Relief filled my voice.

She was weighed with a bag bigger than mine, which was probably for the best. I didn't pack nearly enough things to last long, but I didn't want to raise Richart's suspicion.

"Are you ready?" she asked.

I nodded, unable to bring myself to speak.

"We're going to have to sneak past the guard. Can you do that?"

"I don't know." I had never done anything like that in my life.

"We have to, if you're going to save your baby."

"Right." I had to do this. There was no other choice. I wanted to know that my baby wouldn't be taken to the Sunsire and murdered. "Let's go."

"Once we do this, there will be no going back."

"I know, and I'm certain. Are you?"

"I should have done this years ago."

How old was she? She only looked to be a few years older than my twenty-six. We went forward, behind the buildings, as fast as we could while still remaining quiet. Well, she was quiet. I couldn't say the same for myself. Dead vegetation and rocks crunched under my feet, like there was nothing to do but make noise. How did she learn to be so silent?

The lack of houses and nearing forest stood at the edge of town. The zasin patrolled here. We'd be lucky if we didn't cross their path. They were out tonight, like every night, to keep the town safe—but it was also to keep us in. If they found us, if they stopped us, I'd have no recourse but to be hanged. Not what I wanted for my baby. Not what I wanted for me.

Candui put her finger to her lips and crouched down next to a house. I crouched next to her, grateful for the bushes covering us, even if they weren't leafed. She watched and watched some more. She stared at the patrols going by, leaving no room for me to say anything to her unless I wanted to bring the zasin over to see what was making the noise.

As we watched, I took in the zasin that went by. They were in armor like Richart always was when he got home from a job. Under their armor peeked clothes of black, just like the king's heart. Their boots went up to their knees. At their waist held the most danger, swords and daggers.

At least they weren't the murvor, the king's assassins. They were to be feared even more than the zasin, taking out anyone the king ordered without hesistation.

After too many minutes of watching, she turned to me and nodded toward the guard. She put her mouth next to my ear and whispered, "Follow me, silently, but as fast as you can."

I nodded.

A moment later, the zasin moved out of sight again, and we made a break for it, past the last house and over the bare land that constituted the patrolled area. My feet were crunching on too many things, making too much noise, but there was nothing I could do to stop it. At least I was fast. Growing up with an older brother taught me how to keep up. He was always running away from me, sometimes playing games, other times because he was tired of his little sister hanging around. My sisters would never do such a thing, except perhaps Sizinne.

Candui grabbed my hand and pulled me forward, shoving me across the way into a bush. Moments later, she was beside me, and a man was saying, "Did you hear that?"

"Hear what?"

"I could have sworn I heard something."

"Come on, Jonlop. Let's get on with the patrol before we're caught lollygagging. You know he'll have our heads."

I held my breath, hoping it was enough to make them pass us by. I glanced up at the stars, looking for the right ones to help, but before I could find them, the guard said, "All right. Let's get back to it. I don't want to be responsible for you losing your head."

I breathed a deep sigh of relief. We'd made it out of the village I lived in the last four years.

Maybe there was a chance of me saving my baby after all.

CHAPTER THREE

We marched through the woods all night and well into the day without stopping, except to pull out some bread and cheese Candui had packed. The trees weren't as thick here as they were near Bola. They had a medium-brown bark with dark-green leaves. Pretty to look at, until we had to spend too much time in them. We walked and walked and walked, until I felt like my feet would fall off.

"We should stop," she said after looking at me.

"Do you think we're far enough to be safe?" As much as I wanted to stop, being away was more important.

"Yes. We're a good ways off. They shouldn't find us easily at the rate we've been going. Let's give you and that little one a break."

I slouched and slumped onto the nearest log. It was the most comfortable thing I ever sat on, despite the fact that it had a bump right in the middle of my behind. My feet and thighs throbbed, acting like they hadn't ever seen movement before, though I exercised daily. Mother taught me to, and it wasn't a habit I could break, even after moving away from her. It was the only thing I had to remember her by, besides my star stone.

"Are you all right?" Candui asked.

"I'll be fine. How are you doing so well?" I gave a heavy blink. I was so tired.

"I'm not carrying another life inside me. That alone will wear you out faster. Don't get me wrong. I am tired. Just not as tired as a woman with child. It takes a lot out of you."

"You speak as if you know from experience."

She hesitated. "My mother was the village midwife."

"I didn't know that."

"There's much you don't know about me."

I wanted to ask more but didn't know if I should pry. "Thank you for being willing to come with me. I don't know how I would have gotten here without you. Wherever *here* is."

"We are heading toward the fork in the river. It's as good a place as any to stop, since we're far from Bola but have water from the stream to keep us going. I'm going to make lunch. Why don't you rest while I do so?"

I wanted to protest, but there was no energy left in me. I moved to the ground as she went to fill skins and braced my back against the log I'd been sitting on.

Next thing I knew, she was waving something savory beneath my nose. I opened my eyes. The bowl of soup smelled divine and looked so good, with chunks of meat and vegetables. "Thank you." I took the bowl of soup from her and had a spoonful. "This is delicious."

She shrugged. "We all have talents. Mine happens to be with food."

"Why are you a thatcher? Why didn't you have a cook's job then?"

"You know the government. They put you where they think you can help most, whether it's what's good for you or not."

I didn't say anything. To agree would be treasonous. Of course, I had committed treason by leaving and not obeying the law of the high king. "I agree." The words came out faster and more easily than I expected. After hiding so much my entire life, to say something like that was freeing.

She lifted her eyebrows at me. "You think the high king doesn't know what he's doing?"

I couldn't go that far, but— "I never wanted to be a weaver. That's what they asked me to do, and Cenda needed it. I'm not certain it's fair or that it's the way things should be."

"You don't think they try to do what's best for the people?"

Not always. "What do you think?"

"I think the high king is berserk."

I gasped.

She laughed. "I've gone and shocked you. Didn't think I could do that so well, did you?"

No, I certainly didn't. "It's fine. I never heard anyone speak of the high king that way."

"Well, now you did. You can go on and do so yourself, now that it's the two of us. Speak your mind. You aren't going to say anything that will surprise me."

I bet I could, but I wasn't about to try. "Should we get going?"

She cocked her head to the side but didn't push the issue. "Let's."

I stood, feeling as if I could sleep the rest of the day and night away. Instead, we walked and walked more. We followed the stream, keeping to its winding path as we traversed through the woods. Did Richart know I'd left, or think I was doing a chore or taking an order like I sometimes did in the morning?

What was he doing? What was he thinking? And why did it matter so much? There had to be a reason why I couldn't stop thinking about him. Perhaps it was because I was used to living with him. Being a part of his life. We had created a child together, but the rare times we tried were quick and meaningless. Perhaps it was supposed to be that way, but it wasn't unheard of to grow fond of one another. I couldn't let go and not think about him anymore. I wanted to be in his life.

I wanted my baby to know his or her father.

I had to get out of my own head. "Though we've been washing laundry together for a couple years, I don't know much about you." Not enough to leave my home with her, if I had another acceptable choice.

"There's not much to tell." She kept looking straight ahead. Despite what she said, there had to be more.

"What's your family like? Do you have any brothers or sisters?"

"I had a sister, but she died." Her voice cracked.

I frowned. Too much death in this world. Candui should never have had to lose a sister. I wanted to ask how she died, but I didn't want to pry.

"She was much older than me. I knew her some, but mother would tell me even more stories about her. She felt like a dear friend, who I wish I had a chance to know better. I wish I had the chance." She ran a hand over her straight blond hair, covering one pointed ear. "My parents are both still alive, though I haven't been in contact with them for some years, so it may be wishful thinking. What about you?"

"My parents are alive and well, according to word my mother sends every once in a while. My sisters are getting older and are helpful for the most part. I have an older brother with kids of his own, though grown up enough to not be affected by this all. I miss them. I haven't seen them in over four years. Before that, I never went a day without them. I guess you could say I'm a little home-sick." I gave a soft laugh. "It's a little odd for someone my age, but I will always love home."

She nodded, her head reaching above mine. "I know what you mean. I will always treasure those days with my parents."

We continued on for some time, the silence not as cold as it was in some way and yet colder than ever in another. Neither had anything to do with the actual temperature, which was chilly.

A snap behind us sounded like someone stepping on a branch.

"Did you hear that?" I asked Candui.

"Hear what?" she said, but rushed me along faster.

She moved her hand toward her hip, where a small knife rested. Did she know how to use that thing? I certainly didn't for more than cutting a basic meal.

Before she could grab it, the rustling spread all around us. I glanced up to discover we were surrounded. Elves dressed in all manner of drab colors with arrows and swords aiming at us. No one should be in this part of the forest except perhaps gypsy elves. The moment I thought it, I held in a gasp. When not trading, they were cruel and cunning, and we had been caught by them.

We were going to die.

CHAPTER FOUR

"What are you doing in our territory?" the thin elven woman closest to us asked.

"We're sorry," Candui said. "We didn't realize this was anyone's territory. We'll be going."

She turned around, and I followed suit, only to find our way blocked by the sharp points of swords.

"Or not," I said. "We can stay here and do what you'd like."

The female elf behind us spoke again. "You will come with us."

This was bad. Very, very bad.

We marched forward, the group of elves continuing to surround us, their blades pointed our way. They stayed silent as we went, not giving a clue as to what they were thinking or what they were going to do to us.

Too many thoughts ran through my head. I had to find a way out. Problem was, there was no escaping from wild elves who would sooner gut us for going in their area than take us in. Word about them had spread since I lived in Bola, though I never thought it would make a difference to me.

Candui might be my friend, but she was civilized. Nothing like these wild gypsies. The stories I'd heard since I was a little girl still made me shiver. Were any of them true?

We went deeper into the forest, away from the stream and our only source of life. We made so many twists and turns, I didn't know where we were, with the trees around us always looking the same. I could only hope Candui had a better sense of direction than I did.

What had I been thinking of? Yes, I would have done anything to save my child, but running only led to more problems. More danger, for both me and the baby. What were these gypsies going to do to us? If they'd come to town, it would be to entertain, but since we were in their space, it wouldn't end well.

Blood was in my future.

I forced myself not to touch the star stone at my chest. It would bring comfort and possibly help tonight, if we lasted that long. But for now, it would only give away its existence. I'd gone my whole life ignoring it. Now shouldn't be any different.

It seemed like one moment we were in the forest, and the next we were in a mini village that contained horses and drab canvas covering the wagons. This wasn't what I saw growing up when gypsy elves visited my city. Maybe they were different gypsies. Maybe they wanted to be hidden. Or maybe they only showed their bright colors when they were trying to entertain.

Tall, lithe elves ran around, leaving me feeling out of place. Not that I was short and chubby. For a human I was tall and well-proportioned, but they left me feeling that way. When the elves noticed us, they stopped and stared. They glared at us as if we stole the last of their food. As if we, not they, were the monsters.

We were led to the largest wagon, in the middle of a circle of them, and shoved inside. The woman who spoke with us before we came in was there, surrounded by five other elves, who seemed to be some type of guards.

She said, "Who are you, and what are you doing here?"

"We're passing through," Candui said. "We didn't know you were here. We mean no harm and will be out of your way as soon as you let us go."

"That won't be happening."

I swallowed. We were going to end dead or worse. "Please. We are trying to get away from home."

Shouldn't have said that.

"What do you mean, *get away from home?*" The woman's voice was stern, pressing against us like a hot iron.

"Nothing," Candui said. "We're going to visit friends. That was why we left home. A short vacation."

"Don't speak," the woman told her and looked right at me. "You will talk, and only you. I want answers now. Why are you here? The truth, and I will know if you are lying."

Would she? I doubted she'd use magic, with it being punishable by death. Plus, the rumors about how dangerous and scandalous it was. But then how would she know? Perhaps she was naturally gifted.

"Speak."

"Right." What should I say? "I need to get away from my husband, and that's what we were doing when you found us."

I wanted to make excuses as to why we were in their territory, but I didn't think she'd like them, with the way she treated Candui.

"That is true, but not the whole truth."

"But true enough." I needed her to believe me.

She drummed her fingers on her leg. They were thin and long, like the rest of her. With her imperious eyes trained on me, head held high, she looked like royalty. Her long, white hair was threaded with intricate braids, in a style more elaborate than I'd ever seen.

The longer she waited to say something, the more I worried

over what she would decide about our fate. I glanced around the wagon. The only way out was guarded. I didn't know any distractions that would work in such a small space. If anything, they'd get me in more trouble.

"You will stay with us." She spoke so suddenly it made me jump.

"Stay? What do you mean *stay*?" The words weren't making sense.

"I cannot allow you to leave, but you seem to be a decent enough people to stay with us. I won't kill you."

No, no, no. I couldn't. Not with how close this was to Bola. Richart would find me if we stayed here, and who knew where that would leave these gypsy elves if he brought other zasin with him. They may not be kind to me but they were still sentient beings. A worse thought came to me. What would they do if they discovered I was pregnant?

She must have seen the panic on my face because she said, "You do not agree with my choice? You would rather we kill you both and leave your bodies in the wilderness, for any beast or dragon to find?"

There was no such thing as dragons, but I got her point. I could tell her it wasn't safe for them to keep us, but afraid the outcome would be the same, I decided on, "This will be fine. Thank you."

Candui didn't argue.

The woman said, "I am Nopli."

"I am Candui, and this is Adriella."

She must have felt safe enough to speak. She probably shouldn't have given our real names, but it was too late for anything else. Just as well. I didn't know if I could answer to anything besides my real name.

"Candui will remain in the main camp. Adriella, you will join the smaller one, where our sick are held, and tend to them."

"I don't know anything about assisting the sick." And didn't want to catch anything.

"You will learn."

I wanted to protest, but I also wanted to keep my life, so I stayed silent on the matter. "Can Candui and I still see each other?"

Nopli pursed her lips. "It will be forbidden. Not because of anything either of you did, but because you are human. You cannot catch the sickness but you can carry it. We don't want your friend to become sick herself."

That didn't sound promising. How were we going to get out of this if we weren't together to plan? I couldn't leave without her. I'd like to think she was among her own people, but there were many different types of elves. She didn't appear any more comfortable with them than I felt, the way her movements were stiff and jerky, her eyes wide, as she watched everything. I couldn't leave her behind, but neither would I have a way to take her with.

"You start now." Nopli snapped her fingers.

The guards around us moved in synchronization, motioning us through the small doorway. I glanced at Candui, who had a frown on her face. When she saw me looking at her, she changed it to a tight smile.

That was right; we'd get through this somehow.

I just didn't know how.

CHAPTER FIVE

The camp was full of life as two guards hurried me through it. Elves moved about, doing their daily tasks. Surprisingly, they weren't much different than what I'd seen in human cities. Elves with baskets of laundry headed toward where the river was. More were cooking around the fires. Some took care of horses and goats. There were even a few little ones, and two elves I saw were very pregnant. Pregnancies were rare among the elves. Could either of theirs be the chosen baby? The prophecy only said that it would have a mark on the hand.

One of their children was more likely to be the chosen one than mine was. I never had anything big or important happen to me. I went through life like I should, for the most part, not a person to do anything flashy or fancy. It wouldn't be my baby who took down the high king, which was all the more reason to protect him or her.

An elven girl of about four or five, if she aged like a human, scampered in front of me, chasing a lizard. I smiled at her. Would my child do the same things if the zasin didn't take it to the

Sunsire first? A nearby elf snatched up the girl before I could say hello to her and glared at me.

My grin dimmed. What happened to these elves to make them so hostile of me? Maybe they didn't like strangers.

We headed out of camp, and I asked the two guards with me, "Where are we going?"

Neither answered.

Lovely. We could be going anywhere. They might be going against Nopli's orders and taking me out to kill me. Or better, set me free. I couldn't go without Candui. How far away was the smaller camp?

Someone coughed, followed by another. A groan reached my ears. The noise of sickness filled the air, bringing with it a chill. I clung to my pack, wishing it would give me the strength I needed to deal with whatever was to come.

Unlike the previous camp, this one made its presence known gradually. First the noises, and then a hint of drab colors through the trees, though perhaps this time I knew what I was looking for. The sight came next and left me queasy.

Elves were scattered about, a few up and running from one patient to the next, but most lying in makeshift beds, pale and gaunt. Open sores marred their skin as their coughing grew louder.

What did Nopli expect me to do with this? It hurt my heart to look upon it, but I hadn't a clue how to help. It wasn't what I did; I'd never been around the sick or dying. Never experienced anything more than a cold. Back at my parents' house, Father would sometimes come home with a burn, from his work at the forge, but my mother tended those. Richart came home with the occasional cut, but it would be bandaged by the zasin's healer.

I had no experience that could assist them in any way.

A male elf headed toward us, calling out. "What are you doing here?"

"Nopli sent her to help. We're to guard her and assist as well," the guard on my right said.

Would they get sick? Or were they immune to it?

"Come over here and get to work, then." He hustled over to a patient on a cot next to a wagon. Nearby was a big campfire no one was tending. A kettle hung over the fire.

"Get that hot water over here," the elf said, looking at me before turning his attention to the patient.

I glanced around the fire, searching for something to pick up the kettle with so I didn't burn myself.

"Hurry," the elf shouted.

I huffed, found a thick towel and brought the kettle over to the healer, who instructed me to pour the water in a basin. He tested the temperature before dipping a cloth in it. "I need you to clean the wounds with this."

"I don't know how."

He shook his head, let out an exasperated sigh, and muttered something under his breath. "Get over here, so I can show you."

I moved in closer. The stench of rotting flesh filled the air, forcing me to breathe shallowly. "How come you and the other elves helping aren't getting sick?"

"Some were, that's why I'm all that's left. I'm either immune or will become ill myself soon enough." He wrung out the cloth into the basin and dabbed it on the patient's sores before having me do the same. I did so for several minutes under his supervision. Then he showed me how to cover them in some type of goo he'd made and wrap a bandage around them. After I managed it a couple times, he left me with only the guards for help.

Together with them, I spent the rest of the afternoon and most of the evening going from elf to elf, assisting in cleaning and wrapping their wounds.

Their suffering was great, making my hands work faster. After a while, I got used to the smell and sight and just worked. I tried talking soothing nonsense to those under my care, but either they didn't want to respond or they couldn't.

Where did such a sickness come from? And why did it only affect elves? I was grateful I didn't have to worry over catching it while pregnant, but the questions remained.

THE DAYS MELDED into each other, with me caring for the sick, getting something to eat, and sleeping very little. It wasn't a life I ever wanted, but it did make it easier to forget about my problems.

Late afternoon on the sixth day, while I was wrapping a bandage around a woman's arm, a scream came from the direction of the other camp, followed by a second. I quickly finished up what I was doing and stood next to my guards.

"What do you think it is?" I asked.

"Nothing good," the only guard who ever spoke said.

I bit my bottom lip. What should I do?

An elf came running out of the forest toward us. She called out, "It's the zasin. They're after the babies and pregnant elves. We need help."

My guards glanced at me before taking off, hurrying away from me. They must have decided helping their people was more important than guarding me. Worked well for me. I needed to hide before the zasin caught up to me, especially if Richart was with them.

I glanced around, looking for someplace safe. Was he behind the attack? If he was, I wouldn't forgive myself for leading the zasin to the elves, who lived so peacefully. Well, peacefully except for those who were dying from this mysterious illness.

I started toward a wagon, hoping to hide inside it, when Candui burst from the woods. "Adriella."

I veered in her direction, and she pointed at a massive nearby tree. Thinking I knew what she had in mind, and believing I could do it, I ran toward the tree. She barely beat me there and gave me a boost up, before sweeping the area around the roots with a branch.

"Climb," she said when she saw me watching her.

The limbs were thick and close together, making the first part of the journey simpler than I expected. I ascended, stretching my legs as far as I could and glanced back only once to find Candui trailing after me.

When the branches thinned out, I went slower.

"Quickly," Candui said. "They're coming."

Sure enough, there was a smashing through the woods, and the noise grew closer. I went up six more branches before flattening myself against the tree. Candui did the same. We were high enough in the air that one would have to really be looking to see us. I hoped. And I hoped I didn't carry the illness that would risk her life.

The crashing through the forest reached us, and the zasin came swooping out of the trees into the clearing. I searched for Richart. If he was part of this group, I'd know I was at fault for their being here. He wouldn't stop searching until he found me.

I had never heard of a wife leaving her husband before. Once married, couples stayed together, though not always getting along. What must Richart be feeling after discovering me gone?

Whatever it was, I didn't want to find out because that would mean facing him again.

The zasin swooped through the area, checking the sick only long enough to make certain they weren't big with child—I assumed that was what they were doing from what the elf said the attack was about. I'd noticed no one pregnant amidst the ill, and though there were some teenagers, there were no young ones

—whether because there were so few children among elves or because the sickness didn't affect them.

"Spread out," a zasin called out. "Find the rest of the pregnant women and bring them to me."

That settled it. They were searching for me, despite not knowing it yet.

As a zasin neared the tree we were hiding in, I silently pleaded with the stars to let him pass without seeing us. He slowed the closer he came. I pressed myself to the tree and kept my breathing shallow, so it would be silent.

What was he doing? Why was he stopping? He stared at the ground, which was better than looking up but made me uneasy.

My arms ached from holding myself upright for so long. They shook with exhaustion, but I couldn't let go. Couldn't switch position. Not without alerting the zasin to my presence. The man was many paces from the tree, looking around the area. Searching for me.

No. I hadn't seen Richart. He couldn't know I was here. Even if he was with them, how would they know Candui and I were up in the tree? It wasn't possible.

But the way the man stayed near said otherwise.

A second zasin joined the first and said, "What are you doing? We've got to find the babies."

He didn't mention me. That was a good sign for me, but the reminder they were looking for young ones made my stomach churn. I wanted to vomit, but it would give me away, so I swallowed thickly.

"See these tracks?" The first man pointed to where we had run up from. "They stop. It's almost like..."

"Don't say *magic*. You know that's outlawed. Besides, it's more of a myth than a reality. I don't know why you have to keep bringing it up."

The first man threw his hands up in the air. "Why are you so against it? Imagine if we found someone performing magic. That would get us recognized by the high king."

"And in the meantime, you're making us both look crazy."

"Someone's here. I know it."

My arms shook so bad, I was afraid they'd give out any moment. A fall from a tree—that was the last thing I needed. Between landing in front of the zasin and the fall itself, my life and my baby's would be doomed for certain.

The second man walked away. "Come on. We have to get back to the task at hand, before Dirler has our heads."

The first stood in place, looking at the ground. His head tilted up. Here it came—our discovery.

"Let's go," the second man said.

"Fine. I'm coming." The first man sauntered toward him, muttering, "I'm coming."

He hurried away, and together, they headed back toward the sick camp. Candui and I stayed hidden in the tree, silent, as the zasin continued through the camp. They tossed things out of wagons, yelled at the people, and hit one person before leaving. Disgusting. If this was the way Richart acted when he was on duty, I was glad to be done with him. Disgusting.

We continued to wait after they were gone. And waited some more. The worst thing we could do was come down out of the tree and find them still searching for us.

The sun went down, and one of the three moons, Palo, came out, brightening our way. The Moonska worshiped this particular moon for all that was good and light. I only knew enough about those things to stay out of trouble with both the Moonska and Sunsit. I believed in neither religion, but in Erta, they were your only choices if you didn't want to be hanged by the zasin. Richart thought I was a Sunsit, while he was a Moonska. The differences were part of the reason keeping us from getting to know each other. We tended to change the subject whenever religion was mentioned.

I shivered. I had to stop thinking about him. Having him in my thoughts so often wasn't good for me or the baby when he couldn't be in our lives.

Voices sounded in the woods. More zasin? I braced myself against the tree, preparing to be found. The figures that appeared were taller than most humans. *Elves.* They had to be coming to check on their sick after the raid.

The voices reached us in waves, not clear enough for me to make out specific words, but enough to know they were upset. Who wouldn't be after something like that?

Once they passed us, Candui tapped my foot. I glanced at her. She motioned downward and began to climb out of the tree. Hoping she was right and we weren't about to walk into a zasin or elf trap, I followed after her.

My tender arms strained under my weight, as I climbed from limb to limb. My foot slipped, sending a rustle through the air.

I paused, certain someone was going to come running for us. Nothing. I gave a silent *thanks* to the stars peeking out and continued my descent. I dropped down next to Candui, who had her back to the tree. I glanced at what she was looking at and froze. A group of elves were right next to us, staring.

CHAPTER SIX

Nopli sat in front of us, with no guards. Everyone else was running around, taking care of those injured during the zasin raid. Elves had come over to speak with her a few times while we sat around the fire, but we were alone now, which allowed us the chance to speak.

"Why didn't you go to the zasin when they were here?" she asked.

I didn't know what to say. The truth would be best, but how would she react to it? I glanced at Candui. She nodded. It was up to me, then.

Might as well give the truth a go. "I'm pregnant."

Nopli tilted her head to the side. "I admit this is not what I expected. I thought you were in trouble, but not this kind. Now I know why you ran. Why did you not say as much when we first found you?" When I didn't answer, she went on. "We could still use help, but we always need it. We will have to move our camp, now that the zasin know where it is. I was afraid you led them here, but my sources say it was another elf, lucky for you two. I think it would be best for all if you both left us. If you're running because you are with child, you will only bring more trouble down upon us."

Did she say what I thought she did? She wanted us to go. Wanted us out of her camp. "I don't wish to bring trouble. If you will let us go, we will leave and not return."

"Good. You will go now."

I glanced at the darkness outside of the wavering firelight. "Now?"

"Now," she repeated.

"It's fine," Candui said. "We will get our things, and then we'll be on our way."

"Be safe," Nopli said.

"You as well," I replied. "I wish your people the best."

"And I give wishes that the zasin and Sunsire will never see your child."

I wanted her wishes to come true.

Candui went with me to get my pack before trailing back to the other camp to get hers. All around us, elves scampered about, set on ignoring us, running from one task to another as if it were still day. Worked for me. I didn't want their attention when it might mean delays. It was getting late; I couldn't imagine starting our journey later.

Candui said, "Maybe we should ask them for food."

"We can't. Not with what they just went through and how they treated us." Though we would need it.

"You're right." She sighed.

"Besides, they probably need it as much or more than us," I said. "We should go."

We headed out, moving swiftly. It didn't take long to be covered in darkness, away from the gypsy elves' camp. The night wore on as we trudged through the underbrush. The thick trees made it darker without my stars to guide us.

"Do you know where we're going?" I asked.

"Mostly, sure I do."

Mostly. That was comforting.

We walked and walked, exhaustion creeping in. I didn't want to stop, though. Wanting to get away from where Richart could find me and where the zasin that raided the elven camp were, I didn't feel safe.

I pressed a hand to my belly. Was my baby well? Did all the stress I was going through affect my child? Hopefully not. I didn't know much about being pregnant. Just that sometimes women were sick at first—and I had been a little nauseous but not too bad —and women got bigger around the middle as time progressed. And the fact that pregnancy lasted about three seasons. That seemed like a long time.

"Do you hear that?" Candui asked.

I stopped, straining to listen. If it was another zasin raid, I wasn't sure I'd be able to climb a tree again.

The soft sound of water running met my ears. "Did we find the stream?"

"We did. Let's stop for the night."

"Are you certain it's safe?"

"No, but both of us are exhausted past the point of being able to go on." She sounded as tired as I felt.

We settled in for the night as best we could, and sleep quickly overtook me.

The next morning, Candui was up and about by the time I woke. Once I sat up, she said, "Hungry?"

"Famished." Though my stomach was a little queasy.

She gave me some stale bread, and I choked it down. My stomach felt a little better, despite how old the bread was. "Which way do we go now?" I asked.

"Northwest, following the river. Are you ready?"

Not really. I could have slept longer. "I am."

We hiked for days like that, going as far as we could each

time, before stopping at night to camp. Though the nights were cool, my blanket made them bearable. Food was a bigger problem. We were quickly running out. I should have brought more or done like Candui wanted and asked the gypsy elves for some.

By the middle of the fourth day, my feet were nothing but blisters, and my back ached. I kept my mouth shut, though. I didn't want to complain about it when we had other worries. And where would we go? We couldn't stay in the woods forever, especially with our supplies dwindling, and I didn't know much about living outdoors.

"Do you know where we're going?" I asked Candui.

"Away from Bola."

"Any idea after that?"

She stopped walking, turning her face away from me. "No. Perhaps this wasn't such a good thought."

If she was having doubts, we shouldn't be out here at all. But I couldn't leave my baby in the hands of the Sunsire. "You think we should have stayed?"

"Definitely not." She looked at me, her eyes red and shiny with unshed tears. "But I don't know what to do to keep you safe."

I clenched my jaw to prevent myself from crying with her, though that was all I wanted to do. "We'll figure something out. Where are we?"

"By the river to Windago. On the other side of the river is the road that takes you there, but I've been avoiding it so we didn't run into anyone."

Windago. My childhood home. "I have a notion, but I don't know if you're going to like it."

"What is it?"

"Windago is where my parents live. We could stop by. At least get supplies and figure out where we're going."

She pursed her lips. "You're right. I don't like it. Being

around that many people would be dangerous. It's a huge city. What if you were discovered by one of the many zasin?"

"I'm not showing yet. It would give us a chance to find our bearings and figure things out."

"What about your parents? How would they react?"

"I believe they'd welcome us. Despite the fact that people rarely travel between towns unless they're traders. Especially if I told them I was just visiting and planned on going back to Richart."

"But visiting is forbidden."

"That may be, but there are loopholes. People do it anyway, sometimes. I don't have any better options."

She shifted her weight from side to side. "I'm not sure."

"What other option do we have?"

"It's our only choice. We'll have to sneak around the guard, getting in the city and coming back out. Unless we stay and you know a place you can hide a baby."

Would my parents help me hide my pregnancy and the baby? Mother was the type to be willing, but I wasn't certain about my father. Even if they were willing, though, it wasn't the type of pressure I should put on them. Taking care of a family was hard enough without doing so illegally. Plus, there were my sisters, who all still lived at home, to consider. "Let's get food and supplies from my parents, and we can figure out where to go from there."

And hope no zasin realized we weren't supposed to be there.

CHAPTER SEVEN

I stared at the city gates, watching the guards check everyone who came or went. How were we going to get around them? Did we need to? I wasn't showing yet, so perhaps we could march in—except for the fact that we ran away from our husbands, and if word of that had spread through the guards, there would be danger. Not that I expected any of them to recognize me, but going in there without a plan seemed like asking for trouble.

Mail could travel faster than Candui and I did on foot, what with the mailmen's horses. Not to mention the people traveling on those horses.

I had a backup plan, but should I show Candui? Perhaps it wouldn't make a difference. She knew I was pregnant. What was one more secret?

"This is where you grew up?" Candui whispered as we watched the flood of people go in from our spot in the forest.

"You can only see part of it from here. It goes on quite some distance, though I've been told it's not as big as the capital. But yes, I lived here. My parents are on the other side of the city."

And if it wasn't surrounded by a wall, this would have been so much easier.

"How are we going to get in?"

I don't voice my doubts. "Come on. Let's walk around the city from the outside, and see if we can find anything." When I was growing up here, there were places on the walls guards didn't cover, but that didn't mean they were still there or that we wouldn't get caught.

We backed up quite a ways before curving around to follow the wall. We stuck to the woods, where we couldn't be seen but could do the seeing.

"Guards are everywhere," Candui whispered.

It was true. There were guards every twenty feet or so. Not enough room for us to cross, even if we did have the right equipment. "We'll figure something out."

And that would have to be my tunnel. I couldn't find any other way to get in the city and not be spotted. There were too many zasin for us to risk any other plan. I glanced at Candui. I trusted her with the life of my child. Why not this too? "I know a secret way in, but you have to promise not to tell or show anyone."

Her expression was solemn as she replied, "I promise."

That was the best I could ask for, given the circumstances. "This way."

We weren't far off. I'd been heading that way, but I hadn't led her right to it. I continued through the forest, hoping I could still find the hidden entrance. It had been over four years since I used it. Would it still be there? Had others been using it? Difficult to say. When mother and I used to go through it, we rarely saw others there.

We came to a clearing where the leaf foliage on the ground was still heavy, it being spring. There were some buds on the trees and absolutely no sight of the entrance.

I stepped toward the far side, Candui following so silently after me I almost didn't know she was there. I brushed the leaves off the ground, searching. Nothing but the forest floor. That was all right. It was bound to be here, even if it was covered with more layers of dirt than it used to be. It was probably a good thing, to help hide it.

The ground was bumpy beneath my fingers, rocks lodged into the ground. The longer I looked, the more I lost hope. It was asking too much for it to be undisturbed. Then again, where would it have gone? Even if people stopped using the tunnel, it should still be here—unless someone filled it in.

Was that possible?

"What's this?" Candui was bent down near the ground like I was, dipping her fingers into the dirt.

I hurried over to her. "You found it."

There was the crack of the tunnel entrance. I followed the seam, around to where the front should be then reached forward, searching for a handle. The metal was cold beneath my hand, but it was there and not rusted. Someone was taking care of it.

I lifted the lid, and she let out a little gasp. "Sorry I don't have a light," I said. "We'll have to traverse it in the dark." Because I'd shown her enough confidences for the year or longer.

"That's fine. Elves see better in the dark than humans." She headed over to me and crouched down. "I'll go first."

"Are you sure? I'm not entirely certain what waits for us down there, though I know it ends in the city."

"And that's why I should go first." She dipped down into the hole, darkness quickly swallowing her.

I clung to the lid, pulling it down with me as I followed her. It closed with a finality, bringing nothing but pure darkness. The air was dank and filled with a pressing feeling, the walls barely tall enough for me to stand upright last time I was in here, let alone now. Candui must be hunched over.

"Are you all right?" I asked.

"I'm fine. Let's go." Her voice sounded anything but fine, but I didn't mention it.

"There's only one path, so we should be good to follow it."

"All right."

We went down the way at a slow pace, much like that of a sloth. I bumped into Candui or a wall on the side a couple times, so I put my hands out in front of me, mostly to save my face and torso from impact. I stepped carefully. Softer than I expected, the ground squished beneath my feet until we got farther in.

"How much longer?" she asked.

"I don't know. It's difficult to tell in the dark. We had a light when I used it before."

There wasn't much more to say. We just fought against the dark, damp tunnel we were in. We continued like that for some time before she said, "There's nothing but wall in front of us. Is the exit above our heads?"

"No. There's a secret latch. We'll need to be quiet once I open it." I shuffled around her, knocking into her as I went because of the size of the space. I bent down and felt the side of the wall in front of me, until I hit the latch. I pushed it, and the door swung open, letting in the faint light of the moon.

I hurried out into the barn, taking a deep breath of city air mingled with animal scent. It wasn't as fresh as I'd grown used to in Bola. Something about it was different. A quality of too many people, horses, and close quarters. I sneezed, and cursed myself for not being able to keep it quiet.

Candui followed me out, and I shut the door behind her, making sure it wasn't visible to any casual observer. Then I went to the side entrance of the barn mother and I always used. I opened the door an inch, looked around, and seeing nothing, slipped out with Candui right behind me.

We slunk through the city, waiting until almost dawn before

going to my parents' house. The sky slowly lightened, hiding the stars with the sun's rays. We made our way through the houses, twisting and turning where needed. I was grateful to see others were roaming around despite the earliness of the hour.

They were giving crusty looks to us both, but they seemed more directed at Candui. Why would that be?

Right. She was an elf, in the human part of the city.

I rushed us along. "We're almost there. Are you ready?" I asked Candui.

"Better now than later." She didn't sound any more confident than I felt.

What if my parents didn't want to keep me with them since I was supposed to be with my husband? Or worse, what if Richart sent word for them to be on the lookout for me? I should have thought of that before we stole into the city, but we really did need the food, perhaps more.

"It's this way," I said.

I led her through the streets that were gradually filling with people. My pack felt conspicuous on my back. Did we look as out of place as I felt? I wasn't eager to find out. I wanted to hurry us along, but didn't wish to draw attention.

We were away from the markets, so there was nothing around but houses and a few places of work. The houses were nicer than the one I had back in Bola, but nothing grand in this part of the town. It was familiar. Comforting. Everything would be all right. I grew up here. Things couldn't have changed much in the four years I'd been gone.

"We're almost there," I told Candui.

She nodded but didn't say anything.

"Adriella," a male voice called out. "Adriella."

I turned, dreading who I was going to see. Weaving his way through the people was Edpol, the only man I ever had romantic feelings toward. I forced my feet to plant themselves in place. If I ran, it would look strange. My belly felt prominent, like it would give away my baby, though it hadn't grown much yet. Would he be able to tell anyway? He and I had known each other so well previously...

He was almost to us when Candui whispered in my ear, "Who is that?"

"The man I hoped the combinare would set me up with, when I was younger," I whispered back, and then forced a smile at Edpol.

He was more handsome than I remembered, with his inky-black hair, dark eyes, and fine mouth. The way he carried himself said he knew it too, those legs striding through the crowd like he was the high king himself. Blasphemous thought, but true.

"Adriella," he said again as he reached us at the side of the cobblestone street. "What are you doing in town? Your parents didn't say anything about you coming for a visit."

His voice was warm, like a soothing hot drink. Thinking on my toes, I said, "I wanted to surprise them. Edpol, this is my good friend, Candui Thatcher."

"What are you doing with an elf?" He didn't bother to look at her.

My crush deflated a little. Just as well, since I was now a married woman, and he was probably a married man, but it hurt. "She's a friend from Bola," I said.

"Where's your husband?" he asked.

"He stayed home."

He gave me a sly grin. "I see. We'll have to get together later. I need to work now, but we should catch up while you're in town."

Did I want that? We'd been very close at one time but hadn't spoken since the combinare put Richart and me together. Supposedly, they collected the names of those eligible for marriage, and they picked the couples based on what towns needed. I wasn't sure that was what actually happened. Why couldn't they put me and Edpol together? Did it matter?

"We should. I'd like to hear what job and wife you received."

"Oh. I don't have a wife yet." He leaned in a little closer. "I convinced them to give me a little more time."

How on all of Erta did he do that? No one convinced *them* of anything once they set their mind to something, and he had been slated to get a wife shortly after I left.

"Don't look so shocked." He reached out, pulled my hand into his, and gave it a squeeze.

I waited for the familiar tingle that used to accompany his touch when we were younger. "I'm not shocked."

"Yes, you are. Remember, you can't hide anything from me."

I forced my expression to remain neutral, though I was crumbling on the inside. Did he suspect my secret? There was another I always managed to keep from him. "How is working with the carpenter?"

"Didn't your father tell you? I work at the forge with him now."

Marriage postponed and job changed? What was going on? "Edpol Forger. My father is probably happy about that." Not something I would ever have guessed, though. Why hadn't my mother's letters said anything?

"He is, but he'll have my hide if I'm any later. Can I see you at your parents' house tonight?"

I can't have him coming back into my life when I'm married to another and pregnant with that man's child. Besides, nothing good ever came from playing with the forbidden. But how could I be rude and say *no*? Did I want to see him?

With all my waffling, he didn't give me a chance to respond but pulled my hand up to his mouth and kissed the knuckles. "I'll see you tonight."

I watched him go, trying to decide what the tumult of emotions sailing through me were.

"An old crush, huh?" Candui said, voice neutral.

Oh, stars. This wasn't something I wanted to deal with. "Let's go introduce you to my parents."

She didn't push the Edpol issue, just nodded.

There wasn't much farther to go to get to my childhood home. It was impossible to predict what would wait for me there, but I hoped the reception would be warm for both me and Candui. I didn't understand what she was running from—she kept it locked tight inside—but I wanted her to see my family in a good light. She had been a good friend the past couple of years and was now helping me save my baby's life. I wanted her to be comfortable with my family.

We came up on my parents' street, and I increased my pace, unable to contain myself. We got about a third of the way down when I stopped in front of my parents' house. It wasn't the richest building on the street, but neither was it the poorest. My family was taken care of, and they had what they needed, though not an abundance of it. The memories flooded me so fast it was difficult to grab onto one.

"It seems like forever since I've been here," I whispered.

Candui stayed silent, as I'd grown used to from her unless a strong opinion came to her.

I took a step forward, but before I could go any farther, the door burst open and my youngest sister raced out of it.

"Adriella." She wrapped me in a hug before I realized she was fully out the door.

"Sizinne, how are you?"

She laughed, sounding the way I remembered, but looking much older, with almost a woman's figure. "Better now that you're here. Mother didn't tell me you were coming."

"That's because I didn't know." Mother's voice came from the door.

Sizinne pulled away, and I ran to give Mother a hug. No matter how old I got, I'd never tire of hugging her. "I've missed you." My voice cracked. I worked to pull my emotions in.

"And I you, my dear girl. Come inside."

I turned back to Candui, who'd brushed the hair over her ears, but the tips poked out still. Was she worried what my family would think about her? Now that I took the time to think about it, I was a little too, though not about my mother.

I introduced her and said, "She's traveling with me, to keep me company."

"Welcome to our home," Mother said to her. "Any friend of our Adriella's is a friend of ours."

For the first time since our journey started, a real smile slipped out of Candui. "Thank you."

"An elf?" Sizinne's words of shock reverberated through me. "What are you doing with one of those?"

"Hush, Sizinne." Mother's voice was strict. "She's welcome here. Let's go inside."

Sizinne was in first. I gave Candui a guilty glance, but her expression revealed nothing. Since becoming friends with Candui, I sometimes forgot how prejudiced humans were.

I entered the house of my youth, wondering when it started to feel more like my parents' house than a home.

My other two sisters wove their way between the children my mother tended during the day while their parents went to work and embraced me. Right away I noticed none of their wards were very young. The youngest had to have been at least seven.

As much as I wanted to say something, I kept quiet. I couldn't linger on their ages, with being pregnant myself, though I longed to tell my mother about my pregnancy. She would have been so excited to become a grandmother again under different circumstances.

"Sizinne, would you please take your sisters and the children to the yard to play?" my mother asked.

"I will." Sizinne gathered the nine children and took them out back with my Ulla and Yina, my other sisters.

"Please, sit down." Mother motioned to the couch.

I stepped over a couple wooden blocks, put my pack beside the couch, and sat down with Candui next to me.

"What brings you home?" Mother asked.

"Just wanted to come for a surprise visit." A surprise for us all.

"And Candui, you decided to come with her? I've heard about you from Adriella's letters. The thatcher business must be slow."

I always had someone else read me my mother's letters and pen mine back to her. A friend did the same for her. It wasn't ideal because we had to filter what we told each other, but at least we had a way to communicate. Well, until now. I didn't know what the future would bring.

"It will pick up when spring is fully here."

"We're glad to have you home," Mother said. "Candui, let me show you to our guest bedroom."

It was my brother's old room, from before he got married. I hadn't seen him or his children in too long. While my mother made Candui comfortable, I went to my previous bedroom. Everything was the same as I left it. The bed looked smaller than when I lived here, but that was because I'd gotten used to a bed large enough to share with a zasin.

The quilt was a soft pink one I wove when first learning my trade. The flaws were obvious to me now—I missed colors here, picked up others there—but I was proud of such a big project at the time. There was a window to the left of the bed with space between the bed and the wall. A short dresser, for my things, stood next to the door.

I set my pack on it but didn't unload it. As much as I wanted to stay here forever, it wasn't possible. It wouldn't be long before I showed. This was a short stop before we had to go—something I'd have to keep reminding myself. I touched my star stone beneath my tunic at my chest and pressed back the tears. Crying was not an option.

I sat on the bed and stared out at the children playing with my sisters. Would my child ever get this experience? Ever get to know my family and enjoy life? Or had I doomed him to a life of running and hiding?

Better than letting him die.

At least, I was beginning to think of my child as a boy. It felt right.

The bed dipped beside me as my mother sat down. "I'm glad to see you—don't get me wrong—but I'd like to know why you're not here with Richart."

Or why I was here at all. I sighed. What could I tell her? Not the truth. If anyone could keep it a secret, it would be her, yet I didn't want to concern her when she had so much to worry about and her own to protect.

"He had to stay and work with the other zasin. Couldn't get away, I'm afraid," I said.

"But you could leave your weaving?" Her voice was suspicious.

"I got ahead in my work."

She put an arm around my shoulders. "Are you fighting with him?"

In a way, we were. "I don't know. Even after all this time being married to him, I don't know him."

"Oh, honey... Marriage isn't easy, and feeling like you don't know him will make it harder, but running away won't help. I've been married to your father longer than not, and he's an unfathomable man."

If only I could tell her the real reason I ran away without putting a burden on her. I wished it didn't have to be this way. "I know. This is a short visit."

"I see."

I leaned my head on her shoulder and let myself feel like a kid again, if only for a moment.

"Did you bring *it* with you?" she whispered.

My star stone. And it was back to being grown up. "I wouldn't leave without it."

"Good."

I straightened. My star stone. It had been strange to take it off while I was with Richart, but I couldn't risk him finding it. Wearing it all the time again felt right.

I wanted to ask my mother what it was like to be pregnant with me and my siblings, but that felt too obvious. We never spoke of such things in this house. As a result, I knew so little. It could have been time to change that, but I couldn't without giving her a clue to what was going on.

There was something else I could ask, though. "Where are all the young ones?"

She glanced out the window. "Haven't you heard about the high king ordering all the children to the Sunsire?"

"Richart did mention something about it."

"He must be busy, taking care of it in Bola."

My queasiness returned. Was he helping hand over children, babies, and pregnant mothers to the Sunsire? "He was working extra hard when I left." Though he never said doing what, I could only assume that was what the long hours were about. I should have left him, whether pregnant or not, though I wouldn't have been brave enough to do so had I not been with child. Leaving a spouse never happened, though. Not when it was punishable by death.

The air was heavy with what the high king was doing, but neither of us spoke of it further. Others might possibly hear, and we could be condemned for such things.

Mother said, "He must be missing you."

"I doubt it." Though there did seem to be something missing in my life since I left him. Most likely proper sleep and food.

"You may not think so now, but husbands tend to miss their wives when they're gone."

"Did you ever leave Father, for him to miss you?"

"I visited my parents a few times, before you were born, but then they passed away, and I have stayed with him ever since."

"I didn't know you'd done that."

Her voice grew quiet again—so much so, I could barely hear her. "I never told you, but your star stone came from your grandmother. It was given to her by her mother."

I put my hand on my tunic, pressing the star stone against my skin beneath the material. "Why didn't you tell me?"

"It was wrong of me, but I missed my mother so much, it was difficult to talk about. It still is. But I thought you should know."

"Thank you." Warmth stirred through me.

She gave me a hug. "I'd better go help with the children. They'll be going home soon, and then we'll have something simple for dinner."

I could have gone for a feast instead of simple, but I smiled and nodded. "That sounds nice."

"Good. I'll see you in a little while."

How was I going to leave her again?

CHAPTER EIGHT

S izinne answered the door and giggled. "Edpol, come in."

He entered, and my mother stood to greet him, though my father didn't leave his chair. "Adriella didn't tell us you were coming," he said, his voice gruff. Probably was still upset about finding an elf in his house. That or the fact that he never was a soft person, though something seemed more barbed about him since I returned.

Edpol grinned. "I couldn't help myself. When I saw her in town, I had to visit."

"I see." Mother's words were kind but clipped.

She always liked him but encouraged space between us when the combinare decided on Richart instead of Edpol. That wasn't going to change. "I'm afraid we already ate dinner. Would you like me to warm up something for you?"

"No, thank you." He gaze combed over me. "I wanted a chance to catch up with an old friend."

Father snorted but said nothing.

Sizinne took Edpol by the hand and led him to the couch,

near the chair I was sitting in, and sat next to him. I exchanged a glance with Candui, whose eyebrows were scrunched together.

For me, it wasn't difficult. Sizinne liked Edpol, but he only had eyes for me. Did I still have feelings for him? It'd been so long, and so much had changed. I didn't know anything anymore. Well, I knew one thing—Sizinne was too young for him, even if she wished it otherwise.

The room was silent as we sat there. Eventually, Sizinne launched into conversation, prattling on and on.

When she took a breath, Edpol said, "How are you all handling your father's coming retirement?"

Mother paled.

"Retirement?" My voice came out as a shriek. There was only one thing that happened with retirement.

Death.

If you were no longer useful, only a strain on the crown, you were put to death. I hadn't thought about it much before, since no one I knew had ever retired, but that was changing now.

Candui gave my hand a subtle squeeze. I couldn't bring myself to look at her, but the comfort was appreciated. I might not be as close to my father as to my mother, but he was my parent.

"You didn't tell them?" Edpol looked at my father.

I glanced at him too. His face was red, and lines creased his forehead. "I told you, that's not going to happen."

"It's going to take place. They've only given you until the end of the year. Your family needs to prepare for that."

"Why now?" Mother swayed in her chair, like she was going to faint.

"This is why I didn't tell them," my father said. "Besides, it's far enough away that something could still change."

"You knew and didn't tell me?" Her voice was faint but clear.

My father growled and shoved a hand in Edpol's direction.

"He had to go and tell you, but you might as well know. They trained too many forgers, so they're getting rid of the older ones to make way for the new ones."

Candui shifted beside me. What was she thinking of all this? What was I?

"I'm sorry," Edpol said. "I thought you'd written to Adriella and that was the reason she was in town."

All eyes turned to me. What could I say? "I knew nothing. Just came for a visit."

"You had to know something," Sizinne said. "No one goes for a visit anymore. It hasn't happened for the past ten years."

She was right. The high kingsmen shut that down, but people got around the rule sometimes. Why would I be any different? "Richart is a zasin. He has sway," I said.

She pursed her lips and eyed Edpol hungrily.

Was she trying to make me look bad in front of him? Didn't matter. As much as I wanted to be involved in my family's life, it was a risk I couldn't take, especially not with my father to be retired.

"There has to be something they can do," my mother said.

"There is," Father replied, "which is why I didn't tell you yet."

Some of the color returned to mother's face, though she still didn't look quite like herself. Sizinne took the conversation over, steering away from topics that would cause more problems.

Mother went to the kitchen and returned with treats and a thin smile.

Conversation was stilted. It was difficult to know what to say. How did you comfort someone when they were convinced they weren't going to die, even though it was going to happen? What were Candui's thoughts on all this? She'd been utterly quiet since coming here. She wasn't a chatty person before, but she was even more silent than usual.

After everyone had eaten their fill of dessert, Edpol said, "I best be going. Sorry to have broken the bad news. Adriella, would you see me to the door?"

Not sure what he wanted, I got to my feet and followed him into the hall and to the entrance, wishing I could take Candui or my mother with me. I opened the door and in a low voice said, "Thank you for letting us know about my father."

"I'm sorry you had to find out like that."

"But we needed to know." Even if I'm uncertain what to do about it. Mother will be a widow. At least she has my brother and sisters. I know they'll all help, even if my brother doesn't live at home.

"Thank you for coming, Edpol," I said, leaning against the doorway.

"It was my pleasure." He took my hand, kissed the back of it, and was gone.

Mother came up next to me as I closed the door. She raised an eyebrow.

"What?" Maybe it was better that she or Candui hadn't come with me.

"I didn't say anything."

She didn't have to. It was clear Edpol had feelings for me, but I was married. Even if that wasn't an issue—and it was a huge one —I was pregnant and in trouble with the law. Once Edpol figured that out, his crush on me would end.

CHAPTER NINE

I settled in for the night, wishing Mother hadn't put Candui in the guest room. It would have been nice to talk out our plan. We have to leave soon, despite the news of my father's retirement. It was good to have a full belly and be in a warm bed, but it couldn't last. Who knew how long it would take Richart to search for me here? What was more, I was beginning to tell a difference in the size of my stomach. Others might not notice for a while yet, but it wasn't something I'd be able to hide for long.

How many weeks had I been away from Bola? The days melded together on the trip here. On a good journey, it would take about a ten to fifteen days. A week to a week and a half. Ours had been longer than that. At least three weeks. Thirty days, plus however long I was pregnant before I realized it. Long enough for my stomach to go from flat to having a small bump.

I settled back against my pillow and let my thoughts wander where they chose to. Away from my pregnancy and my father's retirement, both of which I couldn't control.

At first, my mind stayed blank. Lovely and relaxing. But then something began to take shape. Something tall, with broad shoulders.

Richart.

I groaned and buried my face in my pillow. What was he doing here? I left him. I was going through my life without him. I needed to move on. Needed to figure out what I would one day tell my child about his father, if he lived that long.

There was no way to know for certain until the baby was born, but I had a strong feeling that it was going to be a boy. A cute, chubby little baby boy with his father's eyes.

Ugh. I was thinking about Richart again. This was less than useful. If I had to go on without him, I didn't want to continue thinking about him. It would be impossible, though, since I was carrying his baby.

The circular thoughts continued to spiral out of control until I drifted off.

A hand clamped around my mouth, jolting me awake. I tried to scream, but only a muffled *umpf* came out. I struggled against my blankets, attempting to get purchase against my attacker.

Thoughts raced across my mind, faster than I could keep track of them. Who was attacking me in my parents' house? And worse, was it someone who knew about the baby?

I lashed out, clawing at my attacker. My fingers made contact, and I heard a grunt. A man. Not surprising, given his strength. I managed to free myself from the blankets and scrambled away.

A large arm wrapped around me and pulled me. What was he going to do to me? Who was this man? What did he want?

I couldn't let him take me. I bucked against him, to use the momentum to break free, but his grip remained strong. An arm clamped around me, his other hand still on my mouth.

"Stop fighting me," Richart hissed.

My husband had found me, and he sounded mad.

I went limp, hoping to squirm out of his grasp, but he held on tighter. I wasn't getting out of this easily. He dragged me away from the bed and toward the door, which hung open. I didn't want my parents coming out and finding me struggling against my husband. Either they'd take his side and I'd be furious at them, or they'd take his side and I'd be resigned to my fate. Well, mother wouldn't, but she wouldn't be able to do anything about it.

He gripped my upper arm, keeping my mouth covered as we went through the house and out the back door. He dragged me away from the building, but there weren't a lot of places to go with homes all around us.

"I'm going to take my hand off your mouth, and you aren't going to attract any attention to us. Do you understand?" Anger oozed through his words.

I was in so much trouble.

I nodded, and he let go of my mouth. "Why did you leave?" he asked.

"I wanted to visit my parents." Would he buy that?

"In the middle of the night, without telling me?"

Apparently not. "I needed a break."

"A break from what? The perfect life I've tried to give you?"

Heat rippled through me. "Oh no. You do not get to say things like that. I barely know you, despite having been married to you for four years. That's not a perfect life."

He let out a huff of air and rubbed the back on his neck. "Maybe, but I'm trying. It's not my fault the zasin always need me. That's not what this is about, though. We need to talk about why you left. I want you to tell me the truth, and I want it now."

I couldn't. As much as I wanted to, I didn't know him. Didn't know if he could be trusted. "I gave you my answer."

"So your running away has nothing to do with my telling you the zasin are out, hunting for babies and pregnant women?"

"Why would you think that?" How did he guess? If only the two hadn't coincided.

He let go of my arm, but I had no desire to run for the moment. He shook his head. "I had all the zasin in Bola out looking for you, certain something bad happened. My wife would never leave me. Not the sweet girl I know. But you're not so sweet, are you? Is that a front you put on the whole time we've been married?"

"No, I—"

He waved away my response. "I don't want to hear your excuses. Once I thought you might be at your parents, I left, telling everyone I'd be back soon. I was excused from my job temporarily so I could find you. That was when I realized you were pregnant and running. What I couldn't figure out—what I still can't figure out—is why you didn't try to talk to me about it before leaving."

"I was scared you would turn us in." That secret was out of the bag. "And you proved me right. You've got the zasin after me, and now you're going to drag me to them, but know this—I'll be kicking and screaming the entire way. Our child doesn't deserve to die because of your callousness."

He took a step back, eyes wide. "How did you know that babies are being killed?"

"Not because of you."

"I didn't want to tell you, to spare you that horror," he said. "I thought telling you they were taken was enough. But that doesn't matter, does it? Because you didn't give me a chance to see how I would react. What I would do with the news."

I opened my mouth and closed it again. He was right; I didn't give him a chance. With the way he was acting, perhaps that was a mistake. I whispered, "I couldn't risk our child."

"Instead, you risked our marriage. Risked our lives. I would have done anything to keep the baby safe. I still will, but not because of you. You will never have my trust again." He turned and walked away.

What did I do? Why didn't I trust him? I could have had his help this entire time. Candui and I have been stumbling through everything when we didn't have to. How was I to know, though?

He stopped and came back to me. "If this was just about you, I'd leave and never look back, but while you still carry my child, you are stuck with me."

I didn't know if I was all right with that or not. The help would be nice, but what about all the zasin looking for me because of his choice? "What's your plan?"

"Let's get some sleep while I think about it."

Seriously? After all that, he wanted to sleep? I was so anxious I couldn't have slept if my life depended on it. I took a closer look at him under the moonlight. He had dark circles beneath his eyes. He looked worn. What had he been through during these past few weeks, trying to find me?

"Candui has the guest bedroom."

His eyes widen. "Candui is with you?"

"I thought you knew."

"No. Her husband never reported her missing. When she didn't go to work, he said she was sick. I didn't give it more thought at the time because I was looking for you. Does he know she's here?"

"No, and you can't tell him. I don't know what's going on between them, but I get the feeling it's not good."

"At least I'm not the only one with a disobedient wife." He grabbed my upper arm again, less firmly than before. "Come on. Let's get you inside where it's warm."

I hadn't realized it was cold until he said something, but now the chill in the air burst through me, bringing the worst to my unshod feet. I hesitated. "You'll have to sleep in my room."

"Don't worry. I'll sleep on the floor."

As we walked into the house, guilt pulsed through me. He hadn't been searching for me to punish me, but because of worry. How could I let him sleep on the floor after all he'd been through to find me? But I didn't want him in my bed either.

We tiptoed through the house and into my room. He didn't even look at the bed, just grabbed a pack I hadn't noticed, that he must have brought with him. He used it as a pillow and shut his eyes, not bothering to change into night clothes. Thank the stars. That would have been awkward after the conversation we had.

I got in bed and tried not to feel guilty about my husband on the hard floor. Impossible. I ripped off a blanket and threw it over the top of him, so he'd at least have something to keep him warm because stars knew I wouldn't be the one sleeping tonight.

CHAPTER TEN

The next morning, I woke bright and early. Despite worrying I wouldn't fall asleep, I nodded off. The sun hadn't yet risen, but its rays streamed through the sky. I stretched and rolled over to find Richart staring at me.

"What?" I asked.

"Nothing." He averted his gaze, dug around in his pack, and pulled out a change of clothes.

I grabbed my clothes and turned my back on him, changing as quickly as possible. It shouldn't be any different than how we did things before—we'd done enough to create a child, after all—but I was agitated anyway.

Once I had my clothes on, I turned to find him dressed. "Are you ready to talk with my parents?" I asked.

"Do they know about the baby?"

"No. And I'd like to keep it that way, for both their safety and the child's."

He nodded.

"Also, I found out last night that my father is supposed to

retire at the end of the year. There might be some tension related to that this morning. I wanted you to be aware."

"They're killing your father?"

"*Shh.* Not if he can help it. He thinks there's time to do something about it."

Richart shook his head and opened his mouth before snapping it closed. What he was going to say remained unsaid.

I didn't want to say anything further to him, so I hurried out of the room, with him close on my heels. Mother and Father were up, both at the table eating breakfast, but there was no sign of my sisters or Candui.

Mother glanced up and looked behind me. She darted to her feet. "Richart! We weren't expecting you."

"He decided to come on vacation with us and arrived last night after you fell asleep," I said.

"This is a nice surprise. Come on in, and I'll get you both breakfast." She hurried about the kitchen, gathering plates and dishing food onto them.

I sat at the table across from my father, and Richart took the seat next to mine.

Father glared at him. "Still assigned to the zasin?"

"Yes, sir." Richart's voice was full of respect, despite the disdain that oozed from my father.

He grunted. "Suppose someone has to do the dirty work."

I clenched my jaw. I shouldn't say anything, but it would be strange not to come to Richart's defense. I always did in the past, even when I barely knew him, partly because I had to, but there was something more there as well. "Without the zasin, you wouldn't be here, Father."

"Hmm." He took a spoonful of porridge. "Or maybe I would still have a job they didn't want to retire me from and a daughter who didn't sass me."

I sighed as Mother set a bowl of porridge before me. He

didn't use to be so ornery, but he'd grown cynical of life. What happened to him, to make him this way? He couldn't have known about the retirement four years ago when I left. Mother's notes indicated he'd grown worse lately, though, without saying so outright, so perhaps that had something to do with it.

The porridge was hot, steam drifting up from it. My stomach churned at the sight, but eating seemed to help when I felt this way, so I took a small spoonful.

"I'm grateful to see you together." Mother retook her seat next to Father. "When Adriella came home on her own, I was afraid something had happened between the two of you, but of course, nothing has. That would be unthinkable."

I gave my mother what I hoped was a believable smile and took another bite of breakfast. It didn't seem likely things would get any more uncomfortable.

"And of course, she told you Edpol came to visit last night. Good man, that." Father carried on, like nothing had changed.

Richart stiffened beside me. "He came here?"

"Yes," Father answered. "Didn't she tell you? He stayed for some time last night."

Was he trying to drive a wedge between us? Perhaps it was a good thing it was already there. Richart and Edpol hadn't gotten along from the moment Richart came to collect me to marry him. "I didn't get a chance to speak with you about it, since you got in so late," I said.

He didn't look at me, just glared down at his bowl.

The front door opened, and my brother walked in. "I heard my sister was in town."

I jumped up from my chair and rushed over to him, to wrap him in a hug. "*Mivark.* I'm so happy to see you."

"And I you, little sis." He planted a kiss on my forehead, before letting me go. "How long are you staying?"

"We leave today," Richart said from the table.

My brother's expression fell. "But you got here yesterday."

"I know," I said, "and I would stay if I could, but there are things that need taking care of. I'm happy I got to see you, even if it's not for long." So happy. If only it wasn't braced by the bitterness of having to leave and the possibility that I'd never see my family again, especially my father. He might be grumpy, and I didn't entirely understand him, but I still loved him.

I didn't know what was going to happen, but if this was the last I saw of them, I wanted to make good use of it. I dragged my brother to the table. "Come eat with us."

"I already had breakfast."

But my mother got him a bowl, and he ate it anyway. "Vacations are almost nonexistent these days. It's pretty amazing that you were both able to get one at the same time."

"I'm here to escort her home," Richart said. "They gave Adriella much more time than they gave me."

In other words, I didn't have work to go back to, because if I tried, I'd be hanged for leaving my job in the first place.

"We're glad that you got to visit for what time you did," my mother said. "We've missed having you around since the wedding. I wish you'd been assigned somewhere closer to home."

"Silanu, don't say such things," Father snapped.

Mother pursed her lips but didn't say anything. If someone outside of the family had heard her talk like this, it could mean punishment, though she was well-loved in the community. Father was trying to take care of her. At least, that's what I kept telling myself.

The room went silent while we all ate. I didn't dare say anything after my father's outburst. It wasn't that I was unused to outbursts; I'd just forgotten how stern he could be.

"Good morning," Candui said as she walked in the room. She stopped short when she saw Richart at my side.

"My husband decided to come and escort us home," I said. "Isn't that nice?"

"It is." Despite her words, she'd grown pale.

"Candui, this is my brother, Mivark."

She said hello, but he only lifted an eyebrow at her.

Mother got her some porridge and sat her beside Mivark. Candui stirred it around but didn't eat.

"How are my grandchildren, Mivark?" Mother asked.

He had two children, five and seven years of age. Old enough we wouldn't have to worry about the Sunsire taking their lives. Stars be blessed.

"Good. Busy as ever." Mivark grinned, but the smile slowly faded. He looked at me in a way I didn't like. Like he could see every thought in my heart.

The conversation swirled around me. I didn't know what to say that wouldn't give away more than I already had. As much as I loved my family, I was anxious to be away from them. It'd be safer for all of us.

I should have never come in the first place.

After breakfast, Mother helped me pack some food for what she thought would be our journey home to Bola. Where were we going? It didn't matter, I still had to finish up with things here before worrying about it. Shortly thereafter, the children she watched began arriving, and there was no more chance to tell her anything. Just as well. Telling her she was going to be a grand-mother again wasn't a good option.

But I wanted to.

I went to my room, closed the door behind me, and leaned against it with a sigh while I shut my eyes. There was so much I needed to do before we left, but exhaustion was taking over. My body ached with the need for sleep, though I got what I needed last night. Carrying a baby was draining.

I opened my eyes to find Richart sitting on my bed, staring at me. "What?" I asked.

"You look tired."

"Thank you."

"Sorry. I don't mean it in a bad way. I'm wondering what we should do, to keep everyone safe."

I grabbed some fabric from the stash I kept when I was still living at home. I was going to need it before this was all over to expand my clothing size. I placed it inside my pack and sat on the bed next to him. He might be my husband, but he felt like my enemy. He might have come after me, but he had yet to prove himself. I couldn't bring myself to trust him on his word alone. He was still a zasin after all. Except for the common goal we had of keeping the child safe, there wasn't a reason to be around him. I forced myself to remain sitting and not move away. "What are you thinking?"

"I have an aunt in Tosafo."

Wonderful. More walking. "Aren't we going to have the same problem, staying with her, as we are with my family?"

"Yes, but I have connections there that can help."

"Help hide us in Tosafo or help get us somewhere else?"

"Not sure yet."

I held in a grumble. "And you don't have connections here?"

"No. Do you?"

Edpol, but I wouldn't dare ask him for help when I'm pregnant with another man's child. "Not really. Do you trust your contacts?"

"More than I do you."

I winced and turned away.

He sighed. "Look, I didn't know what happened to you and where you went. I didn't want to believe you left me when you discovered what the zasin and Sunsire are doing. It makes it harder to trust you."

"I can see that." It's not like I trusted him either—not when I ran and not now. Not with my heart. Only with our baby. "Are you certain this is the right choice?"

"Do you have a better one?"

I wished I did. "No."

"Then to Tosafo we go."

CHAPTER ELEVEN

I said goodbye to my sisters, who then watched the children so my mother could take her turn. She stood next to my father, a smile on her face, but her eyes red.

"I didn't mean to make you sad," I said.

"Oh, dear one. I'm glad you had a chance to come by. I missed you. I hope it's not long until we see you again."

"I wish so too, but if we're honest, it may not be for a long time." Or ever. The thought made me about to have red eyes of my own, but I kept grinning. Nothing was said about my father possibly not being here when I visited again. I didn't want to bring up the trauma when there was nothing I could do about it.

"You keep a watchful eye out for her," Mother told Richart.

"I will." He sounded determined, but we both knew that it was only because of the baby.

My father surprised me by wrapping me in a hug. "Take care, my girl."

"I'll try." This time I couldn't help the tears that fell. No matter how gruff he was, my father loved me. Was this the last hug I'd ever get from him?

He cleared his throat. "I've got to get back to the forge with Edpol, but you travel safe."

"Nothing will happen to me with Richart and Candui taking care of me."

He grunted and headed down the street. I watched him go, until he turned the corner, wishing things could be so much different. At least I got to see him one last time.

"I should get back to the children," Mother said. "I love you, dear one."

"I love you too, Mother." I gave her one last hug.

She went inside, and I turned to find Candui and Richart looking the other direction. I said, "I'm ready." As ready as I'd ever be. I wasn't certain on how Richart planned on getting us out of town, especially since he had the zasin out, looking for me. It didn't seem like it would go over well. I could tell him about the passageway, but I wanted to see if he had another plan. I didn't want to use the tunnel more than I had to and risk getting it discovered.

We began our journey down the street when someone called my name. Hoping it wasn't someone who'd turn me in, I turned to face them.

Mivark was running toward me. I smiled, grateful to see my brother before I had to go, but he didn't smile back.

Once he reached me, he said to the other two, "May I have a moment alone with my sister?"

"We'll be over there." Candui pointed across the street and down a ways.

"Thank you," I replied, before turning my attention back to my brother. "I thought we already said goodbye, not that I'm sad to see you."

His voice was low and hurried. "I kept thinking about why you would come. I was happy to see you, but no one gets vacation time, without being high up in the ranks or making great dona-

71

tions to the high king that I know you can't afford. So I wondered and wondered. This morning, when I passed a zasin searching for babies and pregnant women, it came to me. You are with child."

The blood rushed from my face. "I'm not."

"It's me we're talking about. I'm your brother. I know what's going on in your life. I've been able to read you since we were children. Don't deny it."

He was right. He'd always been able to read me. I was surprised it took this long. "You can't tell anyone."

He shook his head. "You know I have to. The zasin will come for me as much as they'll come for you if they find out I knew and didn't say anything."

Fear stabbed my chest. "Do you really want your niece or nephew to die because you couldn't keep a secret?" I wanted him to say *no* more than I ever wanted anything in my life.

He was so quiet, I didn't know what he was thinking, but I didn't want to beg either. He hated it when I begged and got whiny when we were children. That hadn't changed over the years.

He said, "I don't want your baby to die—or you, for running—but maybe they'll be lenient on you. Maybe the rumors we've heard aren't true. If they let your baby be born and see that it doesn't carry the mark, I'm sure they'll let it live."

"You may be willing to take that chance, but I'm not. I need to know my child is safe, and I need you to keep quiet about it."

"Adriella..." He sounded exasperated.

"Please. When have I ever asked you something that meant this much? I need you to pretend you didn't guess anything."

"Fine. But if I hang for this with you, know that I'm going to haunt you in whatever afterlife we go to."

"Fair enough." I tried not to let relief coat my words, but it was impossible. "I have to go."

I held in a startled yelp when he pulled me into a big hug. "Stay safe," he said.

"You too. Take care of your children and wife." It would have been nice if there was time to see them before we left, but maybe it was better this way. I needed to move on. Needed to get going, without more distractions from what was to come.

"I will. Now get out of here." He gave me a little shove toward Candui and Richart before leaving back the way he came. I clenched my jaw, hoping he would do as I asked and keep my secret. That he might not was all the more reason to get out of here quickly.

I smiled at the two of them, though it was the opposite of what I wanted to do. "Where are we off to?"

"He knows?" Richart asked.

I let my smile drop. "How did you know?"

"Your reaction when he started talking."

"He won't tell anyone."

"We can only hope. Let's get moving."

My thoughts exactly.

Candui took my hand and gave it a comforting squeeze. "I believe in him. He is your brother."

I wanted it to be so. So much depended on him keeping quiet. I didn't know what I'd do if he gave me away. "Are you all right with..." I nodded my head toward Richart.

"He seems to want the best. Besides, I don't think there's much other choice right now."

No. There wasn't.

"This way," Richart said.

We followed him through the streets. Did he know where he was going? He hadn't spent a lot of time here when we were married, and even that time had been devoted to me and my family, not wandering around.

Richart led us toward the poorer part of the city. I wanted to disagree with where we were going—we stood out too much here —but couldn't bring myself to argue just yet. Perhaps he had a good plan. I didn't understand much of his ideas, so how could I figure out what he had arranged?

How was it that I had been married to him for four years, yet comprehended so little about him? It was strange. I was wed to someone as unfamiliar to me as on the day we met, though we had created a child together. We both did just enough to cover what was expected of us by society, not an inch more.

Soon enough, the baby would be born and then we would... What? Part ways? He'd take the baby from me and raise it on his own? I didn't know. Something I should remedy.

The residents here paid less attention to Candui. Was it because they had more pressing things to deal with than an elf? Plus, the elven part of town was connected with the human part of town in the poor section, so the people here might be more accustomed to seeing them about.

It was strange to think we were only separated by appearance, but that was enough for humans to shun elves. I knew of people who'd never say so aloud, but were jealous of the elves' height and good looks, if not their pointy ears. Was envy what lead to the hate between our kinds? Or was there more hidden? Did elves have some secret to their lifespan I was unaware of? I, for one, didn't mind.

Richart walked up to a man with a cart. The rest of the street was deserted. People had to be off to work.

"Took you long enough to get here." The man sounded put out.

"Sorry. Had an unexpected interference," Richart replied.

So he'd planned this? When did he get the chance?

"It had better not lead here."

"It won't." Richart handed the man a small money bag. "Thank you."

74

"Don't want your thanks. Just your money."

Though Richard didn't reply, his jaw was tense. He wasn't happy about this. What part of it, though? He turned to me and Candui. "Both of you get back here."

I did, not understanding how getting in a wagon where everyone could see was going to help us get out of town. I didn't want to cause a scene, though I hoped I wasn't heading toward some type of trap.

Candui didn't have the same problem. "How is this going to help?"

"We're covering you with straw. It's the only thing I could arrange for during the day on short notice," Richart replied.

She climbed into the back, and I followed her. We lay down, and Richart got in the driver's seat. He set the cart in motion, letting the horses pull us, and we circled around until we came to a field of hay. He pulled us right up to a hay stack and used a pitchfork to pile the hay in. As it showered down on us, I pled to the stars that it was a good idea. I didn't want to be suffocated by hay or be caught by the zasin on our way out.

I put my hand to my star stone where it hid beneath my tunic and closed my eyes. This had to work. Too much relied on it. If we were discovered...

But no. Richart was thorough. We'd be fine.

The hay continued to fall around us until we were covered by it. It smelled a little sweet but mostly of mold, and left me feeling itchy. Despite that, as I lay there, I thought we might have a chance. Maybe.

The soft sound of hay falling continued for a period of time, and the weight on us slowly increased. I wanted to scratch my nose, but stayed still. Perhaps I was the one allergic to hay. I took shallow breaths, attempting to fight off the tickle in my nose.

The cart shifted, and we were moving. It was difficult, lying here, not doing anything, as the fate of my child hung in the balance. The ride was bumpy and uncomfortable, but nothing compared to the pounding in my heart.

Voices grew, though I couldn't make out individual words. They were muffled and mixed together in a way that made it difficult. The noise rose as we continued, and the steady forward movement slowed to a crawl.

My nose tickled more as I kept my breathing shallow. What was going on? How safe was it? Was Richart's plan was going to work? There was no way to know from back here, stuck under all this smelly stuff.

Someone barked out commands. We had to be nearing the gate. I squeezed my star stone and silently begged.

"What have you got there?" a muffled male voice asked.

Richart's voice was just as muffled, but also less authoritative than usual. "Just taking this straw to my brother's farm outside the city."

"Got anything else in there?"

"No, sir. Just straw."

"Then you won't mind if I stab it with a pitchfork."

"Go right ahead, sir. Though if you would make it quick—I've got more deliveries to make today."

I held absolutely still, though my nose was itchier than ever. I needed to do something about it but didn't dare lift my hand to scratch it. What would it be like if the tines skewered us? The nausea that went through me had nothing to do with being pregnant and everything to do with the safety of my friend and child. The straw above us rustled like it was moving, but I didn't feel any stabbing from the fork. It couldn't last, though. Any second I expected the pitchfork to slice through me.

"All right, then," the gruff voice said. "Get a move on."

"Thank you, sir," Richart replied.

The cart moved again. I let out a relieved sigh, and then the worst happened.

I sneezed.

I silently cursed myself and waited for the guard to attack while I switched to breathing through clenched teeth.

"What was that?" the guard asked.

"Just sneezed, sir."

"Sounded like it came from your cart."

"Feel free to check it again if you'd like."

"Get on with you." The guard sounded exasperated, but I'd never been so grateful to hear those words.

The cart continued on for some time. I sneezed three more times and was beginning to feel rather itchy as we went. I bit my cheek so I wouldn't move and tried to concentrate on the pain instead of the need to scratch.

What felt like hours and hours later, we finally stopped. I didn't change position. Didn't know if it was safe. Maybe we'd been spotted. Or maybe it was time to get out. Or maybe the guard at the gate realized the sneeze did come from inside the cart and sent a load of zasin after us. Whatever the case might be, I held still.

There was a sound of metal scraping against metal and then straw falling. Richart said, "Come on out. It's safe."

I clawed my way out of the straw, sneezing like a banshee. It didn't take long for me to spot Richart's angry expression.

"Sorry. I didn't mean to—" A sneeze exploded out of me, followed by another.

"I know you couldn't help it. Look at you—you're covered in red bumps." Richart's angry expression melted into one a little more sympathetic.

"Guess she's the one allergic to hay, not I." Candui came up beside me on the cart and helped brush the hay off me.

"I had no idea." I sneezed again. I never spent much time around hay before. It wasn't needed until now. Wish I had known beforehand.

"We should get you rinsed off," Candui said. "Is there any water around here?"

"There's a stream not far from here. We need to hurry away from this house, though, in case they send someone after us."

I sneezed. "Let's go. I can wash off later."

"Are you certain?" she asked.

"It's either that or get caught. I can be miserable for a little while to remain free." Though dipping in water sounded blissful.

"Let's get going, then." Richart lifted me off the end of the cart like I weighed nothing, my sides warming where he held onto me.

He set me on the grass, reached for Candui, and set her beside me, despite the fact that she was taller than me. He was a lot stronger than he appeared.

He led the way, and we followed, keeping silent and glancing around to make certain we weren't being pursued. I tried not to scratch, but everything itched so much, I couldn't help it. I sneezed several more times, but that calmed with time. My itching didn't.

We hiked for what the sun said was about an hour before Richart said, "Let's get you washed up."

"Do you think we're far enough away?" I asked.

"Doesn't matter. If you keep scratching like that, you'll start bleeding." He helped me take my pack off. "I'll find you a change of clothes and have Candui bring them to you."

I raced off to the sound of gurgling water, anxious to soothe my skin. At the riverside, I looked around and couldn't see anyone, though I knew Candui and Richart were nearby. I took off my shoes, but I'd have to wait for the rest. I couldn't risk leaving my star stone away from me, even hidden in my shoes, but neither could I let Candui see it. She might not recognize it for what it was, but I couldn't chance it. Drat and double drat.

I took my time, hoping Candui would hurry with the clothes.

I tried not to itch. My skin was begging for relief, but I couldn't give it without unleashing my deepest secret, which I wasn't ready to do.

The soft thud of footsteps sounded behind me. I turned to find Candui striding toward me. Disappointment struck me at my core, but I wasn't certain why.

She handed me a tunic and pants with a cake of soap on top. "Do you need help with anything else?"

"No. Thank you."

With a nod, she turned and left. As soon as she was out of sight, I stripped down, except for my star stone, and cleaned the rest of the straw from my body. The water was icy, raising goosebumps on my arms and legs. Despite the cold, it was a relief to wash off the uncomfortable feeling. Once I was fairly clean, I pulled on my clean items and scrubbed my straw-covered ones. I was focused on my work, my hands wrinkled with water, when I heard footsteps again.

I froze, not daring to move, in case it was someone I shouldn't be seen by. Did the zasin follow us? Did they find me? Were they going to take me away and kill both me and my child?

Though I wasn't showing yet, so we might get away with more than if I had a rounded belly, but since we weren't supposed to be traveling, it could mean trouble. Even an excuse like my father retiring wouldn't be enough to go against the law.

I wasn't going to go easy. I silently set down the wet clothing and soap and felt around for a rock about the size of my fist. The footsteps grew nearer. They were heavier than Candui's. Was she already taken?

I licked my lips. This was going to be a one-chance thing. The sound grew nearer. I whipped around, flinging the rock toward the noise, and bent my knees to run. The rock sailed to the right of Richart's head as he reached for me.

He yanked me to his side. "What do you think you are doing?"

I huffed, ignoring the warmth blossoming from where his arm pulled me close to him. "Your footsteps were heavier than Candui's. I thought you were a zasin."

"I am a zasin, but not one you need to throw rocks at. Good thing your aim is bad."

I struggled to get out of his hold, and he let me go. "I wish it was better, so I could knock some sense into that thick skull of yours." Not that he hadn't shown sense, I was just irritated. Though I probably shouldn't take it out on him, it was too late to take back the words.

"We can improve it, but only if you promise not to attack me anymore." There was a hint of a smile on his face.

He shouldn't be too mad, though I was upset with myself. "You can help me throw better?"

"I can."

A new thought hit me. "I want more than that. I want you to teach me to fight."

"I'll protect you."

"But what if there is a moment you can't? I should have the skills to protect myself and the baby, in case something happens to you."

He mulled this over, taking on a far-off look. When he returned his gaze to me, his expression was no longer waffling. "You're right. We should give you some skills that will protect the baby."

"I'm sorry. Did you just say I'm right?" I teased.

His expression remained serious. "If it saves my child, I will do whatever it takes, even if it means admitting you're correct."

The response stunned me so much, I stared at him. He moved over toward the river, to look at the clothes caked in soap. "Are you going to finish those, or do you need help?"

"Oh. Yes." I hurried over to them, determined to finish up quickly, so we could be on our way and the zasin wouldn't find us here. As I scrubbed, I asked, "What is your aunt like?"

He sighed. "At one point, after my parents died, she was like my mother. I didn't stay in touch with her like I should have, though. I hope she isn't angry with me, for not keeping her better up to date."

"Why didn't you write her after you left Tosafo?" When he came to marry me. It wasn't like he had a choice in the wedding any more than I did. He did read and write, though, unlike his uneducated wife. It was part of what was required of a zasin leader.

He sat on a log beside the river as I cleaned. "Let's just say I had a hard time leaving. She was the one who convinced me it was the right thing to do."

I turned to look at him as I kept moving my hands. "You didn't want to marry me?"

He cringed. "It wasn't like that. I didn't want to leave Tosafo. And though I'm suited to be a zasin, if the truth is told, it's not what I wanted to do with my life. Besides, I didn't think I was ready to get married. I was older than most grooms-to-be but still felt like a kid."

Perhaps that explained why he was so cold with me when we married. It wasn't like I was warm with him. "Were you a zasin in Tosafo?"

"After I finished my apprenticeship, yes. I worked there for a few years. That's one reason I was surprised to get a wife from out of town and be sent to another village."

Did he love another? Was that why he was reluctant to marry an outsider? Did he have someone he was close to before we met, like I was close to Edpol? I pushed the thought aside but then realized I was his wife. Even if we didn't get along the best, I did have a right to know if we were walking back to a love interest who might interfere with things. Interference could mean danger for my child. "Did you leave a lover behind?"

His brow creased. "What? No. Why would you think something like that?"

"I was curious." And strangely relieved there was no one besides me. I didn't have a right to feel that way, but I did, all the same.

Though there wasn't even me. Not really.

"Well, I didn't. I've never loved anyone."

Ouch. I couldn't complain, since I never loved him either, but it didn't take away the sting. I swished water through my clothing before ringing it out. "We should get on our way."

"Are you ready to walk until dark?" he asked.

"If that's what it takes."

Because it was going to take that and so much more.

CHAPTER TWELVE

A fter a quick breakfast of bread and fruit, we got on the road. I didn't sleep well last night, but Candui and Richart both looked like they slept worse. They took turns standing watch, and when I offered to help, they insisted the baby needed me to rest.

It was strange to think how I had two people looking out for me—well, for my child. I wasn't accustomed to such attention and usually did things for myself, like the rest of Erta.

"How long will it take to get to Tosafo?" Candui asked as we walked.

"Longer than it would have taken on the main road. This back road isn't used much, for good reasons," Richart replied.

"What other reason besides not being used much?" I asked.

"What makes you think there's another?"

"Because you said *reasons* with an *s*. Pretty sure that means more than one." And I didn't like the sound of it at all.

He sighed. "There have been a couple of animal attacks on this road, but I'm sure with the three of us, we'll be fine. It's not like we're traveling alone, though I would feel better if we had horses."

"Why didn't we bring the horses, then?" We left them at the farm we stopped at.

"They weren't part of the deal, and I wasn't going to make the man I dealt with angry by taking them. That would be the wrong move."

"Animal attacks?" Candui asked. "That doesn't sound good."

"Like I said, we'll be fine. We're making enough noise to warn the animals away, and we'll keep our fire bright at night."

"Which will lead people right to us," I said.

"Unless they're zasin on the lookout for you, we should be fine."

"That *should* is so reassuring." I was feeling a little too sarcastic that morning, but it was hard not to when things looked so dismal and I had to stop to use a tree every ten minutes.

After another such break, we continued on our way, walking with me in the middle.

"Tell me more about your family, Candui," I said. "I know some about Richart's, but I don't know much about yours." Because I needed to know more about this woman who insisted on risking her life to run with me. I should have asked her more sooner, but I was self-absorbed and worried about the zasin catching us. I still was.

"There's not much to tell." Her words were curt.

"What about your parents? What are they like?"

She livened up. "They are good people. I grew up in a good home with loving parents. They taught me much since I don't have any living siblings left."

"I'm sorry." I wished I knew what else to say.

"Don't be. You've been so kind to me since you moved to Bola. I couldn't have asked for anyone better."

Heat rose to my cheeks. "All we did was wash laundry together."

"And you talked to me. Didn't avoid me, like so many humans do."

"Do humans really have problems with elves?" I knew we weren't always on the greatest terms, but I hadn't thought things were that bad either.

"Some do. It's likely why those gypsy elves were so harsh with us."

"What gypsy elves?" Richart asked, voice sharp.

I winced. "We may have had a run-in with them. But we were fine. There was a raid on their camp, looking for babies, and we hid. Afterward, the elves had too much going on, so they let us go."

"You came across a camp of gypsy elves, and they let you go? They never let anyone go."

I shrugged. "I don't understand it any more than you do, other than the fact that I helped take care of their sick while there. Perhaps they appreciated my work with the ill." And Candui hasn't seemed to get sick, which was my biggest worry over the whole thing.

"I overheard them talking," Candui said. "They did think Adriella was doing a good job. They were surprised she didn't try to run away."

"What did they have you doing?" Richart asked her.

"They kept me locked up until the attack, when my jailer freed me, saying he didn't want to see something bad happen to me because of the raid. I think he felt sorry for me, since I was a fellow elf."

"That makes more sense than what happened to Adriella." Richart went silent.

My legs were aching from the walking, from the back of my thighs all the way down to my calves. I thought I'd gotten accustomed to it, but Richart set a faster pace than Candui and I had before.

Despite the chill in the air and the extra layer of clothing I was wearing, there were buds on the trees and bits of green were popping up in the dirt. It helped me keep walking when I focused on those bits of color rather than thinking only of myself.

I was looking at one such green plant when I heard a noise behind us. "What's that?"

Richart didn't respond, just grabbed my arm and yanked me off the road.

Candui followed.

We went far enough into the trees, to hide in some brush.

Richart said, "Others on the road. Quiet."

I held still and didn't say anything, like he requested. Was it zasin coming for me or travelers taking the back road, like ourselves? Neither would be very good. Who would come the back way if they weren't looking for something or trying to avoid something? Unless it was another pregnant woman or someone with a child, which I had a hard time believing. Then again, maybe many were trying to escape. I couldn't be the only one.

A wind picked up, shaking the branches of the trees. I shivered but didn't drop my gaze, keeping it trained on the part of the road the noise was coming from. Soon enough, a group of five people on horseback came sauntering into sight. They were three men and two women, wrapped up well against the cold. Because there were women in the mix, I doubted they were zasin, but it was difficult to tell with how well they were wrapped up.

Their pace was so leisurely. It was going to take a while for them to ride by. I settled in to wait. It was stressful, watching without being able to do anything. With them on horses, it wasn't like we could run. If something happened and they headed for us, we were done for.

My legs ached from being crouched for so long. I didn't know how much longer they would hold, but there was no other option. Slowly, I put my hands down on the ground, to give me some support. The ache in my legs didn't go away but eased some. I'd make it now.

They were almost in line with us when something tickled my fingers. I held in a scream as I looked down and saw a giant spider. It was huge, bigger than my hand, with fangs an inch long. Despite trying to stay quiet, I must have made some noise because Richart looked over. When he saw the spider, he tensed beside me.

It stayed there, sitting on my hand as the group continued on by. I didn't know its species, but if it decided to bite me, I was done for. This was so very, very bad. I couldn't handle it biting me. I wasn't ready to die. I had to give life to my child. Live mine in a way that would bring me and those I cared about joy and comfort. Up until now, I hadn't done much. I needed to change that.

"Stay still," Richart whispered over the sound of horse's hooves clacking.

Like I planned on moving. But I obeyed him. I didn't want to do anything to risk being bit. It moved forward little by little, and I grew hopeful it was going to get off me without a problem, until it stopped next to my thumb and drummed its leg against my skin.

I couldn't help the whimper that came out of me. It burst forth unheeded to my wishes to not let it sound. Luckily, the group passing by didn't seem to notice over the noise they made. The group was getting farther from us, though they were within sight. Out of nowhere, Richart smacked the massive spider off my hand. I barely kept from calling out my surprise at the sting of being hit.

It didn't hurt much, but the shock had me wanting to yelp. I bit my bottom lip and let out a small grunt. It was all I allowed myself.

The group was soon gone from view.

We didn't get back on the road, but Richart said under his breath, "That was close."

"You didn't tell me there were enormous spiders in this forest. That thing was big enough to eat a bird," I whispered back.

"I didn't know."

Candui put an arm around me, comforting me like a sister would. I didn't know how I stayed in place for longer, until the horses' noise was long gone, but I forced myself to. Once Richart stood, I went running from the patch we had hidden in, back to the road, brushing myself down as I went.

I patted myself down to make certain there were no more little critters on me and shuddered. "That was disgusting."

"Not to mention life-threatening," Candui said. "I don't know how you stayed so calm."

Me either. I didn't feel calm at all.

Richart came over to us, a frown clouding his features. "I hate to be the bearer of bad news, but we need to travel off the road."

"With more of those spiders?" I said. "I think not."

"If there are more people on the road, we are going to have to keep hiding, and if something attacks you again, we may not be as lucky."

He had a point. That didn't mean I had to like it. "What about the creatures out there? Aren't they going to cause us a problem?"

Candui shivered.

"I'll keep my sword ready and the fire bright tonight. We'll be fine."

I hoped he meant better than we were when we had to get off the road, because things weren't looking that great.

CHAPTER THIRTEEN

He wasn't joking about the fire being bright. It was huge, the heat coming off it in waves. He lit it in a large clearing we found, the trees tight around us, but not so close together that someone couldn't see the flames.

"Are you certain someone isn't going to see this from the road and come looking for us?" I asked.

"No," he said matter-of-factly. "But we should be far enough away that it won't matter, even if they see it, and it will protect us from the animals."

"If you're sure..."

"I wouldn't risk my child." He sounded so confident, it was difficult to do anything but believe.

Where was this confidence while we were married? I hadn't seen it. He wasn't cowardly, just not this self-assured. It was a whole new side of him I never knew before.

And if I had to admit it, I liked it.

"What's for dinner?" My stomach rumbled at the thought of food.

"Same thing that's going to be for dinner until we reach Tosafo," Richart said.

Candui groaned. "I can't wait until we can eat something besides hard cheese. I'm getting so tired of it."

"I could go for something sweet and salty. Maybe even a little sour," I said.

She giggled. "You're definitely the pregnant woman in the group."

I blushed. "I can't help it if this baby is craving things I can't have. It sounds so good, though. Perhaps a light sweet bread with frosting lightly covered in salt and a fresh squeeze of lemon, not that we'll find any around here." I'd only had lemon once before. At the time, I didn't like its sour taste, but now it sounded perfect.

"Now you're making me want some," she said.

"Maybe we can find us both some in Tosafo," I replied, not that they'd have the much sought-after fruit. "What should we expect once we get there?" I asked Richart.

He stopped gazing at the darkness around us to focus on me. "Only a little better than this, I'm afraid. At least we'll be inside, but Tosafo is a poor town. They aren't going to have much good food. My aunt is nice, though. She'll take care of you the best she can."

I tried to hide my disappointment. It's not like I had to have light sweetbread—but oh stars, did it sound good. Better than any cheese or hard bread I'd eaten in the last while.

I stood and paced around the camp fire. Lots of pebbles and some medium-sized rocks were buried within the dirt. No spot was without them.

"What are you doing?" Richart asked.

"Looking for the place that looks the softest to sleep. Unless you're going to let me help keep watch tonight."

"Not tonight."

Or any night. All I'd be able to do was scream. That had to

change. "When are you going to start teaching me how to defend myself?"

He looked at me thoughtfully for a moment before striding closer. "Why don't we start now?"

"Now?" It wasn't what I had expected. What my body wanted was to sleep, but I needed to learn skills that could someday possibly save my baby's life. If only I never had to use them.

"Yes. Now would be good." He reached down to his belt, pulled out a small dagger, and handed it to me. "We'll start with this. It will be the best thing to use to defend yourself while you're pregnant. The sword is going to become too unwieldy."

I felt the weight of the dagger, the metal cool but warming in my hand. "Is this big enough to protect myself?"

"It will get the job done, as long as you know how to use it. And while we're at it"—he turned away from me and faced Candui—"you should learn too."

She took the proffered dagger, swung her arm, and let the weapon go. It sailed through the air and came to rest in the trunk of a tree on the other side of the fire.

"Amazing." I had no idea she could throw a blade like that.

"Pretty good," Richart said. "Do you know how to use it in hand-to-hand combat?"

"Well enough." She stalked over to the tree and pulled out the dagger with some effort.

"You can help me teach Adriella, then."

"I'd rather not." She strode back over to us and held the dagger toward Richart, hilt first.

"You keep it. You may need it at some point."

"No, thank you." She pushed it closer to him.

He slowly took the weapon. "If you change your mind, let me know, and you can have it back."

"I won't, but thank you for the offer." She settled down beside the fire, her back to it, looking out into the forest.

What was her story? Why didn't she want the dagger when she knew how to use it so well? I wished she'd open up to me and tell me how things were. It wasn't like I'd tell anyone else, even if I did have someone to tell. Besides, it would do her some good to let her feelings out.

Richart came next to me, grabbed the hand I had closed around the dagger, and repositioned it, his fingers calloused but gentle with mine. "You'll want to hold it like this. It will give you better aim and a good grip."

I nodded, trying to ignore the way my skin tingled where he'd touched me. That sensation was always there, but it wasn't something I could pay any heed to when we had so many other things going on.

I tried to tell myself that anyway, but my thoughts kept straying to it.

"What now?" I asked.

"We'll start with you protecting yourself in close quarters, because if the attackers are far enough away, I want you to run as fast and as far as you can while I deal with them."

"Is that really the smartest move? You could teach me to help."

His expression grew stern. "I don't want you anywhere near a blade that could injure you."

Well, then— "Guess I'll be running."

"If you have to fight, I want you to jab for the weak spots. Places where you aren't going to be blocked by bone or will do the most damage. Which can you think of?"

I didn't want to think of them at all, but if it protected my child... "The stomach?"

"Right. The gut is a good soft spot to embed your weapon in but oftentimes blocked by your opponent's weapon. Trained soldiers tend to block their vital parts. Can you think of anywhere else?"

"I don't know."

"Think hard."

I cringed. "Under their chin?"

"If you can get to that, it will do the job. Aim upward, and you may have a chance. Another thing you can do is try to hit their clavicle. I know I said don't hit bone, but this one will work for you. If you damage that, their arm won't work well, giving you a better chance at getting away."

I groaned. "I can't do this. It all seems so violent."

I thought he was going to bark at me, about how I was being weak. Instead, he said, "I know it's difficult. I had a hard time with it when I was first ordered to be a zasin. Honestly, I still struggle with it. But sometimes you have to do what's needed to protect yourself and the ones you love."

It was a true statement but surprised me coming from him. I didn't expect him to struggle with hurting people and being a zasin.

He came around behind me and said, "I want you to practice stabbing like you're attacking someone. I don't have a dummy for you to work on—we'll figure something out later—but for now, go through the motions slowly."

It felt awkward, but I did as he asked and stabbed forward.

"You need to put your whole body behind it, not only your arm. Try again."

I did so, feeling even more awkward.

"That's a little better, but try this." He moved forward and pressed up against me, bringing his hand down onto my own.

My breath hitched as I struggled to focus on his words. Why was I reacting like this? We were married, for star's sake. We made a child together, and he never affected me the way he was now. Granted, something was different about this closeness.

Something that had me wanting to lean back into him. Not that I did.

"Are you paying attention?" he asked.

"Sorry. I'm not used to holding this dagger."

"I know you're more accustomed to working with a loom, but you need to pay attention so it becomes more comfortable." His hand ran up and down my arm, sending a shiver across me, despite the jacket over my bare skin. "Now, hold your arm steady. Don't let anything sway you from your decision. You need to be focused and certain of what you're doing."

I was sure I didn't want to move, but that wasn't right. He was the enemy. "Like this?"

"Right. Now, plunge the dagger upward and twist your wrist."

"Why twist?"

"Trust me on this."

"No, really. Why do I need to twist my wrist? What good will that do? It seems like a lot more work."

He sighed, his front pressing into my back. "It will do more damage to your opponent."

Made sense, but I didn't want to have to do it. I remembered the baby and forced myself through the action.

"That was better, but you have to be certain. Swift and sure." He grabbed my hand, brought it straight out, and swiveled like we were punching someone in the stomach. "Like that."

I tried again, with his hand still on me. "How was that?"

"Better." He sounded breathless, like he'd been training. He took a step back, the lack of his presence leaving me chilled. "Try it again, by yourself."

We worked for a while longer, before he said I did a good job and we'd practice again later. I turned to give the dagger back.

"You keep it," he said. "As much as I hope you're not going to need it, you should be prepared. We'll get you a sheath while we are in Tosafo. Be careful with it until then."

"Thank you." Though I wanted to give it back, I understood his reasoning. I went back to my search for a spot to sleep. When I found a place that didn't have as many rocks, I grabbed my pack and pulled out a blanket.

"Candui and I will take turns sleeping by you when we're not standing watch," Richart said.

"I'll be fine by myself." He insisted one of them sleep by me every night, to keep me warm. "With the fire, I'll be plenty fine."

"We'll sleep on the side not facing the fire."

"I don't want you guys to be cold because of me."

"We'll be fine," Candui said, coming over to us.

I sighed. "If you insist."

She and I settled in for the night, after clearing some rocks while Richart paced around the fire, keeping watch on the darkness. When he was on the opposite side, Candui whispered to me, "I think he likes you."

I snorted. "He likes his baby."

"No. It's more than that." She went quiet as he approached us. Once he was farther away, she continued. "There's a spark in his eyes when he looks at you."

"A spark of anger that I ran away from him."

"Not the kind of spark I mean. You watch him, and you'll see."

He came around again, and we went silent.

Did he really like me? Most of the time, it felt like he tolerated me. I would take his protection for my child, but that was all. There would never be anything more between us. Nothing had developed in the years we were married, and then I ran away. No, Candui had to be mistaken. It wasn't me he liked; it was the fact that I carried his baby.

But could she be right?

CHAPTER FOURTEEN

"We should reach Tosafo in another day or two," Richart said. It was midday, and we'd been walking since morning.

I held in a groan. I didn't know if I could handle even more. The walking seemed to never stop. I always thought I was in good shape, until we came on this sun-forsaken journey. At least we hadn't run into any strange creatures.

We continued forward, not stopping or resting except at night. Every day I seemed to get a little stronger, but every day Richart seemed to push us a little more.

The sun moved through the sky as we trudged on. And on. And on. It was when the sun was low in the sky that the sound of a growl had me freezing in place. "What was that?"

Richart withdrew his sword. My dagger was in my hand because he'd insisted I hold it the entire time we were walking. The growl sounded again, from the left of me.

"Get behind me," Richart said.

I raced to get behind him, but before I could do so, a large, dark creature jumped out between us. It stood as high as my waist and looked almost like a boar, but it had reptilian skin, a bigger tail, and wicked-sharp teeth.

"What is that?" Candui said from my right.

The creature turned its head toward her. It eased forward, saliva dripping from its mouth. Whatever it was, it wasn't something we wanted to have a run-in with. It dived for Candui.

Instinct took over, and I went at it with my small dagger. The blade pierced its leathery skin, but only just, before falling to the ground without being deep enough to stick. The creature rounded on me, grunting and growling, its putrid breath making me gag.

"Hold real still," Richart called out to us. Then— "Over here, you stupid animal. Come on, you stupid, ankock."

That thing was an ankock? I thought they were stories, told to children to frighten them into being good.

This was no story.

It bounded for Richart. He swung at it, but barely missed. It lunged for him. Candui leapt closer, striking it hard between the eyes from behind with nothing but her fist. It reared at her, snarling.

Richart lunged toward it. Candui stumbled backward, tripping and falling with a cry. The ankock was on her. I had to do something, but what? I had no weapon. Nothing to fight with, except my body.

That was it.

I kicked at it, and at the same time, Richart dived for it with his sword. It turned toward me, causing Richart to miss.

Oops.

It faced me, Candui on the ground and Richart recovering. It ran for me, jumped on my chest, and knocked me down. I fell with an *umpf,* pain ratcheting through my body in an array of agony.

The ankock snarled down at me, baring its teeth next to my

cheek. I turned my head, wincing. This was the end of me, but the body went limp on top of me.

What happened?

The weight left, and Richart's face popped into view. "Are you hurt?" he asked.

Was I? I felt all in one piece, just very sore. Was the baby going to be all right after I'd been knocked to the ground and practically stood on? He had to be. I couldn't handle it if something happened to him because of my stupidity. "No. I think. Candui?"

Richart checked the carcass next to me and turned to my downed friend. I struggled into a sitting position and watched as he checked Candui over. She was awake—that was something— but her face was scrunched with pain.

I got to my feet, ignoring my aches and pains and worries over the baby, and hurried over to her. "Where does it hurt?"

"Ugh," was all she said.

"That doesn't sound good." I turned to Richart as she pointed to her right leg.

I glanced down and hurried to look away. It was swollen and bent in an unnatural angle.

"She has a broken lower leg." Richart said.

"From the ankock?" I didn't remember it going near her foot.

"Stumbled. Over. Rock." Her words were laced with pain.

"I'm sorry." This was my fault. If I'd done what Richart asked, he would have killed the beast at first try and not missed.

"Don't. Worry."

Richart gave me a look that might as well have been the worst glare. I was in serious trouble with him. I didn't think he'd forgive me any time soon.

I put a hand to my star stone. Could I...?

"I can set your leg, but it's going to hurt." Richart put a hand on each side of her injury.

98

I was looking at it again. I forced myself to glance away. I couldn't watch that without my stomach churning. I focused in on her face. She grimaced, and then screamed. It resounded through the woods. Birds took flight, screeching.

"Sorry," Richart said.

She whimpered.

The air filled with a sound that made my hair stand on end. Grunts and growls reverberated around us through the forest, sounding like the ankock, only a lot of them. Way too many.

Richart was on his feet, sword in hand, before I finished processing what was going on. He whispered, "Grab your dagger, Adriella, and stay with Candui."

I snatched it and moved back by her side. A quick glance at her told me she was out cold. If we had to die, she wouldn't feel any pain. If only there was something I could do. A way to help. I touched my star stone, but nothing came to mind with all the ankock coming into view and my brain shutting down. It'd been too long since I practiced.

Richart was on the move. "Stay still and silent." Once he was farther away, he shouted, "You stupid beasts, I'm over here. Come and get me."

I stared in horror as the forest came to life with varying sizes of ankock racing toward my husband, and there wasn't a thing I could do about it.

I held still as could be, not daring to disobey him this time after what happened before. As they neared him, they slowed down as he swung his sword long enough for me to take count. A good eight of them, the largest one smaller than our original attacker and the smallest about the size of a medium cat. That one I could handle, if its skin wasn't as tough as the last one, but the rest I wasn't so sure about.

I bit my bottom lip to keep from calling out. I needed to assist Richart, but I also needed to heed him. Besides, I didn't know what I could do. He was more on his own than I wanted him to be, but maybe if I held still long enough, it would be fine for me and Candui.

Losing my enemy should be fine, but he was the protector of my child for the time being. More than that, I didn't want to lose my husband. Not now, not ever. It was a surprise revelation, but there wasn't time to think on it.

I bit harder as I watched the ankock tighten the circle around him. He swung his sword around the circle, breaking them up. One yipped at him from behind. I wanted to call out a warning but remembered his warning to stay silent as it bit into his calf.

Moments later, the creature was sliced through. The rest jumped forward, and I knew without a doubt I'd lost him forever.

CHAPTER FIFTEEN

C andui moaned, and the animals on top of Richart stopped their snarling and switched their gazes to her. This was bad. One by one, they left Richart's body only to come at us. I didn't want to know what was going to happen to us.

She moaned again, and they snarkled. I stood with my dagger at the ready as they stalked forward. I might not live through this either, but I wasn't going to go down without a fight. Richart hadn't. Candui hadn't. I wouldn't, either.

The first one reached me. I slammed my arm down on its head and twisted, like Richart taught me. I pushed aside my surprise when it dropped to my feet, and somehow managed to keep hold of the handle of my dagger this time.

A second creature jumped for Candui, and I jammed my body against it as it went past, knocking it off course but also falling to the side. I tumbled to the ground and landed on the ankock. It grunted and squealed, wiggling beneath me. I grimaced and slammed my dagger into it.

More of them came at me. I swung the dagger, attempting to keep them at bay as long as possible. They were all coming toward me now, instead of Candui. As long as she didn't make another sound, she might make it. Though she wouldn't be able to do much, with her leg.

There wasn't more time to think about it. I hit toward anything that moved close to me, but they came faster and faster. I couldn't keep them off much longer.

I cringed. This was the end. "Sorry, little one."

A yell filled the air, and Richart burst forward, slicing through the creatures going for me. One after another, they fell to the ground, until the remaining ones turned and ran back to the forest, squealing as they went.

"Richart?" I asked, voice small. "I thought you were dead."

"Not yet."

He bled from a dozen scratches. "Why did you give up?

"What?" His words didn't make sense.

"You said *goodbye* to the baby. Why did you do that?"

"Because I thought I was dead. No one was going to make it."

"Don't do that ever again. Never give up." And then, he passed out.

I crawled over to him, wondering how I ended up in the forest with two people down, worrying that the ankock would come back any moment. It didn't look good, but Richart was right. I couldn't give up. Couldn't back down from the challenge.

I double checked Candui. She was still breathing, her pulse steady, beside the fact that she was out cold again and her leg was messed up. There was nothing else I could do for her at the moment. She'd be all right.

I turned my attention to Richart, ignoring the creatures' carcasses I had to wade through to get to him. He still held on tight to his sword, unwilling to let it go even in unconsciousness. His chest didn't seem to be moving. Maybe he was—

No. I wouldn't think that. Not again.

I put my head next to his mouth, to listen for breathing while

I watched his chest. Nothing. I clamped my jaw shut against the well of emotions, and as I did so, I felt a warm caress of breath across my cheek.

He was alive.

I turned to my pack, grabbed the first material I could find, and shredded it into strips with my dagger. I dabbed at his wounds before tying up the ones I could. I wanted there to be more I could do for him, but that would require the star stone, night, and more skills than I had. Though dusk wasn't far off, it was distant enough that I didn't know if it would do much good.

After making certain I'd done everything I could for him, I stood and took in our surroundings. I didn't know what to do, but we'd need a fire. We wouldn't be going anywhere any time soon.

I dragged the dead ankock aside and gathered as much wood as I could, before pulling flint and steel from my pack. We each had some, but I hadn't used mine yet. Luckily, I'd started the stove enough times to know how to do it.

When the fire was going, I wanted to make certain none of those things would come back. I built it as high as I dared and then gathered more wood to throw on as the fire died down. I adjusted Candui and Richart to make them as comfortable as possible, putting their packs beneath their heads and covering them with their blankets.

Then I sat and waited, holding onto my dagger with a death grip. I wouldn't let anything happen to them again. Not on my watch. Richart had done so much for me these past several days, and Candui even longer. I wasn't about to let them get hurt now.

Despite the soreness of my body and the growing dark, I stayed awake and moving. When my stomach grumbled, I ate. And I watched, waiting for them to wake up.

Candui groaned again. This time, no creatures came running for her. I went to her side, hoping she'd come around and have some ideas as to how to help Richart. He was so quiet. So still. It would have been better if we had a run-in with the zasin than those moon-blasted ankock.

"Candui? Can you hear me?" I asked.

She moaned and fluttered her eyes open. "Water," she rasped.

I got a water skin for her and helped her drink. Once she had enough, I asked, "How do you feel?"

"Like my leg is on fire. What happened?"

"We were attacked by ankock, and you did something to your leg. I think it's broken. Richart would know better than me, but he's..." I glanced at his still form.

She turned her head toward him. "What happened to him?"

I described the attack while she kept her gaze trained on him.

"He's breathing, you say? And you wrapped up his wounds?"

"Yes. What else can I do?"

She closed her eyes. "Just give him time. He'll wake when he wakes."

That wasn't comforting. "*When*, though. Right? Not *if*?"

She sighed. "It should be *when*."

Should be. None of this was comforting. "Can I get you anything?"

"I'm fine."

"You don't want anything to eat?" I was hungry, even after eating dinner, and she'd had nothing.

"Definitely not."

I settled in to wait again, wishing there was more I could do. Two of the moons appeared in the sky, lighting up our little patch of fire brighter. I closed my eyes without meaning to. That was a bad sign.

I stood so I wouldn't fall asleep and paced around the fire, making sure to stay close to Richart and Candui. The two of them had me on edge.

She drifted in and out of sleep through the night, asking for some herbal powder we had mixed for pain a few times through-out, but not much else. At least she was lucid, even if she was in torment. The longer Richart was out, the more I worried about him—the more I wanted him to wake up and say something, even if it was to chew me out.

Still, nothing.

I watched the three moons move across the sky and the stars twinkle in their brightness until they were lined up just so. I looked to Candui, to make certain she was asleep, and then went over to Richart. I took my star stone out from under-neath my tunic and pressed it against his palm. I needed this to work.

I focused in on the magic held within the stone and the align-ment of the stars, using them to heal him. As I used the magic to assess his wounds, I found that he'd had major blood loss. I did what I could to restore him, using the correct stars to guide my stone and let it pull the power from them.

Richart groaned. I hurried to put my star stone back under my tunic, making sure it was well hidden. He blinked and looked up at me.

I couldn't help but stare into his eyes and give him a faint smile. "Welcome back."

"Why is it dark?"

"You've been out for a while. It's almost morning. I was worried you wouldn't wake again."

He grunted. "I'm fine. Why don't you get some sleep, and I'll stand watch?"

I couldn't help the laugh that sprang from me. "You're in no condition to keep watch. You've been unconscious for hours."

"It can't have been that long."

"It was."

"The last thing I remember is seeing you protecting Candui with your body."

"And then you protected me with yours, almost losing your life in the process."

He was silent for so long, I didn't think he was going to reply. "You exaggerate," he said.

"Not hardly. What do you need?"

"A big dose of pain powder."

"I can do that. Been helping Candui with it all night, so I should be pretty good with it about now."

As I started to put the powder in some water, he said, "She's all right?"

"Awake off and on, but in a lot of discomfort. Her leg is really bothering her."

He didn't say anything further. Was he thinking what I was thinking? Was Candui going to be able to walk in the morning? I didn't know how to fix a broken bone with magic. I was lucky I knew what to do for Richart. My mother had taught me so much, but without people to practice on, it was difficult to learn.

After I gave him the medicine, he fell back asleep, though this time I was more confident he'd wake back up.

Time dragged on, taking too long in bringing about morning. There were no further animal attacks, but I wasn't sure what was going on either. They could be waiting for me to fall asleep so they could attack unhindered. I didn't think they were that smart.

I needed to use the bathroom but didn't dare leave them both while they were down, so I did a little dance, waiting for the sun to rise. But it wouldn't matter. There was still a problem. The ankock attacked during the light last time. What would keep them from doing so again?

I made a break for it and took care of my business as quickly as I could, then hurried back to them.

Richart was getting to his feet, sword in hand. "Where were you? I thought something bad happened to you."

"I needed to use a tree."

He sighed, dropped his sword back on the ground, and plopped down next to it. "You can't leave without telling me."

I bristled. I saw his point, but what was I supposed to do? "You weren't awake, and I needed to go."

"Then wake me up."

"When you were just attacked by a bunch of ankock. Right."

He settled back down, lying on his pack and pulling the blanket over him. "I can see I'm not going to win with you."

"Not this time."

He grunted. "I'm going to stand watch now."

"You do that from right where you're at."

"You need sleep."

"Not as much as you do." Though he was right. Exhaustion was pulling at me. Sleep would be a welcome relief, but I couldn't give into it yet.

"I'll be up in a minute, to take over."

I didn't say anything, just let him drift off to sleep as I continued to keep watch.

CHAPTER SIXTEEN

A t some point, Richart woke and convinced me to rest while
he stood guard. Well, more like lie guard.

It took some time to fall asleep, despite being exhausted,
because I worried about him and his ability to stay on his feet. He
seemed steadier now that he'd had some rest, though. Between
sleep and my magic, he was doing better.

With that thought, I was able to get some rest. I woke to
voices and dark sky. I'd slept the day through. I stretched and sat
up to find that Richart was keeping watch on his feet and talking
to Candui, who sat propped up against a log.

"Evening, sleepy head," Candui said to me.

"You're one to talk," I replied. "You slept most of the night
and day away. How are you feeling?"

"Like an ankock bit my leg, instead of me tripping over something to break it."

I cringed. It didn't sound good either way. "I'm sorry. Do you
need anything?"

"Richart has kept me well-medicated."

And he had wrapped it up some way too. "Need something to eat?"

She chuckled, though I could hear the pain laced within it. "I'm not hungry at all, but I'm sure you're famished."

I laughed. "That's not hard to guess. It's difficult to be anything but hungry lately." And tired, but I wasn't about to admit that.

I pulled an apple out of my bag and munched on it. The juice was sweet, but only just. Otherwise, it was flavorless. I ate it anyway. There was only so much food; I couldn't afford to be picky.

"I still can't believe ankock are real," I said.

"Me neither." Candui shifted positions, her face lined with pain. "Next thing we hear will be that magic isn't the most disgusting, evil practice in all of Erta."

I forced my expression to remain neutral, though I wanted to clench my teeth or run away screaming. The tales told about magic were darker than any story you could hear about trolls, orcs, dragons, or any other creature. Anyone with magic was hunted down, flayed within an inch of their life, and left to rot, chained up where the public could see. If that didn't finish them off, the crowd would.

My stomach churned. I didn't want to think about it. I might know magic to be good in the right hands, but everyone else believed it to be of demons. Something vile and evil. Maybe I shouldn't have risked healing Richart, but I couldn't very well sit back and do nothing.

"Magic is evil," Richart agreed.

If they expected me to concede... I changed the subject as soon as it felt comfortable to do so. "What's the plan from here?"

They both grew silent. This wasn't a good sign. Finally, Candui said, "You should leave me behind. I don't know how I'm going to be able to travel through the forest like this. It'd be better for everyone else if I stayed."

"I don't think so," I said.

At the same time as Richart said, "Now wait a minute."

She held up a hand to stop our protests. "I know you don't like the idea, but we've got to get Adriella out of the woods and to somewhere safe. This is the only logical solution."

"It's completely unacceptable," I said. "We'll figure something out. I'm not leaving you in the middle of these woods, at the mercy of the ankock and whatever other monsters are on the prowl."

"But—"

"You won't fight me on this." I made my tone firm. When I glanced at Richart, he gave me a half-smile and a nod. He agreed with me, even if it might put the baby in danger. What was the point of saving my child if I inadvertently killed my friend along the way?

"Then what do you propose?" she asked. "We don't have enough food to stay in these woods forever. Besides, with the creatures in here, it wouldn't be a safe idea anyway."

"I could carry you out," Richart said.

"The entire way?" She lifted her eyebrows. "And what if we were attacked again? You'd be bound up by me, which would mean the death of us all. I'm not seeing any good options here."

"What if we made you crutches? If we found two sturdy limbs that were long enough, you could use them to help you walk. Then you'd come with us without tying up Richart." It should work, even if it would be slower than any of us would like.

She didn't say anything for a moment. "I don't know. Won't that take too long?"

"It's a good idea. I'm not certain how to make them, though," Richart said.

"I can, with your help." I'd seen my father make things out of

110

wood before, and he taught me a few tricks along the way. I stood. "I'm going to go hunting for the right pieces of wood."

"Not in the forest alone, you're not." His voice was firm.

"I went in there many times alone when you were unconscious."

"But there are beasts out there," Candui said. "Here we at least have the fire, which seems to have scared them off."

For the time being. Who knew if it was the fire, or if they were still licking their wounds from the fight?

She must have noticed I wasn't convinced because she said, "Please stay with me, Adriella. I'd feel more comfortable if you were here."

With a sigh, I sat back down. "Don't you want Richart and his sword to protect you?"

"He won't go far, and I'll know you and the baby are safe."

"It's settled, then," Richart said, not giving me a chance to fight. He brought his sword over to Candui and used it to measure how tall she was. "Hopefully, it doesn't take too long for me to find something the right shape and size."

"It doesn't have to be perfect." I didn't want him gone longer than he absolutely needed to be.

"All right. Holler if you need me. I won't go far." He grabbed an ax that hung on the side of his pack and headed for the woods.

Once he was out of earshot, she said, "Thank you for staying."

"You've got to tell me something."

Her voice took on a note of caution. "What is that?"

"Why do you care so much about me and the baby?"

She got a far off look in her eyes. "You have a right to know."

I didn't say anything, though I desperately wanted to.

"You know elves don't conceive as often as humans. Well, I'm one hundred and twenty-three."

She looked more like twenty-three, though I wasn't surprised she was older. I was surprised she was over one hundred. It felt more like she was my age of twenty-six, maybe just a few years my elder. Not in her hundreds.

"Through twenty-one years of marriage, I didn't get with child. I started to think it wasn't possible. That maybe I was one of those elves who never had a baby of their own. Shortly after I gave up hope, I realized I was pregnant. I was thrilled, my husband not so much. Not like I expected him to be. He went into a rage, saying he'd tried to prevent it, and I should never have gotten pregnant. I don't know how I missed it, but he hated children, never wanted one, and had been taking herbs to try to stop us from conceiving." She gave a sigh.

My heart was heavy for her. If only there was a way to show her my sorrow. To grieve with her, but I didn't think she'd welcome it. To make matters worse, I had a horrible feeling this was only the start of her story.

"Throughout my pregnancy, I tried to avoid him as much as I could, but it's difficult when you share a small house. I thought when I had the baby he'd change his mind. That he would come to love our child," she said. "I was wrong. So very wrong."

A tear streamed down her cheek. I pulled out a handkerchief and handed it to her.

She wiped the moisture from her skin. "After the baby was born, he pretended like he cared about him enough that I thought he was all right with him. My sweet little boy was about six months old when he made it to childcare before I did. I didn't think anything of it and went home, but no one was there.

"I believed maybe he stopped to talk to a friend or had an errand to run, so I started dinner. When it was done, they hadn't shown up, and I was starting to worry, but I kept going. As I got dinner on the table, my husband came in alone. Our son was not in sight." Her expression grew stoic. "When I asked him about it, he said he got rid of the problem. Gave him away."

"Oh, Candui." I put my hand on her shoulder. What could I do to help with that type of heartache?

"Now you know why I hate my husband so much," she said. "Why I had to get away from him. I tried to find my son—tried so hard to figure out who he'd given him to—but there was no sign of my child. No one knew where he went. No one cared. My husband had every right to do what he wanted with him, and there wasn't a thing I could do about it. I was expected to stay by his side and be happy with the choice he made, but I hated him from that moment on."

"How long ago was this?"

"Seven years ago."

I held in a gasp. "And there's still no sign of him?"

She shook her head.

I couldn't imagine how she must feel. Richart and I might not be on the best of terms, but he cared about our child and would never do anything to harm him.

I couldn't make this better. Couldn't fix what happened. But I could be there for Candui, and that was what I did. While Richart continued his search, sometimes coming back to ask if this branch or that limb would work, I sat with her and let her know I was there for whatever she might need.

CHAPTER SEVENTEEN

The crutches worked—mostly. Candui was slower than she liked. Really, than any of us would have liked, but she was moving forward.

We'd left early that morning, making very sluggish but steady progress. Being away from the fire had me nervous, though. I didn't like feeling like the ankock could come back any moment.

"You should go on without me," she said. "I can catch up later tonight."

I wasn't having any of that. "First—no. Second, even if we did let you, it's likely that you wouldn't be able to find us in this mess of a forest. I'm not sure how Richart knows where we're going."

"Easy," he said. "See those mountains to the west?"

"The Breka Mountains?" I'd heard nothing but horror stories about those, much like about the ankock. If the ankock were real, how much of the rumors about the Breka Mountains and Umpi Forest next to it were true?

"The very ones. We're keeping our distance from them and the Tower Line, though the closer we get to the Tower Line, the sooner we'll reach Tosafo."

The Tower Line was exactly that. A group of towers lined up across the entrance to Umpi Forest. I didn't know much about it other than monsters got through sometimes. I used to think that was a something to frighten children. Now I wasn't positive. "I didn't realize Tosafo was so close to the Tower Line." There was nothing like the stories I'd heard about it.

Richart looked right at me. "Scared?"

"Not hardly." I was too busy being petrified.

"You should be. Tosafo is right next to the Tower Line, and occasionally, things get through."

"Things?" I asked. "What type of things?"

"I'm not sure you're ready to hear about them," he said.

"Tell us." I'd rather hear it now, than see it later and not be expecting it.

"Orcs, ankock, trolls, yipra, griffins. You think of anything scary, and it's past the Tower Line."

"Next you're going to tell us there are dragons in there." Though if there are ankock, maybe the others are just as real. I was pretty certain orcs were real since people spoke of seeing them sometimes, though I'd never seen one. What else could Erta be filled with that I had never seen before?

Richart went quiet.

The *thud, thud, thud* of Candui's crutches filled the air. It was difficult to watch her struggle and not be able to do more than lift a tree branch out of her way. And not a heavy one either. More than wanting to help her through her struggles, I wished there was something I could do about her missing child.

What type of husband and father would do something like give away his child? I couldn't fathom it. My parents weren't perfect, but they loved me. Richart wasn't the best husband, but he appeared to care about our child. Even my brother, who'd teased me mercilessly growing up, took good care of his children and was willing to keep my secret about the baby. It was all I could think about.

"THIS IS TOSAFO?" I asked as we looked upon a village that was tinier than I imagined.

"There are more houses a ways off than you see here. People like their space in this town, but yes, that's Tosafo," Richart responded.

"I can't believe you grew up here. It's so small."

We crouched behind some bushes, looking on the one and only dirt street of the small village. And *small* was an understatement. There had to be fewer than one hundred people living here. How did they function? It existed mostly to help support the Tower Line, but this seemed not nearly enough.

"Now you know why I was surprised they pulled me to a different town. I always expected to become a zasin, but I thought they'd need me here, helping guard the town and taking my turn on the Tower Line."

"Why did they move you to Bola?" Candui asked.

He shrugged. "I have no idea."

Probably because he was more skilled than he gave himself credit for and they needed someone to be in charge of Bola. He wouldn't admit it, but the other soldiers always praised his skills and leadership, at least the few times they spoke to me.

"Here's what we're going to do," he said. "I'll go into town and make certain no one's come here looking for you two. Once I'm positive it's safe, I'll come back for you."

At this point, they were most likely looking for him as well, but neither I nor Candui mentioned it. "Be safe."

"And bring back something for Adriella to eat," Candui said. "I can hear her stomach growling."

He chuckled as my face heated, then said, "I'll be back soon."

We watched him go and sat down to wait, hidden as we were.

"How long do you think it will take him?" I was hungry but also worried for him. If the zasin were looking for him and he walked right to them here, it wasn't going to end well. I had no doubts he would keep quiet about Candui and me being here, but we'd lose everything despite that. We had no way to rescue him or replenish our food sources. No way to get away from the zasin that would come looking for us.

Candui couldn't move fast, and though Richart was training me when we stopped for the night, I was no match for zasin who'd been working at their skills since they were fourteen or earlier.

"Stop worrying," she said. "Everything is going to be fine."

"How did you know I was worrying?"

"You were biting your lip."

I sighed. I hadn't realized I was doing it. "Being anxious is my specialty. Especially since I became pregnant."

"It's hard not to, but Richart will take care of things."

I was biting my lip again. I made myself stop. "What if his aunt doesn't like me? What if she suspects? Worse, what if the zasin are already here, after us?"

"You know, stressing about those things doesn't mean they're not going to happen. What will be, will be. They're not worth stressing about, though that's easier to say than to do."

"You're not afraid?"

"I'm petrified, but gnawing on it won't do any good."

She was right. Of course, she was. But that didn't mean I could turn off the worry. I could attempt to redirect it, though. "How's your leg?"

"It's good."

"Liar."

She shook her head with a little laugh. "How do you know I'm not telling the truth?"

"Because it has to hurt. I can't imagine it not. Besides, your forehead is wrinkled and has been for the past couple hours." It got that way the longer into the day we went. It must have been hard on her, to keep pace and deal with the pain.

"Fine. It hurts. Nothing I can't handle, though."

That I was certain of. She was tougher than I ever expected.

"He's coming back."

I glanced up, and a tightness I didn't know was in my chest loosened. He wasn't chased by zasin and didn't seem upset. Now, if only he had good news...

He went around the forest, not walking straight for us but getting here quickly, anyway. He said, "No one is looking for us. Let's go meet my aunt."

The tightness in my chest returned tenfold. "You're sure?"

"Positive." He helped me to my feet before turning his attention to Candui.

Once she was leaning on her makeshift crutches, we headed away from town, to the south. "My aunt lives away from most folks, like a lot of people around here prefer. Seems backwards, being so close to Umpi Forest, but they're a tough people."

I wanted to ask more about her, but I didn't know what to ask, to prepare for this meeting. I never met any of his family. She wasn't there for the wedding ceremony. It took place in Windago, where he came to pick me up, and she couldn't get away from work. My family was lucky to get away for an hour to see the Sunsit leader wed us.

We walked a ways before a house came into view. It was the smallest house I'd ever seen, even tinier than the building I lived in with Richart back in Bola. "How does someone not get claustrophobic in such a cramped space?" I asked Richart.

"My aunt doesn't spend much time inside. She's usually out

in the town or tending her garden, which is bigger than her home. Besides, it's just her. My uncle passed away years ago, and I built this place for her when I was old enough to know how, with the help of my friends after we'd get off work."

"You built this place?" I had a newfound respect for him. Despite its small size, it looked well constructed, the logs close together, filled with something to keep the wind and other natural elements out. The chimney at the top of the building puffed smoke in a steady stream that curled up in the air.

"With help." He stopped and faced us. "Listen. My aunt can be a little strange at times, but please be kind to her. She's the only family I have left."

"I wouldn't dream of doing anything to hurt someone you care about," I said.

"Just me," he muttered.

"What was that?" Candui asked.

"Nothing," Richart and I said at the same time.

"R—right. Let's get going, shall we?" she said.

She had to be ready to sit down and see if his aunt had any medicine that would help her feel better, or at least take the edge off.

Richart lead the way and knocked on the door. After two more tries with no one answering, he said, "Let's try around back."

We followed him past the building, and a massive garden came into view. A gnarled woman tended to the part that was close to the house, so it was no surprise we hadn't seen her on our way in. She looked up, her weathered face wrinkling even more, but becoming more charming as a huge grin graced it. "Richart. What brings you here?"

Her voice was clearer than I expected, with her lined features and stooped shoulders.

"I wanted to bring my wife and a friend by," he responded.

"It's been too long since I was married, and you didn't get to meet them."

"Good thing you did. I've missed you terribly. Before I get to your bride, come give me a hug."

He strode over, bending down to wrap his arms around her. She appeared so thin and frail next to him. Once they pulled apart, she said, "And I've been anxious to see this wife of yours."

"This is Adriella."

I stepped forward. "It's a pleasure to meet you."

"And this is our good friend, Candui," he continued.

Candui stepped up beside me and gave a similar greeting. I waited for his aunt to say something negative about Candui being an elf, but she said not a word.

"This is Scerta, my beloved, wise aunt."

"You flatter me, boy."

He smiled at her in a way I'd never seen before, that had me wishing that smile was meant for me. "I said nothing that isn't true, aunt."

She hobbled over to him and patted his cheek. "You're a good boy." She faced us. "I don't have much room to put you up in, but you're welcome to stay with me. It may mean sleeping on the floor, but it's better than outside."

Which was what we had been doing. "I'm certain it will be fine," I said.

"Come on in, then, and bring your things. Looks like you traveled light."

"I'm afraid it's because we can't stay long," Richart said. "We'd love to spend the rest of spring and summer with you, but we can't be away for that amount of time."

"Just as well. I probably won't be alive that long."

He shook his head. "You've been saying that for years, aunt. If I didn't know any better, I'd say you had some elf blood in you."

"You and the rest of the town, but I'm only an old human.

You know elves and humans don't mix." Scerta grabbed a cane I hadn't noticed leaning against the house and headed around front. She opened the door and hobbled inside, and we followed.

She lit a lamp. "It's not big, but it's perfect for me. You can put your things under the bed."

The bed was more of a tiny cot. Being small, she didn't need anything bigger. We put our packs beneath it and looked around the room. Beside the bed, there was a stove. Near it was the smallest table I'd ever seen, with one chair.

Despite how tiny everything was, it was well constructed, the wood floors worn smooth beneath our feet, and not a flaw to be seen. Granted, I didn't build houses, but it looked like Richart and his friends had done a good job providing for his aunt. There wasn't much room on the floor for us to sleep, but at least the wind wouldn't be tearing at us all night long.

"This is lovely," I said.

She grunted. What was that about?

Richart pecked her on the cheek. "I hate to run so quickly, but there are a few things I need to take care of in town. Are these ladies fine here until I get back?"

"I'll put them to work."

He chuckled. "I'd expect nothing less."

He nodded at both me and Candui and then left the house. I listened to his footsteps crunch away, wishing I could go with him rather than stay here. I wasn't certain what to do or say. Thankfully, Candui took over for me as Scerta took a seat at the table.

"How do you like it in Tosafo?" Candui asked.

Scerta looked from her to me and back again. "It's a town. I live and work in it, much the same as anyone does." She smacked her lips. "I suppose you'll be wanting something for dinner."

"Only if it's not too much trouble," I said. "We can manage if you'd like."

Not that we had anything left to manage with.

"Can't let Richart bring guests into my home and not feed them. Bring that bowl over to me." She spent the next hour ordering me about, but it was well worth it for the smells coming from her oven. Freshly baked bread. When was the last time I had that? The scent was warm and homey. It made my stomach growl in anticipation.

After she had the bread in the oven and a pot of beef and vegetables going, she settled back down, leaving Candui in charge of checking the food every so often to make certain it didn't burn.

"What did my nephew need in town?" They were the first words she'd spoken that didn't have to do with preparing food.

"He said he was going to talk to a friend," I responded. It seemed a safe enough answer.

"Ah. Aphier. They were the closest of boys growing up. The two of them could only be separated at bed time. Even then, it was questionable. There never were two happier children, until Richart's parents died."

I wanted to ask how that happened. I understood they were no longer alive, but I didn't know how they passed away. Richart never spoke of them, except once to tell me they weren't with us anymore. It didn't feel right to ask, though. If he wanted me to know, he'd tell me himself.

"He'd better be home in time for dinner if he wants anything to eat," she said. "I remember the time he made mud pies for a meal. Smashed them into a wee girl's face when she wouldn't play along with him."

"Richart?" That didn't sound like him at all.

"He was a little rascal, always getting into one mischief or another. I think that's why they chose him to be a zasin. Used it as a way to channel his energy. Moons know he didn't listen to anything I had to tell him. It worked, though. Look at him now, leader of the zasin in Bola, with a wife pretty enough to please any eye."

I glanced down, my cheeks heating.

"If only they had stationed him closer to home... But it's probably for the best. He's better able to grow away from here. Away from tragedy and memories we would all rather avoid." She shook her head. "Listen to me go on. You girls must have much more interesting stories. Tell me about your lives."

What could we tell her that wouldn't give away the fact that we were on the run? I didn't want to put her in danger or give away secrets, but that was what my life was lately.

"I grew up in Cenda," Candui said. "It was much bigger than this village and Bola, where my current residence is, but I like the smaller towns better. There's something homier about them."

I didn't realize that. It was nice to talk to someone else so I could better understand my own friend. Though it also made me realize I had a lot to chat about. Sure, I couldn't talk about what was going on right now, but there was a history with her nephew she might be interested in.

"That's a good choice," Scerta said. "I like my space, roaming away where the high king cares little for influencing the people. And don't go and look shocked. I shouldn't talk that way, but no one out here cares. We all like that we're given freedom because we're too small to make a difference. We're left in peace, and I wouldn't have it any other way. I think the bread's done. Will you check it, dear?"

Not certain if she was talking to me or Candui, I said, "Sure."

The oven let out waves of heat when I opened it. I knocked against the hard crust of the bread, and when it sounded hollow, used a thick towel to pull it out. The front door opened as I put it on the table next to Scerta, and Richart walked in with another man.

"I knew you'd bring Aphier home with you," Scerta said.

"You'll have to eat standing up, but I had the girls make enough for your big appetites."

Scerta was in the only seat, and Candui was propped up on the cot. With the men in the house, it was downright cramped.

"Thank you, Aunt." Richart went over to the stove and dished up while Scerta sliced the bread and passed it around. Soon everyone had food. I dived into mine like I hadn't seen food in a month, though I tried to remember my manners. It was difficult with how much my stomach was growling.

While we ate, Richart introduced us to his childhood friend, Aphier. The man nodded at us. "It's good to meet you, ladies." He was a little shorter than Richart, though still big for a human, not as tall as Candui. He had a sandy-brown head of hair, clear brown eyes, and a well-rounded face. Fairly neutral features.

His gaze continued to stray to me as we ate. Why? He was a little shorter than Richart, though still tall.

"What work are you a part of?" Candui asked.

He glanced back to her. "I'm a zasin like Richart. At first, I thought it was so they wouldn't separate us, but then he went and got assigned a bride." He looked back at me. "And she looks like quite the bride, Richart. She's glowing."

Richart caught my eyes, a look I couldn't understand in his. "She is."

How could he just admit that? He might as well have told them both I was pregnant. Everyone knew pregnant women had a glow about them. I couldn't be pointed out like that, but then maybe he felt so comfortable around these people that saying such a thing was natural. I wasn't looking to excuse it, but Aphier wasn't calling me out for being pregnant and no one was running to the other zasin. It would be all right.

The discomfort knotted in my chest said otherwise.

CHAPTER EIGHTEEN

The rest of the evening went more smoothly. Aphier and Richart reminisced over stories from when they were children. I tried to focus on what they were saying, but my mind kept dozing off. After dinner, Aphier took his leave, and we settled on the floor to sleep. The wood beneath me was hard. Despite that, I fell asleep quickly.

I woke to the sound of whispers. I blinked and stretched. Light streamed in the window.

"Your wife, the sleepyhead, is finally awake," Scerta said.

I yawned. "Sorry. I didn't mean to sleep so long."

"Don't worry about it." Richart handed me a plate of bread and an apple left over from fall.

I downed them both, followed by a long drink of milk, before I picked myself off the floor. After using the necessary out back to the side of the garden, I came back in to find Aphier was back. Scerta headed out to her garden. She didn't say anything as she passed me on the way out, closing the door behind her.

Everyone was silent for a moment before Aphier said, "So you want to tell me what's going on?"

"Can't an old friend come for a visit?" Richard asked.

"Not in most of Erta. The high king has much tighter control over Bola than he does here. A visit wouldn't be allowed."

Candui, Richart, and I exchanged glances, but no one said anything.

"Just tell me," Aphier said. "It can't be that bad, unless you got your wife pregnant."

I clenched my jaw and avoided looking at anyone.

Aphier gave a low whistle. "That's it, isn't it? You're going to be a daddy."

"You can't tell anyone," Richart said.

"I'll keep your secret, but why come here? What are you hoping to accomplish?"

I glanced at Richart, who said, "Honestly, it was the only place I could think to run to. They're probably going to be on our trail soon, if they aren't already. I don't want to bring them here—hopefully, they don't come—but I had to do something. If it was your child, would you let the Sunsire kill it?"

The strength in Richart's voice made me stand straighter.

"No," Aphier replied softly. "I wouldn't. But you have to have a plan. You can't stay here. Nowhere in Erta is safe."

"Then we leave Erta," I said, surprising myself.

"Erta is everywhere," Candui replied. "Where do you think we should go?"

"Umpi Forest."

She hissed. "You want us to cross the Tower Line? Do you know what's out there?"

"It can't be any worse than the ankock we faced."

"You faced an ankock?" Aphier asked, respect in his voice.

"Several." More than I ever wanted to see.

"Well, I'll tell you this," he said. "You might be able to handle them, but there's more in Umpi Forest than ankock. There are things darker than you could have ever imagined in those woods.

Without a guide who knows what they're doing, you're dead within a day. If you make it that long."

That sobered me. If we couldn't go into the forest, there was nowhere else left to run. Not unless we made it north to Nortu and crossed the waters, but that came with perils of its own.

"Don't worry," Aphier said. "I know just the person to guide you."

"I don't think so." Richart's voice was curt.

"What? You don't think I can help you through the forest?"

I stared at Aphier. "You want to lead us?"

"Yes, ma'am. I can take you in there and keep everyone safe."

"Until the baby is born? Even then, we'll have to continue to hide for many years." Hope flickered inside me, though I tried to dampen it.

"No," Richart said.

"You got to give me more than that," Aphier replied.

"Fine," Richart said. "No, you aren't taking us into the forest. You have your own life to consider. It's dangerous, who knows if we'll survive, and even if we do, anyone who walks into that forest and comes out again will forever be an enemy of the high king. Adriella, Candui, and I already are. I can't put that on you."

"Too late. I've already done things the high king would have me put to death for if he found out about." Aphier tapped his chin with a finger. "I'll take you. I know how to live off the land. I've spent more time in Umpi Forest than others I know. If someone can keep you safe there, it's me."

"What have you done?" Richart asked.

Aphier shrugged. "Doesn't matter. What does matter is that you have a pregnant wife when the high king is on a vicious hunt to murder the one meant to kill him. In all likelihood, with the number of babies out there, that's not your child, but he doesn't care one way or the other. He'll take out everybody who's a threat to him. I'm against anyone who kills children."

We were all silent until Candui said, "Aren't we all?"

"No. Not everyone is," Aphier said. "Which is why it's more important than ever to get out of here as soon as possible."

"I can't let you do this with your life," Richart said.

"You don't have a choice. I'm coming, even if I have to hunt you down because you snuck out without me."

Was this a good turn of events or a bad one? It had to be good because I knew no other way to get through Umpi Forest. "Are we going to reside in the woods for the next few years, or try to make it over the Breka Mountains?"

"And face dragons? Are you crazy?" Aphier said.

"Dragons aren't real. Everyone knows that." At least, I thought they weren't. After the past week, I wasn't sure of anything anymore.

"Right. Well, I don't know anything about the Breka Mountains. I only know about the forest, so I suggest we find a place to live there."

"Is there going to be enough food for everyone? Will we be safe? Will we be able to raise a child? To have one born there?" Richart asked.

I studied Aphier carefully, anxious to hear his response.

"Safer than here or anywhere else in Erta. I'm confident we'll be able to uncover some place safe for the little one."

If only I shared his confidence, but at the moment, it was all we had. "When do we leave?"

"The sooner, the better," Richart said. "I'm going to give my goodbyes to my aunt. Can you find food in the forest?"

"I will," Aphier said.

Richart nodded. I was grateful for his friend's help, but we were placing so much trust on Aphier. Everything was happening too fast.

"I should go with you." I didn't want to, but it felt like the right thing to do. She'd been kind to let us in her home and share her food. I should thank her for that. The only reason I didn't wish to was because I wanted to interrogate Aphier more. I wanted all the information I could get about the forest, but that wouldn't change things. If Richart trusted him, I'd have to, as well —cautiously.

"My aunt would appreciate your doing so," Richart said.

"I'm going to go pack. I'll meet you where we used to play as kids." Aphier was out the door before anyone could respond.

"I'll get our packs together," Candui said.

I glanced at her crutches. No one had mentioned those or her coming with us in that condition, but I couldn't imagine leaving her behind; it would be too dangerous for her. But how would she manage through the forest?

We'd be slow—that was certain. Once we were in the forest, though, it wouldn't matter. As long as we didn't run into any creatures we needed to hurry away from. I wouldn't leave her to them. She'd done so much for me. I would stick by her side whatever it took.

"Thank you. We'll be back in a moment." I couldn't imagine it taking longer than that.

She nodded.

Richart reached over and handed me a sheath. "Keep your dagger in this. It will be within easy reach but safe."

"Thank you." I took it from him.

He led the way out of the house. He was silent as we moved around back. I kept expecting him to say something. Anything. But he didn't. Then again, neither did I. Instead, I hoped for a future that was brighter than it felt.

How was I going to raise a baby in the Umpi Forest? It was an impossible feat, yet I'd accomplish it. It would work. I had to be positive about it. We'd make it, and my little one would grow up knowing how to take care of himself in an environment like that. It had to be a good thing.

We found Scerta in much the same place as when we came yesterday. Richart was the first to speak. "Thank you for your hospitality, aunt. I'm afraid we have to be going now."

"Already? You just got here."

"Yes. We have some other places we need to visit, but we were glad for the chance to see you."

"And I was happy to meet you," I added on.

It was clear she wasn't taking to it, though. Her eyes showed her mind working. It was strange that we'd come so far and stay only a day, but we couldn't afford to linger longer under the circumstances. Letting her think we were peculiar was a much better option.

She turned her attention away from me and focused on Richart. "I'm grateful you came by, boy. I wish they hadn't taken you away from me."

"I wish the same." He gave her a hug.

"Thank you again, for all you've done for us," I said.

She pursed her lips and nodded.

That was it, then. We walked back toward the front of the house. I expected more. Not sure more of what, but something. It seemed strange to have such quick *farewells* with his only living relative when it took much longer with my family. Perhaps it was just their way or the fact that my family was bigger.

When we reached the entrance, I expected Richart to go in, but he turned to me. "Thank you for doing that. My aunt really appreciated it."

She had a funny way of showing it.

He grabbed for the door handle, but I spoke before he could open it. "Do you really believe we can do this?"

"I believe it's our best option."

"But you don't think it's going to work."

He rubbed the back of his neck. "The truth is, it might work, but it's going to be tough. I grew up next to this forest, and it was

130

never easy. I imagine going into it is only going to be harder. But compared to our other choices, this is by far the best choice."

That wasn't very comforting.

He put a hand on my shoulder. "It's going to be fine. I promised you I would do everything in my power to take care of the baby, and that's not changed. I'll make certain the baby is well cared for, even if he has to grow up in the Umpi Forest."

If we lived through it. I sighed. "Thank you. That means a lot. I'm just worried."

And it was difficult to put those worries away. They multiplied. But we had a plan. I only hoped it worked.

CHAPTER NINETEEN

By the time we got to the spot out of town, where Richart played with Aphier as a child, Aphier was there with a giant pack on his shoulders. "Took you long enough."

"It's my fault," Candui said. "I slow everything down."

Even now we had to walk more slowly to keep up with her. But if it meant she could come with us and stay safe, it was worth it.

Aphier stood. "That's all right. We need to wait for dark to cross the Tower Line anyway."

I bit my bottom lip. I couldn't believe we were going to pass over it. It seemed like a feat greater than I could accomplish. What was more, the Tower Line was supposed to keep the wild things out. What were we doing, going toward those savage beings?

"I managed to grab some food on my way out," he continued. "It won't last long, but it will give us a chance to find resources in the forest. I have some ideas of where a few are, but we're going to need more and deeper in."

"How far in have you gone?" Richart asked.

"Far enough to know my way around parts of it. We'll be fine. It's not nearly as bad as everyone says."

And yet, the Tower Line existed for a reason. He was trying to comfort us, but there was small comfort in it.

"If we're going to wait," Candui said, "maybe we should have had lunch with Scerta. That would have saved us a meal."

Richart and Aphier shared a look I didn't understand. When neither of them said anything, I asked, "What is it?"

"My aunt is sweet and would give her home for any wanderer, but it's the end of spring. She's got meager supplies this time of the year. We're lucky she had what she did."

"And we probably shouldn't impose on her more than we have to and leave those supplies even smaller." It made sense—yet another reason we hurried out of there.

"Right." Richart gave a faint smile.

Life was different out here than in the city. It was hard to remember that. It'd be more difficult to adjust to life in the forest, but I was determined to do it.

"Why don't we sit?" Aphier asked. "It's going to be a long while."

I helped Candui to the ground, where we took off our packs and set them together. We talked but about meaningless things. How nice the weather was for this time of spring. How it was likely to turn sour, and we might get caught in some snow while in the forest. That last part hung me up. I'd never been in the snow before. Not when I could go inside a house.

When I voiced my concern, Aphier said, "We'll be fine. Wet and cold, but fine. I have a few tricks up my sleeve that should help."

That didn't sound all that comforting.

We waited a while longer, the sun dipping past the mountains, its rays shooting up and over it until they too were gone.

Aphier passed out some food, and we ate in silence, the night growing darker. Something howled in the distance. I clenched my jaw, hoping whatever it was would be not in the Umpi Forest, or that it was more harmless than it sounded. I wasn't going to hold my breath, though.

We finished eating and cleaned up dinner. This time we waited in complete silence, other than the sound of life around us. Only the hooting of owls. They weren't something I was accustomed to before running away, but now they told me it was time to sleep.

I yawned, ready to lie down and rest until it was time to go when Aphier said, "Let's move."

Of course. I should have taken a nap earlier. We gathered up our packs.

Aphier said, "You need to be quiet from here on out. Do exactly what I tell you, when I tell you. If the zasin on the Tower Line catch us, we'll be hanged. Not to worry, though. I've done this more times than I can count. We'll be fine."

But not with an elf on crutches. This was going to be interesting.

We hurried forward, keeping pace with Aphier while I kept an eye on Candui, to make certain she kept up with us all right. Both luckily and unluckily, two moons were out. That meant it was easier to see where we were putting our feet, but we'd also be easier to spot at the Tower Line.

We walked quite some distance, the towers growing bigger the closer we got. They were huge, much bigger than I expected, with giant bonfires at the top. I could only hope those fires would destroy the guards' night vision and make it harder for them to see us.

We got to a cluster of trees, and then the path before us cleared. A pair of zasin were walking toward the closest tower and soon went out of sight. I expected us to make a mad dash for it, but Aphier only stood, watching. Waiting.

Not moving bothered me more than I dared to admit. It was more nerve-wracking than trying to go forward. What felt like a couple minutes later, another pair of guards went by. If they turned their heads and looked hard, they'd see us.

Then a worse thought hit me. If they were able to do that, what was watching on the other side of the clearing where we'd be shortly? It had better be nothing, or this would be the shortest trip into the Umpi Forest ever. Not that there were many trips into the Umpi Forest.

Still, we waited. Richart put a hand on my shoulder. I didn't want to admit to him how much comfort it gave me, but I was most grateful for it.

Finally, after a pair of zasin went by, Aphier turned and whispered to us, "Richart and Adriella, I want you two to go first. I'll help Candui through at the next chance after this. When I tell you to go, run as silently as you can to the other side. I'll find you. Richart, take Candui's crutches. I'm going to carry her across."

Candui opened her mouth, but Aphier put a finger to her lips to stop her. "Silence."

She didn't argue, only handed her crutches over to Richart. He carried them, looking over at me. I wasn't certain exactly what he wanted, but I gave him a nod. That seemed to satisfy him until he took my hand. Apparently, we were running across the clearing hand in hand. Not sure that was a good idea, with him carrying the crutches. I tried to pull away, but he held on firm.

Before I had more time to think about it, Aphier said, "Go. Now."

We broke into a sprint across the clearing. It was bigger than it looked, each second leaving me feeling exposed, like an arrow was going to be shot into my back. I tried to keep my feet quiet, but they thudded against the hard-packed ground. Even my breathing was loud.

Richart squeezed my hand when we were about halfway

across and pulled me on faster. I stretched out my legs, willing them to go faster. I had to be stronger than I ever had been before. My body complied for a moment, until I hit a rock with my left foot and went tumbling down, Richart's hand torn from mine.

My heart pounded in my ears. I couldn't handle this. We were going to be caught. Richart bent to help me up, dropping a crutch in the process. As he picked it up, I hurried to my feet.

I wanted to glance around, to see if anyone was coming, but I didn't dare. Richart grabbed my hand again, and we rushed forward, crutches waving in the air. I bit my cheek as we reached the other side. We weren't out of the clearing yet. We still had to find a place to hide.

We went in between the trees some distance before finding a large patch of bushes to hide behind. We'd barely made it when the steady sound of marching feet met my ears.

We'd almost been caught.

But we weren't. We were as safe as we could be now that we were officially in the Umpi Forest. Though we still had to wait for Aphier to carry Candui across. If he'd been the one to fall, there was no way he'd recover in time.

I pressed my hand to my hidden star stone and willed him and Candui to be safe.

I glanced up at the stars and searched. There was no alignment that could help. Just as well. Showing my magic would be the worst thing I could do. I put my free hand on my growing belly, grateful my tunic was loose and comfortable. I couldn't do anything to jeopardize him.

The zasin went past, not looking to the right or left. I let out a relieved sigh they weren't searching for us—a silent one.

I'd feel better when the other two were on this side as well, not only because I cared about Candui and their fates, but also because I'd need them to survive in this place. It was a selfish thought, but true nonetheless.

Richart put a hand on my back. The reassurance was comforting. I wanted to lean into him. Wanted to feel more of that comfort, warmth, and security. But he was only touching me because I carried his child, so I kept my gaze trained on where I thought Candui and Aphier were waiting.

The soldiers passed once. Twice. Three times. Still the others didn't come. The longer they took, the more I felt like pacing. Despite that, I kept myself crouched down and silent.

Richart made little circles with his hand on my back. I couldn't resist any longer; I leaned into him. He stiffened before relaxing and wrapping his arm around me. Where we stood as far as our relationship went was a mystery, but we did have a child tying us together, and it looked like we were going to raise him together, at least for a couple of years. Time to stop thinking of all the things that could tear us apart, and start thinking of what would bring us together, to rear a baby.

A flash of movement caught my eyes. I strained to see, with only the light of night to brighten the path. The movement grew more defined and was coming straight for us. It looked like someone carrying another person. Aphier and Candui.

Unfortunately, they weren't going nearly as fast as they should be, given the space between zasin watches. Was I about to see my best friend get caught? What was I going to do about it?

I slipped out my dagger. The pressure around my shoulders increased as Richart gave me a reassuring squeeze. He might think everything was going to be all right, but I wasn't so certain. They moved so slowly across that gap.

The footsteps that marched through the clearing grew closer. Both them and the noise Aphier made with each step. It wasn't good. If I heard him, so could those on watch.

I expected the zasin to quicken their pace and shout for my friends to stop, but nothing happened. My friend and helper were only about halfway across, though, and the zasin grew ever closer. They weren't going to make it at that pace.

Richart must have thought the same thing because he whispered in my ear, "No matter what happens, stay here."

Before I could protest, he was up and gone, leaving Candui's crutches behind. I looked for him in the darkness of the forest, but his form had disappeared.

Aphier still had some distance to go, and the marching footsteps were quicker and faster, like the zasin knew something was wrong. I bit my bottom lip, my grip on the hilt of my dagger so tight my hand hurt.

I wanted to save them but didn't know what to do. Besides, Richart said to stay here, and I had the baby to think of. What was he planning on doing?

The thoughts were churning in my mind when a crashing sound came to my left. It was large, waking the whole forest to sounds. Birds took flight. Something roared in the distance.

Aphier pushed out a burst of speed, but no zasin or animals appeared within sight. What had Richart done? Had he created the diversion? I couldn't have him getting caught either.

Would the zasin search the forest for whatever caused the noise, or would they ignore it unless it came out into the clearing? Hopefully the latter, but I feared the former.

Aphier crossed over into the trees. I popped up so he could see me, and then crouched back down as he drew near.

He set Candui beside me before joining us. His breathing came in hard gasps. "Where's Richart?"

"He left. I think he made that noise."

Aphier shook his head and cursed under his breath. "That noise was not Richart."

And all the worries I had increased tenfold.

CHAPTER TWENTY

"We can't stay here long," Aphier said. "The zasin probably won't search the forest, but the creature that made that noise might be hungry."

I pressed a hand to my belly. "We can't leave him."

"I know." Aphier sounded frustrated.

A couple of zasin crossed the path ahead of us while we sat there. And then another. They were coming in pairs more frequently. We wouldn't have stood a chance of making it across had that creature made a noise before we came over. Of course, we were stuck with it over here, where it could attack us at any moment.

After too short a while, Aphier whispered, "We have to go."

"No. Richart." What would I tell my child? That I left his father to be eaten by one of the Umpi Forest's dark creatures? No. That was completely unacceptable.

Aphier sighed. "Fine. As soon as the next watch passes, I want you ladies to head straight back into the forest, away from the noise. I'll find Richart and bring him to you."

"How will you know where to find us?" Candui whispered.

"I'm familiar with this area of the forest," he replied. "Can you do that?"

I nodded.

"Good."

We settled in to linger another moment or two, before the next zasin couple came into view. They went by and out of sight.

Aphier opened his mouth, and another loud *crash* came from closer by. "I can't leave you two," he said.

I had a feeling that wasn't what he was going to say before. I shook my head. "I'm not leaving Richart."

"Look—I don't like this any more than you do, but given those sounds, he's probably dead."

"What?" The life drained out of me. It couldn't be. Aphier had to be wrong.

"I'm sorry, Adriella, but that thing sounds big, and it went in the same direction Richart did. It's not a good sign, but he'd want us to keep moving. To get away from danger."

He was probably right, but everything in me screamed to find my husband. To make certain he wasn't dead.

"The zasin passed. We have to go." Aphier helped Candui to her feet and handed her the crutches. I stood, ready to follow them, even though I couldn't feel any parts of my body. Everything was numb.

"What are you still doing here?" Richart asked, appearing from my left. "Run." He picked up Candui and sprinted deeper inside the Umpi Forest.

I was so shocked by his sudden appearance, I just stood there. Was he really alive?

Aphier grabbed my hand and yanked me forward.

My feet kicked into movement though my head was still struggling to think. I followed Richart while Aphier brought up the rear.

We were making too much noise, crashing through the forest

like we hadn't a care in the world, instead of being silent and stealthy. Moments later, it didn't matter. There was a great roar, and the trees to our left started moving.

Whatever did that, I didn't want to find out. I put on a burst of speed, and soon caught up with Richart. I grabbed Candui's crutches from him. I didn't think it would help with whatever was out there. Why did we think this was a good idea?

"Faster," Richart said between breaths.

I strained myself, stretching ahead of him. Now that I wasn't following someone, I wasn't sure where I was going, but wasn't a concern at the moment. I hurried through the foliage, doing my best not to trip again. I would stay on my feet. Even more than last time, I couldn't afford to fall again. What if I'd already hurt the baby because of it?

"Leave me," Candui said from somewhere behind me.

"Not happening," was the only response Richart gave.

I didn't know what it was costing him to carry her, but I didn't care. I was grateful he wouldn't leave her behind. She deserved more than to be devoured by a wild beast.

I ran and ran. It took some time to realize the crashing noises were fading. They were still there, but closer to the Tower Line than to where we were going.

I slowed to a stop, needing some guidance. Something smacked into my head and knocked me to the ground.

Whatever it was, the thing was huge. And silent. I hadn't heard it coming. My face ached, but it didn't matter. Richart, Candui, and Aphier were there, waiting for me.

"What was that?" I asked.

"Bird," Aphier said as he grabbed Candui from Richart.

"Some bird," I muttered.

"Follow me." Aphier took off, running.

Richart helped me up from the ground and prodded me to run in front of him. I ran more than I had in my entire life. My legs ached, and my vision struggled to keep up with how fast we were going in the dark. Every once in a while, Aphier would look behind him, to make certain I was still there. I would do the same, checking to see if Richart was still following me, though I could hear the branches snapping as he went by. The sound didn't matter. I needed to see him. Needed the reassurance. Needed to remember that he was alive and well.

We stopped. Richart set Candui gently on the ground, and I knelt beside her, laying her crutches to the side. "Are you all right?"

"I'm fine. You're the one who had to run the entire time."

I gave her a faint smile before turning to Richart. "I thought you were dead."

"Why would you think that?" His eyebrows knit together.

I pointed at Aphier. "He said you were probably gone, since you were in the vicinity of the creature."

Richart tilted his head to the side, raising his eyebrows. "It was huge and had enough teeth to do me in."

"You saw it?" It was hard not to let fear coat my words.

"Correction," Aphier said. "You saw it and lived?"

"I did. What was it?"

"Depends. What did it look like?"

Richart shook his head. "Like nothing I've ever seen before. It was huge. Tall as three or four men, and as wide. It had razor-sharp teeth—three rows of them—and claws the size of a large dog."

"It was a yipra."

I gasped. That couldn't be. "How many creatures that I thought were tales are real?"

"You're going to discover all sorts of things you didn't want to in this forest," Aphier said.

"Now you tell me."

"I would have told you sooner, but then you wouldn't have wanted to come, and this is the safest place from the high king."

"But not the safest place for people to be, from the sounds of things." I tried not to be frustrated at the situation the high king had forced us to put upon ourselves.

"Is this location safe?" Richart asked.

His sword was out. How long had that been the case?

"It's secure enough for now," Aphier said. "Let's get a fire going. That will help with most creatures."

"Most?" Candui sounded as skeptical as I felt.

"You can't scare away everything. There are some pretty intelligent creatures in this forest."

Probably more than he wanted to admit. This wasn't starting off well. My stomach rumbled, sounding like a creature of its own.

"Let's get the pregnant lady something to eat," Aphier said. "We'll save the little bit I was able to bring with me for emergencies. I'll go hunting around here and see what I can find."

Curious about what he was looking for, I said, "I'll come with."

"Are you sure? I'll be killing things."

"I know where food comes from." Even if the thought of killing an animal turned my appetite sour.

"Keep her safe," Richart told Aphier.

"I can take care of myself." A little bit, anyways.

He turned to me. "Your skills are getting a better, but I'd be more at peace if I knew he was keeping an eye out for you and that nothing was going to happen while you were out there."

I swallowed back my emotion, a strange twist of pleasure and disappointment. "All right."

"It's settled, then. Richart will set up a makeshift camp, and Adriella and I will go get food."

"And I'll sit here and try not to feel useless," Candui said.

"You can help make dinner when I get back." She was much better at it than I was. Hopefully that was enough because I didn't know how else she could help. It was true that, for the most part, she would be more of a burden than a help, but that was fine. We'd make it somehow.

She nodded.

If only I could heal her without giving myself away. It's too bad I didn't know much about how the stars affected broken bones. If I did, maybe I could sneak some healing on her slowly, when the others weren't looking. I knew enough about magic to understand it would take the right alignment of stars, which was different for every illness. Exactly why I couldn't heal her. Too many choices and very little knowledge.

I trailed Aphier out of our little clearing and back into the forest, this time at a much slower pace. Despite that, my legs wanted to give out beneath me. They were tired. I was tired. I wanted nothing more than to sit down and relax, but that wasn't going to happen.

We went a ways, me following him, when he motioned me to his side where there was a bush. "See the way the leaves are shaped and the hue of purple they are?"

"Yes."

"That means they are the hippaberries, and they are not poisonous." He pulled a pouch out of his pack; it was a good size when unfolded. "Fill this with as many as you can. I'm going to look for more food but keep you in sight."

"Sounds good." I took the pouch and picked berries. It was a slow, tedious process, but I was doing something useful. For every handful of berries I picked for the others, I ate some. They were tarter than I was accustomed to, but they were food. Unfortunately, they made my stomach growl harder. Hopefully, Aphier was having better luck.

I glanced around, expecting to see him. There were trees,

bushes, and more trees. No Aphier. I went to call out his name, but then remembered something else could be in the forest with us. I didn't want to draw attention to myself with the creatures that were here. I didn't know the way back to camp either, though. I should have paid better attention. This was so not good.

I should call for him.

I opened my mouth, and someone clamped a hand over it from behind, preventing a scream. I jabbed my elbow backward, aiming for my attacker's stomach.

"*Ugh.* It's me," Aphier said. "I was trying to catch a rabbit that went by without scaring it, but we can rule that out. At least we know they are here. I'll set up some traps for them, and with any luck, we'll be having rabbit stew for breakfast."

Once my heart slowed back to its normal pace, I said, "Rabbit soup with berries. Yum." The truth was I'd eat about anything, even if it was fruit in my soup.

"Can't be picky this time of year, but you're going to need lots of nutrition for that growing little one. We'll do what we can to find it. How's the berry bush coming along?"

"It's getting to be sparse pickings."

"Good. Come help me with this other bush I found. Same berry, bigger stash. We're lucky they're ready to be picked this early in the year. Usually they'd take another week or two."

I followed him to a second patch, where he handed me another pouch to fill. After we'd worked a while, I asked, "What's in this for you? Why are you helping?"

He picked a berry and studied it closely. "It's a fair question. One I'm not sure I have an answer to."

"You gave up your entire life. You have to have some sort of answer." And I was dying to know. People didn't leave to help save their best friend's child for no reason. Especially when it meant death for them.

Candui taught me that reasons can be complex, but there's

always a reason. I hoped his wasn't as devastating as hers, but there had to be something hiding in there.

We picked berries in silence while I wondered more and more what he was thinking. I understood everyone else's reason for being here, but I couldn't understand his. Perhaps if I'd known him longer, it would make more sense, but we just met.

Finally, he spoke. "Part of it is a sense of duty toward Richart. We are friends, but did you know he saved my life?"

"No. He didn't tell me that." I popped a few berries in my mouth.

"He was set on me never speaking of it to anyone, so I'm not surprised he didn't tell you. He's bashful about it. But I always wanted to tell everyone. Let everyone know what a great person he is."

"So what happened?"

He sighed, focusing on his task instead of me. "We were in our early teens. We'd been called up for zasin training, and that was rough. Unless you've been through it, it's kind of hard to understand how tough it is. Every day is like a lifetime of never-ending torture. It was exhausting, and he knew I hated it. Don't get me wrong; I'm grateful for the training now, because it allows me to do things like come into this forest with ease. But at the time, it was the last thing I wanted to do."

"What did you want to do?" I asked, hoping it wouldn't change the subject too much.

"I don't know exactly. I always enjoyed creating things. Something about making beauty out of an everyday object was a delight, but of course, the high king would never stand for someone making things simply because they were beautiful. Unless, of course, it was him. Sorry. Does it shock you to hear me talk this way?"

"Only because I'm not accustomed to it. No one ever talks

bad about the high king. I thought he was a wise ruler, if a little strict at times."

He shrugged. "Most people would agree with you, but I've always hated him. Now that he's doing something as horrid as having babies killed, my hate is justified, and I hate him more. Though it doesn't affect me personally—or didn't until I met you —I knew it was wrong. Not something we should put up with as a society."

He tossed a few berries in his mouth. "Anyway, Richart and I thought it would be a good idea to take a break from our training one night. We trained at Elvia. The capital was enticing. Everything a young boy could want. But we never got to go explore it because of our duties. It was straight in when we arrived and straight to work."

"But you didn't stay at work?" His story was pulling me in. How did Richart save his life in a city full of people? I'd never been to the capital, but I'd heard stories.

"No. One night we snuck out after we were supposed to be asleep. I'd studied the guard rotations for weeks, determined to find a way out."

"You seem to be good at that," I said.

He gave me a cocky grin. "Definitely a trait I admire in myself."

I laughed.

"We snuck out and explored the city. There was so much to see and do. I wanted it all—everything to be mine. I wanted out every night after that. Richart wouldn't let us go that often, but once a week, we would continue to escape. Only, the last time we went, it didn't end well.

"We were walking down the street when we were attacked by robbers. They tried to take everything from us, but we were poor soldiers. We didn't have any money or anything worthwhile, except our weapons. They tried to take those, but Richart and I both knew, if we showed up the next day without any weapons, we would be whipped within an inch of our lives."

My body was tense. "What did you do?"

Aphier shrugged. "I thought we would be able to fight them, but they had a knife to my throat before I could stop them." He turned to me and lifted his chin in the air, placing his neck in the light of the moons. "I have a scar still, where he dug that knife into my skin."

Indeed, he did. There was a white line, faint but thick.

He lowered his chin again. "I thought I was dead for certain, but before any of us knew what happened, Richart flew into action. He dived for the knife and turned it on my attacker. It wasn't long before the robber's own knife was at the robber's throat. Don't think I've ever seen someone so shocked before. That robber looked like he was going to wet himself.

"Richart didn't let them go, though. We couldn't take them to the zasin because we weren't supposed to be out. Richart demanded all of the money they'd stolen from people and took their weapons before setting them free." He gave a mirthless laugh. "As soon as they were gone, I thanked Richart to the Sun and back for saving my life, but then I got cocky. Told him we were rich now and could do whatever we wanted. You know what he did with that money?"

"I'm guessing he didn't spend it on himself."

"Nope. He sure didn't. He donated it to the Moonska. We passed by one of their holy places, and he slipped it in the donation box. Every last coin."

That was amazing. I knew he was kind, but not that kind, generous, and brave. It was hard to fathom how wonderful he was. And he was mine.

Or he should have been. Maybe I'd lost my opportunity with him, but he was here with me, ready to stand by both me and the baby. Our baby.

"How did you feel about that?" I asked.

He laughed. "Oh, I was mad. We could have been rich, and he went and gave it all away. Couldn't complain, though, since he'd saved my life."

"I bet."

"You can't tell him I told you this story. He'd be embarrassed."

"Of course. I promise, my lips are sealed."

We picked for a while longer, until our pouches were all the way full, before heading back to camp. When we got there, the fire was blazing, bringing with it warmth. Richart was in the light, half of his face brightening up with the flickering. My heart pattered, giving me an unfamiliar feeling.

It was good that I'd promised Aphier I wouldn't say anything, because I wanted to. I wanted to let him know how great he was, not only for saving his friend's life, but also for giving the money to a religion that would hopefully use it for the people. The Moonska were always known to be generous. They probably were that time too. What did they think of the high king and Sunsire's taking the lives of little ones? The Moonska had a place in the palace, like the Sunsit, but there hadn't been any word about the Moonska taking any action for or against the killing of babies. It was curious.

My belief in the Starda never belonged in the palace. Not ever. Those who sought power from the stars were feared and hated, not given a place of honor.

Richart glanced up at me, his forehead wrinkling. "Are you well?"

I realized I'd been standing here, saying and doing nothing, for too long. "Fine. I'm thinking." About how lucky my child is to have him for a father. "Are you hungry? We found some berries and set snares. There should be meat in the morning, but berries are better than nothing."

He waved me away. "Feed Candui first. She needs the strength to get better."

"That doesn't mean you can't eat," Candui said. "You need energy as much as the rest of us, especially if you're going to take a turn on watch tonight."

I handed him a full pouch, ignoring his protests, and took the other to Candui.

"Don't you have one for you?" she asked.

"I ate my fill, back at the bushes. They're tart, but you get used to them after a while. Though my mouth is a little sore, after eating so many."

"You ate more than anyone I've ever seen eat of them at one time," Aphier said with a laugh.

"The baby likes them," I said in defense.

Everyone laughed.

We finished setting up camp for the night, the cool air seeming to shrink around us the longer I was near the fire. It seemed backward but gave a respite from the heat of the flames.

I looked forward to morning, though. The dark was oppressive. I needed the light of day to feel comfortable in this place.

CHAPTER TWENTY-ONE

I was wrong. The light of day was worse than the night. It revealed the trees with dark bark, pressed together. They lent an ominous feeling to our surroundings. The trees were different here, unlike any I'd seen before. Instead of leaves, they had thin, needle-like foliage. All the trees I knew had just begun to show their greenery or budding.

Aphier caught three rabbits in his snares. Granted, they were scrawny after winter, but better than nothing. I ate my meat, wishing it had some vegetables to go with it. I didn't dare voice my thought, afraid they'd take it to heart as something the baby needed and go looking for it right that moment until they found it.

"What are we going to do now?" Candui asked.

I was grateful she spoke the question I'd been thinking of. We were in the woods, surrounded by who–knew-what, with me—a pregnant lady— and a woman on crutches. We needed a plan. And a miracle.

Richart muttered something under his breath.

"What was that?" I asked.

"Nothing." He looked to Aphier.

"For starters, we'll look for a place we can set up a more permanent camp. We're only a few hours' walk from the Tower Line, but though we can still see it, as long as we don't go climbing any trees—which you don't want to do in these type of trees—we don't need to go much deeper. Phew. That was a lot. Any questions?" Aphier said.

"Why don't we need to go deeper in?" It should be safer away from the Tower Line and the dangers associated with the zasin, and we were already in the forest, so what difference did it make?

"Good question. We'll go a little deeper, but I don't know what's in there after that. I don't want to risk unknown dangers when the zasin are too frightened to come into the forest anyway."

"But you come here. Plus, you'll be missing from your post by now. Isn't that going to create problems?"

"Nah. The rest of them are too scared to come into the forest. After last night, I wouldn't be surprised if they thought I was eaten by the yipra."

"But you weren't supposed to be anywhere near the Tower Line last night, right?" Candui asked.

He shrugged. "Maybe not, but around here, even hearing the call of a creature from the Umpi Forest can mean a disappearance."

"That makes me feel so much better." I let sarcasm coat my words.

"We'll be fine. I know a spot a few hours from here with a clearing, an abandoned cave, and a stream that runs past it with little critters like more rabbits. I think we should settle there."

"And the monsters?" Richart asked.

"Last time I checked, it was an empty area." He sounded so confident. I wanted to believe him.

"When was last time you checked?" I had to ask.

"About six months ago."

Candui scoffed.

I pursed my lips.

Richart said, "Six months is a long time. Are you sure it's still safe?"

"We'll check it before we make any final decisions, but I'm sure it'll be fine."

It would be nice if I had his same confidence. Accepting that future was difficult.

"Look," Aphier said. "I'd scout it out before we went there, but the prime option is to stick together. I don't want anyone to get hurt, and the best way to do that is to stay as a group. Once we get close, I'll scout it out, but we'll be fine."

"If you're sure," Richart said.

"Positive."

"Let's clean up camp, then, and get going." Richart grabbed his blanket, folded it, and stuffed it in his bag.

The rest of us followed suit, putting together what few things we had and taking the rest of the hippaberries with us, to snack on as we walked. Sadly, there was no more rabbit left. Aphier scattered the ashes from the fire a little, before we left, but otherwise we left things as they were. A yipra could enjoy our camp when we were long away from here.

As we hiked, I tried to help Candui by holding back branches for her and cutting down on the amount of foliage she had to hobble her way through, but it was tough and slow-going.

At some point, she tumbled to the ground, and I barely caught her.

"This isn't working," she said as Aphier came to a stop ahead of us and Richart caught up from behind.

"Slow is fine," I said as I helped right her. I made sure she was stabilized before helping wipe the mud from her tunic. "Is your leg causing you problems?"

"No." She didn't look at me.

"Well, I'm tired. Can we take a break?"

The rest of the day continued like that. Short bursts of walking, followed by small breaks. Despite the downtime, Candui seemed to be flagging. I couldn't imagine how hard it must be on her, traveling through the forest on what was essentially two sticks.

Night was coming on fast, the sun dipping behind the mountains. I wanted a fire and food. The berries ran out hours ago, and my stomach felt like it was trying to digest itself. "Can we stop for the night?"

"We're almost there," Aphier said. "We should be upon it any moment."

"*Should?*" I didn't like the sound of that.

"We will be upon it at any moment."

"Do you want to scout ahead while I stay with the women?" Richart asked.

"It'd be faster if we all stuck together."

"But you said you were going to scout it out for us before we got there," I said.

Aphier sighed, running a hand through his hair. "The truth is we should have reached it by now. I'm not lost, per se, but I'm not as confident as when we started out. I think it's just up ahead, but I'd hate not to be able to find you in the dark. If that happened, it might not be until morning that I saw you again, and I don't want to leave you alone that long."

We were all silent for a moment. I didn't know what the others were doing, but I was trying my best to keep my anger and frustration in. How could he do this to us? We were lost in the Umpi Forest, with who knew what creatures out there? I didn't like it one bit.

"Why don't we camp here for the night?" Candui asked.

"There's not enough room to set up a very good camp,"

Richart said. "If we started a fire without a clearing, the trees might catch."

"What do you suggest?" I tried to keep the bitterness out of my voice but failed. I was tired, hungry, and angry. A very bad combination.

"Let's go a little farther and see if we find a better clearing. We can sort the rest out in the morning," Richart said.

Sorting it out in the morning better not include finding food then. I didn't want to say anything and make things worse, though. We could worry about that once we had the camp set up.

"Let's get going, then," Aphier said. "The longer we stand here, the more light we're losing."

"Is everyone ready?" Richart said.

There was a chorus of *yes*.

"Good. I'm curious when you all stop jabbering," said a deep voice.

Before I had time to worry about where the voice came from, something darted out of the darkness around us, yanked me up in the air, and brought me to its giant nose to sniff, making my stomach sink. I gagged over the stench of rotten meat. Its nose was massive, almost as big as my face but squat. "Smells like we got dinner, boys."

A cheer went up through the air, whooping and yelling ringing through the forest, like the noise was going to tear the forest apart. I swung through the air in the massive paw, trying not to scream, though it rippled at my throat. At least I was going away from those wicked teeth, but I wasn't being set back on the ground.

I didn't know how many our attackers were, but they sounded like at least three. If they were all as huge as the one that carried me, we were in heaps of trouble.

Looked like dinner was coming, but not for me.

CHAPTER TWENTY-TWO

I swung back and forth in the creature's hand as it walked, similar to a human. I squirmed and kicked to no avail. I was stuck. He hoped he didn't squeeze hard enough to hurt the baby. It wouldn't matter if he was going to eat me. I shivered. It wasn't a way I ever thought I'd go to the stars.

Instead of wasting my strength fighting a hold I couldn't get away from, I lay still, the movement making my stomach churn. Perhaps it was a good thing we hadn't had dinner.

Some ways off, Candui screamed, "Put me down, you big brute."

"Candui?" I yelled, panic clawing at the word.

"I'm here."

"Are you well?" I attempted to keep my voice calm despite the fear twisting my gut.

"Other than this meaty hand wrapped around me. But I lost my crutches."

We wouldn't be walking away from this, even if the giant beasts somehow fell asleep before dinner. How could we ever escape them with her not being able to walk? A bigger question was how we were going to escape at all? It was hopeless, but I wouldn't quit trying until breath left me for good.

I wanted to call out for Aphier and Richart, but something stopped me. I didn't hear either of them. What if they managed to get away? More likely, they were busy trying to get out of these giants' clutches, but just in case, I kept quiet.

The other possibility of what could have happened to them was unthinkable. I tamped it down before it could surface, but it kept gnawing at me.

What if they were dead?

It didn't take long for the giants to stop and drop me to the ground. I tucked and rolled, trying to protect my stomach. I glanced around for somewhere to run.

Before I could find a way out, the giant who caught me said, "No going anywhere. If we have to chase after you, I'll tear your arm off."

Good enough for me. Another giant dropped Candui to the ground, and I sat down next to her, Next was Aphier. Where was Richart? I opened my mouth to ask Aphier, but he shook his head. I clamped the words down before whispering the second question on my mind. "What are these things?"

"Trolls," he said.

"Trolls that hear good," the one who caught me said. "Shut up, before I show you what it feel like to lose arm."

Hear good but don't talk well. I kept my mouth shut. I wasn't going to risk being one-armed for the little bit of life I had left.

They shoved us next to a pile of wood that couldn't be for a good purpose. Once we were pushed back onto the ground, they surrounded us, and one of them lit a fire with the stack of wood.

"Scrumyummy for my tummy," the one closest to me said, drool dripping down its chin.

"Wait till they cooked," a second said. "Last time we eat no cook, they stringy."

"Stop bickering," the troll who caught me said. "Go get spice for new food. I keep watch."

The other two grumbled but left, heading out in different directions. The troll who stayed behind squatted and stared at us, licking his lips. The firelight flickered over him and the area. The clearing was wide, with what looked like a cave in the back. Everywhere else was tight with trees. How did the trolls move so quietly through the woods?

I searched the clearing with my gaze, looking for any sign of Richart. What happened to him? It didn't sound like they ate him, but neither did I see anything that would reveal his presence. He was smarter than to appear where the troll could see him, but it would be comforting to know where he was.

I swallowed down bile. I couldn't believe we were about to be food. After all that running, we found an area safe from the high king, only to run into trolls. I knew the Umpi Forest wasn't going to be safe, but I didn't expect us to be in danger so soon, and I certainly didn't expect to be eaten—at least not by things that spoke.

Next to me, Candui's eyes were wet. I wanted to cry right along with her, but I couldn't. I had a baby to think of. I had to do my best to get out of this, even if it was impossible.

The troll plucked me from the ground and held me level with its eyes. Putrid smells came from it as it said, "You no escape."

Not sure if I should answer or not after being told to keep quiet, I said nothing. I stared him right in the eye, trying not to show my fear. I clenched my jaw to keep it from shaking and wished my dagger was within reach, not that it would do much against such a large creature. Doing anything with it would enrage the creature. No wonder they didn't bother taking it from me. They could use it as a toothpick.

The troll set me back down, and I landed close to Candui and

Aphier. This situation wasn't ideal, but better than being in the troll's hands. I just hoped the baby was all right.

Soon, I would be in his mouth. I shuddered.

What could I do to get out of this? Clearly, looking for a way to escape drew negative attention from him. With his enormous eyes on us, he didn't miss much. No matter how hard I thought, I couldn't think of any way to get out of this.

Richart was our only hope.

Though I couldn't imagine what he could do against three giants by himself with only a sword.

Time passed, the moons moving across the sky while the troll continued to watch us. It took much longer than I expected for the others to return, the flames of the fire burning down to coals. This wasn't good. Coals were perfect for cooking things.

"Urp. Nark. Where are you?" the troll called out suddenly.

So they were supposed to be back by now. Hope fluttered through me. Maybe Richart did something to them.

The troll called out their names again, this time taking his gaze off us to look in the woods. As soon as he turned his head toward the forest, there was a wet sound, followed by a cry from the troll. He swung around, blood dripping from its back.

Richart was there, fighting the troll. I couldn't make much out with the troll in front of me, but I could tell the troll was losing a lot of blood. At this rate, he wouldn't last long. The question was would he hurt Richart in the mean time? I couldn't let that happen.

I jumped forward, dagger in hand, and slashed at the tender spot just above the troll's heel. The troll hollered, whipping around to face me. I scrambled back as he came at me. Before he could reach me, he fell to the ground.

Richart stood behind him, holding his sword.

I stood there, too stunned to do anything.

"What were you thinking, woman?" Richart asked. "You could have gotten yourself killed."

That snapped me back to myself. "I was helping you."

"I didn't need any help."

"And yet you made the killing blow after I distracted it."

"I made the killing blow the first time I sliced into it. The troll just needed time to bleed out, and I was making sure that happened. I didn't need you to risk yourself."

I didn't know whether to feel ashamed or irate. I landed somewhere in the middle. "Sorry. I was trying to help."

Finally putting his sword down, he sighed and walked toward me. The troll jerked toward him, leaning heavily on the side that didn't have the damaged heel. Richart swung a final time, taking it down.

My heart hammered in my chest. Was I going to pass out? "Is it dead this time?"

"It's dead, and I killed the others too." Richart checked the troll over and then strode over to me. His voice came out much softer. "Don't do that to me again. I thought something was going to happen to our baby. Are you hurt in any way? Is the baby all right?"

It took a second to process what I was feeling as the adrenaline wore off. "I think everything is all right. I'm just a little sore. I don't know much about being pregnant, but I believe the baby is well."

His tight features fell into a relaxed pose. "Thank the moons for that."

I never heard him invoke his religion before. He must be really relieved.

I whipped around to face Aphier.

"*We'll be fine*, you said." Anger oozed through my words. "That was anything but fine."

"Sorry. I didn't know trolls had moved into the cave," Aphier said.

"That's not good enough."

Richart put an arm around my shoulder, taking away some of my anger. I couldn't help but add on, "If it wasn't for Richart, we'd all be dead."

"I wouldn't go that far," Richart said.

"I would," Candui said.

"What are we going to do now?" Aphier asked. "Should we move the body and make camp here?"

"How are we going to move a body that big?" I wouldn't be much help, and Candui couldn't assist at all.

"Good point," Richart said. "Let's sleep over here, to the side."

"Only for the night. I don't want to remain here." It might not be fair to the others, but I really couldn't stomach a location where trolls tried to eat me.

"It's the best clearing around to live in for a ways," Aphier said.

"Maybe that's why trolls moved in," I countered. "I don't want a place that's too attractive to others. Can't you think of a better area?"

He threw his hands up in the air. "This is the best part of the forest."

"Let's continue this in the morning," Richart said.

"That's a good idea," Candui added. "We should get some rest and get an early start."

"Very well, but I'm not staying here any longer than I have to." And I meant it. This was too much of a draw for other creatures and now held bad memories.

CHAPTER TWENTY-THREE

Morning arrived much too soon. I groaned but pulled myself together because of the gnawing in my stomach. I had to eat something. Dinner was skipped last night, and I was starving. If it was just me, I could have dealt with it, but I needed to get the baby something, especially after what I dealt with last night.

"Morning, sleepy," Richart said.

I sat up and found Richart and Aphier standing around a small fire while Candui sat next to it. The sun was higher in the sky than it should be, given how exhausted I felt. "Ugh. How did I sleep in so late?"

"You're carrying a little one. That's how," Candui said. "Wait until you get toward the end of your pregnancy. You'll still want lots of sleep, but you'll wake up every hour or two."

That sounded great. Not.

Richart took a few steps toward me. "I've got some food for you. It's not much, but Aphier found mushrooms and roots this morning and made a breakfast soup out of them."

"Yum." That sounded disgusting. I was too ornery for this

late in the morning. I needed to get a hold of myself. "As long as there's no troll in there."

"They're poisonous to eat," Aphier called to me.

And they talked. I couldn't imagine eating something sentient. I took the proffered food, grateful I wasn't going to eat something that tried to eat me, and slurped up a spoonful, ready to gag. It wasn't as bad as I expected it to be. It was almost good. "Thank you."

I hurried to finish my food, wishing there was more the instant it was gone. I stood and glanced around, trying to look like I had enough to eat and wasn't searching for more, but didn't succeed.

Richart said, "Sorry, there's no more."

"We'll find some food as we walk," Aphier said.

"Does that mean you agree that we need to find a different place to live?" I asked.

He sighed. "It does. We talked it over this morning while you rested, and that'll be the best option. The cave here is clear, but it's been compromised. I don't know what we'll find out there, though. Anything could be as risky as staying here."

"Except we know this area will attract creatures," I countered.

"Perhaps. If you're ready, we should get going."

"What about Candui's crutches?" I asked.

"Aphier and I will take turns carrying her, until we find something that will work." Richart moved to where I'd slept and folded up my blankets.

"You don't have to do that," I said. "I can get it."

"Too late." He put them in my pack and held that out to me.

I put the pack on, thankful for his help. Sure, I could have done it myself, but it was nice of him. Thoughtful. I didn't remember him being this way the whole time we were married.

Did I miss it? Or was it just now coming about? Either way, I liked it.

"Are you ready?" Richart asked Candui.

"I feel bad, having you carry me. What if you need to fight something?"

"Then I may drop you. But with predators coming after the troll meat, those that can digest it anyway, getting away from here is more important than finding you crutches right now. We need to go," Richart said.

"I know we talked about this, but I feel bad," Candui said.

"Don't. I'm happy to help."

"Besides," I added, "we'll get you back on your feet in no time."

"I suppose," she said.

He swung her up into his arms, and a strange knot formed in the pit of my stomach. I wanted to be in his arms. Which made no sense. I wouldn't want a broken leg, and I'd much rather walk myself. These pregnancy emotions were getting to me.

We strode through the undergrowth, Aphier leading the way while I held back branches for Richart to pass. How long could we walk like this? Candui wasn't big, but she was tall, and carrying around another person didn't seem easy. So I kept my eye out for something I could use to fashion another pair of crutches.

While we walked, I thought about the troll that stared at me for so long it gave me nightmares. I might have them again, but I begged silently that they wouldn't. I needed to focus on other things, like how to survive for the next ten or more years away from people that could help and civilization in general.

The sun rose high in the sky before falling back down. It was past time to eat, my stomach growled loudly, and there was no food.

"Look," Candui said from Richart's arms. "There's a berry bush."

I glanced over to where she was pointing and ran to a bush full of plump, ripe berries. I gathered a few before Aphier came over and swatted them out of my hand.

"Don't eat those," he said. "They're poisonous."

I sagged. I needed something to eat, and I needed it now.

He watched me. "Maybe we should take a break from hiking to find some food. I'm not used to eating often while in the forest, but we should change that for the sake of the baby."

Thank the stars. I couldn't handle waiting much longer.

Richart gently set Candui down next to me, and I tried to make her as comfortable as possible. There wasn't much I could do, but I tried by making sure she had a blanket to rest on.

"You don't have to fuss over me," she said.

"Of course I do." I waved away her concern.

"Why don't you keep watch, and I'll go hunting?" Aphier said to Richart.

"Sounds good."

Aphier headed off to my right, quickly disappearing from sight through the thick trees. Richart scanned the forest.

I stood and went to him. "Do you think there's anything dangerous close by?"

"I'm not certain, but it's best to be safe."

I clasped my hands together, not sure what to do. How best to help. I couldn't keep watch, and I couldn't go looking for food in the forest—I wouldn't know what to look for. I should have asked to go with Aphier before he left, but now there was no choice but to sit and wait.

"Why don't you lay your head on my lap?" Candui asked me. "You look tired."

"I'm fine. I got more sleep than anyone else."

"But you're growing a new life. That takes an extreme amount of work. I'd feel so much better if you rested."

I sighed. She was right; I was tired. I pulled my blanket out of my pack and lay down next to her, using my pack for a pillow instead of her lap. It wasn't long before I was asleep.

I awoke to someone yelling, "Bear!"

I was groggy, but I jumped up. I pulled out my dagger and glanced around. Richart was looking at something behind me, his sword out, so I turned around. Moments later, Aphier streamed out of the forest, panting. "Bear. Coming."

Richart nodded and went ahead. He raised a hand to me. "Stay behind me."

No problem. I'd never seen a bear before, and I was curious. They weren't as mythical as most animals believed to inhabit the Umpi Forest, but they were still an oddity.

A large brown animal came racing through the woods on all fours. Richart raised his sword, hollering in a deep voice. The bear slowed but continued forward.

Aphier joined Richart, yelling and waving his sword in the air. The bear stopped, got up on two feet, and bellowed back at them. The noise made me cringe. After living through a yipra and a group of trolls, we couldn't be done in by a bear.

I didn't move up next to them, but I screamed with them, adding my voice to their own. I wasn't clear on why we were doing it. My only guess was we were trying to scare off the bear.

It growled at us again before getting back on all fours and sauntering away.

I loosened my hold on my dagger. I hadn't realized I'd tightened it. "What was that about?"

Aphier was trying to catch his breath. After a couple more moments, he said, "I accidentally stumbled onto the bear's den. I think she had cubs, but I didn't stick around long enough to find out."

"We should leave," Richart said.

"At least I found more hippaberries." Aphier handed me a light pouch. "Go ahead and eat these. We'll find more food tonight. I'm sorry it's not more."

"Thank you." I held the pouch like it was more precious than jewels. I'd never held jewels, but I'd seen them at the market before. I put the pouch out to Candui, "Would you like some?"

"You eat them."

"Are you certain?"

"I am."

I turned my attention to Richart. "What about you?"

"Not hungry."

"Liar."

"Maybe, but I'll be fine. Please eat."

Aphier hefted Candui off the ground as I gathered my blanket and stashed it in my pack. He led us through the woods while I popped berries into my mouth. It wasn't long before I was enjoying their tart taste. Anything would taste good right now, but these seemed extra good.

I reached for another handful, only to come up with a few of them. That didn't last long. I savored the last of the berries and stashed the pouch.

The walk was monotonous going forward. Aphier switched out carrying Candui after some time. I wanted to ask how much farther we were going to go today—when we could stop and search for more food and rest—but I didn't want to be more of a burden than I already was.

I put one foot in front of the other, focusing only on that and on following Aphier. A step. Then another. And another. It was boring. I would much rather be at home, weaving, but then, who knew if I'd still be alive or what would happen to my child.

We continued until almost dark. It was Richart who finally said, "Let's stop here."

I'd been in a numb stupor, but his words pulled me out of it enough to look around and see what was going on. Aphier came to a stop as we entered a large clearing. There was no evidence of other beings around, but then there hadn't been any yesterday either when we were caught by the trolls.

"I'm going to check around and make sure there's nothing milling about," Richart said, placing Candui on the ground beside me. He straightened and said to me, "I'll be back."

"I'm counting on it."

I watched him go before taking in the rest of the clearing. There was the gentle sound of a brook or some sort of stream nearby. The trees weren't as thick in this part of the forest, but they were still dark and ominous.

I plopped down next to Candui.

"How are you holding up?" she asked me.

"I'm alive."

"Yeah. I feel about the same, which is strange, because I didn't do any walking today. I shouldn't be so tired and worn, but being carried uses different muscles than I'm used to. Or something. Whatever it is, I can tell I'm going to sleep well tonight."

I wanted to say I wouldn't—not with being in this forest—but I would anyway with how tired I was.

Aphier asked, "Do you ladies need anything?"

Food. But I wasn't about to request that until Richart came back. How long would it take him? There was no way of knowing. I pleaded with the stars that he returned. I shivered and forced my thoughts to something nicer.

"Nothing," Candui said. "Except maybe for something to eat, but we can find that when Richart returns."

I'd be forever grateful to her for asking that. It was hard enough that I was constantly hungry and tired and couldn't do anything about it.

"I can do that," he said.

I turned to him. "Do you know this part of the forest very well?"

"Not as well as others. I've been here a few times, but not often and never for long."

"It is safe here?"

He shrugged. "After the trolls, I'm not certain anything is safe, but the woods feel more at peace here than they did last night."

"What do you mean?" Because that sounded awfully strange.

"Can't you feel it?"

Candui and I shook our heads.

"Well, I can. It's strange, but I've always felt it. I don't know why I didn't get us out of the situation with the trolls before it happened yesterday. I guess I was more concentrated on finding our way than I was on the woods around me. But now I'm focused on it. It's like a soft hum beneath my skin. I don't know how to describe it. There's the sound of birds and life in the forest. Not something you have when a predator—especially a large one—is around. We'll be fine here for the night, but we'll wait and see what Richart says when he gets back and keeps a good watch going."

It almost sounded like magic, but magic didn't work like that. You had to have a star stone for magic to work. What was more, you had to harness the power of the stars, which was harder when they weren't out yet. They'd appear soon; I could almost feel them coming to brighten the night sky. It was like Aphier said about the forest, but different.

"What are you thinking about?" Candui asked me.

"Oh, nothing much." Nothing I could tell her without frightening her. "Why do you ask?"

"You had a far-off look on your face. I wasn't sure if you were thinking of the home we left or your family or something else."

I sighed and slouched down before stretching my body out.

After a yawn that was much too wide, I said, "I do miss my family. It's strange, though—I don't miss Bola. I wasn't really living while I was there. I wasn't my true self. I was a woman walking through the motions of what the high king expected of his subjects." I'd hardly cast any spells since getting married, for fear of Richart catching me.

"I know what you mean. It's almost like going to sleep while your body keeps going. I was that way until my baby came along." Her eyes glazed over.

I wish there was a way to help her find her child, but I'm having a hard enough time protecting my own.

"The area seems clear." Richart came back into the clearing from close to where he left it. "I circled several times, going farther out each time, and while I found some critters, there was nothing harmful."

That was a relief. Maybe we could make it through the night without any adventures, though I wasn't holding my breath.

"Good. Thank you," Aphier said. "I'm going to go look for food. The women are hungry."

"Good luck," Richart said. "I'll keep watch while you're gone."

Aphier headed out in the direction the brook was babbling from. I didn't know much about tracking food, but it made sense that you'd find food near water. It would be good if he would come back with more than he did at lunch time. I couldn't handle sharing, and I was hungry.

Despite that, I was restless. I roamed around the clearing, as Richart kept a good eye on things. Candui fell asleep at some point, leaving me and my husband more alone than we'd been in some time. I wanted to talk to him but didn't know what to say. How did I explain to him I was developing feelings for him after four years of being married, especially when he had condemned me and was only sticking around because of our child?

"Richart?"

He focused his attention on me. "Yes?"

"I've been wondering something for a while, and I'm not sure I should ask, but..."

"Go ahead. Ask away." His words were warm and open, but his eyes were wary.

I bit my lip. I really wanted to know. "What did you do in Bola, after the profecta was found and the high king issued the order to gather up the women and children? Were you...?" I gulped down the rest of my question.

"Was I turning in women and children to be killed by the Sunsire?" He ran a hand through his hair. "No. I was trying to figure out how to avoid it without rebelling. Wasn't having much luck, though. Another day or two, and I'd have to either gather them up or forfeit my life."

"Do you know—that is to say..." Why was this such an awkward conversation? "Would you have turned them in?"

He came closer, shaking his head. "I honestly don't know. I couldn't imagine doing it, but at the same time, I never thought of running, like you did. You were the brave one."

"It was Candui's idea."

A grin tugged the corners of his lips. "Why am I not surprised? Still, you ran. You did what you needed to in order to save our child's life. The truth is I'm rather in awe of you."

Heat blossomed across my cheeks. What did I say to that?

He tucked a strand of hair behind my ear, the slightest touch of his skin against my ear making me shiver.

"I would have given my life for those women and children, but I worried about leaving you behind."

My words came out quieter now that he was closer. "You should have said something."

"I should have, but I didn't know you well. The truth is I

feared you turning me in as much as you feared me turning you in."

And yet, here we both were, running for our lives but getting to understand each other better than we ever had the previous years we kept to ourselves. "I would have sided with you."

"I know that now." He leaned in, and my pulse amped up before he pulled away. "I should get back on watch. I don't want anything sneaking in here, to harm us."

"Right." I got the need to ensure our safety, but I wanted that kiss instead of him being responsible.

A while later, Aphier came back, carrying his pot in his hand —a good sign. He said, "Found a few roots we can eat. There's no meat, but I set up snares, so hopefully we'll have more tomorrow."

"I should have gathered some wood while you were gone." I jumped toward the forest, new life in me now that food was on the way.

"Don't worry about it. I'll hel—"

"I'll help her," Richart cut Aphier off. "I know the type of wood we need to build a fire. We'll stay within sight."

Aphier gave him a knowing look. What was that about? I needed to bring firewood and get dinner cooking, so I didn't worry too much about it.

I stood and walked next to Richart. We went into the trees but could still make out the forms of the other two in the dying light. We worked side-by-side, picking up logs and carrying them back to the clearing, where Aphier started building a fire.

There was something peaceful about the job as the sunlight died off. I wanted to stay by my husband's side for a lot longer, but Aphier said, "We have enough wood for tonight and tomorrow morning."

"I guess that means we're done." Richart looked at me, the firelight flickering across the side of his face.

"Guess so." But I didn't move. We were close enough to the

others without being right next to them. Something in me was reluctant to return to them. I didn't have an excuse for staying, though. My mind was blank as I tried to make sense of the way we studied each other.

"I should help with dinner," I said.

He glanced at the fire. "Oh. Right. We should." But he didn't move.

"Thank you for helping me collect the wood."

He met my gaze again. "The pleasure was mine, I assure you." He paused a moment before saying, "Why weren't you more like this when we were married, before all this happened?"

Shame washed through me as I glanced at my feet. What excuse could I give? Better than that, what was the truth? "I think I had a hard time leaving my family. Life away from them wasn't what I expected. When the combinare put us together, I was sure my life was over. I would never make it back to the big city. But I found myself married to you and weaving.

"I knew for a long time I was going to be a weaver, but it wasn't what I dreamed of doing. And if I'm honest, you weren't the husband I dreamed of having. It was hard, adjusting to an existence I didn't expect. I shut myself off from the world." I finally looked at him. "From you."

He reached out, cupping my face with his hand. "You don't have to shut yourself off from me anymore."

My throat tightened, like a lump of root got caught in it. I swallowed hard, watching the light dance across his lips.

We had kissed—of course we had—though not much. What would it would be like to kiss him now that I knew him better and actually wanted to kiss him? That there'd be emotion behind the action?

But would he kiss me back? Was it a risk worth taking?

His gaze lured me in, making me lean forward.

"Dinner's ready," Aphier called.

Richart winced, taking his hand from my face. "Guess we should go eat."

Without his touch, everything felt foggier. Did I truly want to kiss him a moment ago? Did he want to kiss me?

I thought so, but I couldn't be certain, and without being certain, I didn't want to kiss him. I needed to know he wanted to and that I wasn't going to be alone in my emotions. Enough of my heart had been tattered about ever since I left my family. It was time to keep it safe.

CHAPTER TWENTY-FOUR

"This clearing looks like a good spot to make a home." The sun was up in the sky but not at its peak. Breakfast was over, and for the first time in a while, my belly was full, thanks to the food Aphier had caught in his snares. "It's got plenty of food and water. The clearing is big enough we could make some type of shelter." I didn't really know much about those things, but it sounded good.

"I agree," Richart said. "What do you think, Aphier? Is this area safe from predators? Are we going to have problems if we move in here?"

"As we learned with the trolls, I don't know everything about living in these woods, but yes, I do think this would make a good spot to live. I'd prefer a cave, but most of those are taken by predators, and we probably wouldn't want to kill one to get one."

"What's your opinion?" I asked Candui.

"I would be happy not to have to be carted everywhere." She gave a half smile.

It would be easier if she didn't have to be carried. And if we weren't walking, we had a better opportunity to search for branches we could turn into crutches. "We should stay, then. Everyone seems in agreement."

The mountains could be seen from where we were, still towering over us. The Tower Line wasn't within sight. If we climbed the trees, we'd be able to see it, but I wasn't planning on doing that any time soon.

"What do we need to do to make this place livable?" I asked.

"We should get started on a shelter right away," Aphier said. "It would be good if we made sure our food supply was steady too. The air is warming with the coming summer, and food will be more plentiful then, but we'll need a way to preserve food for winter. A place to store it all that won't attract more bears or anything else dangerous."

"We should do a wider perimeter check, to make sure the area is still clear," Richart said. "I don't trust that nothing came through in the night. I'd feel a lot better if we knew things were safe."

"I'll do a sweep while I'm out looking for food and setting more traps. In the meantime, we're going to cut down some trees to make a cabin. Maybe make a temporary home until we get the log cabin built."

A log cabin. That sounded cozy. How would we make it? I had no skills that were useful without a loom. My husband, though, seemed to have better skills at such things.

Richart had left the skins of the animals out to dry, and we still had a small stash of food from this morning. It would have to be a good enough start, but we needed more.

I jumped to my feet. "What can I do to help?"

"Why don't you rest? I'll figure things out." Richart's voice was kind but sent me flaming.

"Just because I'm going to have a baby doesn't mean I can't do anything. I want to help out. The more hands we have working on this, the sooner we can get things going and be prepared for anything that comes our way."

Richart's eyes were wide. I never spoke to him like that before, and it clearly caught him off guard. If I was honest, it caught me a bit off guard as well. I glanced at Candui, who held a hand to her mouth like she was holding back a laugh. It was a little funny.

"I'm sorry," Richart said, sounding sincere. "I wasn't thinking. Of course you can do things to help. I'm not used to taking care of a pregnant woman. Forgive me for wanting to keep you safe, and I will do better in the future to include you."

My anger sizzled the rest of the way out. "Apology accepted." Never thought I'd hear one from him. "What can I help you with?"

"Why don't we see about using blankets to make a temporary shelter? It won't be the best option, but it will help until we can build something better. One of us should always be on watch, so it only needs to be big enough to fit three of us in it at a time, plus our things."

I went to his pack and started to open it.

"I'll grab that." Richart hoisted it away from me. "Do you have any rope?"

Strange. "I don't."

"As a matter of fact, you do," Candui said. "I put some in the bottom when I helped pack up bags at Scerta's. There's not much of it, but it should help get the job done. There's also some in my bag."

"Thank you for thinking ahead." That would have never occurred to me.

She shrugged. "I packed a few extra things I thought might be useful."

"Better to be prepared." I shifted through my pack, removing things as I went, except my underthings. I didn't want those to be displayed before Richart. The thought had me blushing. I pulled out the rope before putting my things back.

Candui handed me her pack, and together, we went through it. I said, "There are a lot more things in your pack than mine. It's practically bursting."

"I didn't want you to strain yourself carrying too much. You still have a lot in your pack, though, so don't get too carried away."

Was I angry, like I got with Richart? Perhaps a little, but I understood where they were both coming from. I wanted to take care of the little one too. It would be nice when he was born; I could see him and move him around, others could better help, and I would do more. But then, I always know where he is at now, and I'm not afraid for anything except what happens to me. It would be a trade-off. And I had months to get used to the idea of him being exposed to the world.

"Where should we set up this tent?" I asked Richart.

"Over here. It's going to be in the sun in the morning, but the shade in the afternoon, which will be better with the coming summer."

I walked over with him. "Have you made many like this before?"

"A few. It's something you do in zasin training. We should have brought a couple tents. They would make things a lot easier. Of course they'd be a lot heavier as well, and we had enough stuff to carry."

"I'm sorry," Candui said. "I wish I could walk and didn't have to be carried everywhere. I don't like being a burden."

"Don't worry about it." He turned to her. "I'd rather have you here than be able to bring more things."

"But I'm such a bother."

"You aren't," I said. "Besides, you'll make up for all of it when you get better. Knowing you, you'll be working twice as hard as the rest of us in no time." I turned to Richart. "She used to finish her laundry long before me and then would help with mine. So yes, she's washed some of your clothes." I laughed.

He raised an eyebrow at me as Candui blushed.

"I wanted to help," she said.

"And you did. I would have spent a lot more time washing without you. That means a lot, but especially this past winter, when it was so cold."

"I'm surprised the river didn't ice up," she said.

"Me too." I frowned at the memory. I hated doing laundry in freezing temperatures, but Candui made it more bearable.

"I didn't realize how close you two are," Richart said.

I glanced at her, and she looked back. "Not as close as we should be," I said. "Not while we lived in Bola. I've learned a lot about her since we've begun this journey."

"And I have learned a lot about you." She propped her pack up behind her and rested against it. "It would be nice if we knew more about how long it was going to take my leg to heal. I can't handle this. It's driving me nuts."

Richart threaded the blanket over a thick tree limb. "I wish I could tell you. From the little training in injuries we got as zasin, I'd say it's going to be some time yet. The more you rest it and stay off it, the better it's going to be."

That was going to be so hard for her. I sent her an encouraging smile and held the rope for Richart as he used it to string the material up and together. It took less time than I expected to have the makeshift tent up. It wasn't perfect, with only a back and no front, and barely big enough for three of us and our stuff, but it was much better than what we'd been dealing with.

For a brief moment, I wanted to be at home, where I had a nice soft bed I could use and lots of blankets I'd made myself. But the thought was quickly gone. Not only had I saved my child's life by escaping into the Umpi Forest, I'd also gotten to know Richart and Candui better. They were good people I should have known them well in the first place. I was grateful for the opportunity to do so now. Hopefully, Aphier would turn out to be of the same caliber. He seemed so, as far as I could tell, but I needed more time to test it out for sure.

"We should start gathering more wood for our fire, and see if we can find a couple crutch-like branches for Candui," Richart said.

I followed him, though we stayed within sight of Candui at all times. I gathered wood—mostly smaller pieces that could be used as a starter, but some bigger ones as well—and went back and forth to where we stored it beside the tent.

Richart brought in giant pieces that needed to be cut with his ax.

"How did you carry that in the first place? It's so big," I said.

He turned and gave me a grin that had my stomach doing flip flops. "I have my ways."

And that was all he would say about it.

When he went a little deeper into the forest and brought out a whole trunk, I watched his muscles strain against his shirt. He was far stronger than I would have expected. And I expected a lot of strength from a zasin.

"This should be good for now. There's still a lot out there that's fallen, but I don't think we need it yet." He pulled out his ax and told me, "Keep looking for something we can use for crutches, but stay in sight. I'm going to work on this. Be extra aware of your surroundings at all times. Candui, will you help me keep an eye out for nasties?"

"Certainly." Her gaze was already on the forest, but now it was sharper than ever. I heard once that elves could see better than humans. Was that true?

I wandered around the edge of the clearing, looking for

anything that would be of good use to her. I kept getting distracted by the noises in the forest around me. A crack here. A chirp there. My senses were on alert. Everything seemed so harmless, but I knew better than to think that.

As I was making the rounds, I came across another bush of what looked like hippaberries, though I didn't dare try one without Aphier clearing it. "Richart."

He stopped his steady chopping to glance up at me and wipe his brow.

"I found a berry bush over here. We should tell Aphier about it when he gets back."

"Excellent. Anything that would work as a crutch?"

"Not yet, but I'll keep looking."

He nodded and went back to swinging his axe, the rhythmic noise filling the air.

The day passed slowly, and it was far past time for lunch. My stomach was growling when Aphier returned with five bunnies strung up in one hand. "Found food. And all looks clear. We shouldn't have any problems—at least not right away."

It had better stay that way.

After pointing out the bush to Aphier, I sat by the fireside to watch him prepare food. I'd never skinned animals or dressed them—I bought them from the butcher taken care of— but I was determined to learn. To do as much as I could to help out.

As soon as he pulled out his knife and put it toward the creature, I ran as fast and far as I could before heaving up my breakfast. A moment later, Richart was at my side, water skin in hand.

I wanted to hide under the dirt or behind a tree. Anywhere but where he could see me. I couldn't believe I vomited in front of him.

Still, I took the proffered water and rinsed my mouth a few times. I straightened, dabbing my mouth on a handkerchief. The water skin was almost empty. "Do you want me to fill this back up for you?"

"Nah. I have it. Are you feeling better?"

I glanced back at camp, where Aphier looked down at his work, Candui watching him. They were a ways off, trees between us, but I could still see them. "Yes. I guess I couldn't handle cleaning the animals." My stomach churned when I thought about it.

"You don't have to do that, then. Don't worry about it. There are enough of us here that others can do that chore."

"I'm sorry." And mortified.

"Don't be. It's one of those things that comes with being pregnant."

"Where did you hear about that?" I was barely learning stuff like that, and I was the one carrying the child.

"My aunt talked to me about it before we got married."

"I see." I wished my mother had too. Maybe then I wouldn't feel so lost as to what to do. Maybe she planned on it, but it never happened. Or maybe she was so busy teaching me magic in our hidden together time that she didn't get the chance.

"Is there anything you'd like to know? I can share what little knowledge I do have."

Still embarrassed over throwing up in front of him, I couldn't bring myself to look at him.

"If you want to know, ask." He started to reach toward me but pulled back.

I handed him the water skin, and together, we walked back to camp. I avoided looking at what Aphier was doing but managed to say, "Sorry."

"Forget it." He had the rabbits roasting over the fire. I tried not to glance their way, so I didn't have a repeat of the previous moments.

When they were cooked, I took some to Candui and ate

beside her, attempting not to steal peaks at Richart. I enjoyed being drawn to him, but it also left me wondering why I hadn't been before. Had I been so wrapped up in myself and losing my family that I hadn't taken the chance to really see him?

Whatever the case was, I wanted to see him now, and for a good long time.

CHAPTER TWENTY-FIVE

A fter waking to a freezing morning and eating more berries for breakfast, I was aching for something real. Though I wanted to be kind, I felt snarly and agitated. It was probably because all my clothes were snug.

"Do you need me to do anything? If not, there's a couple things I wish to attend to," I said.

Richart was close by, clearing an area for our new home to go while Aphier was in the forest, bringing in wood.

Richart said, "Go ahead and do what you need to. I can get your help later."

I went to my pack in our makeshift shelter, where I'd been warm while being in the middle, until the others got up. I took out some extra fabric I'd picked up from my mother's house, grabbed some needle and thread along with some outfits, and went to sit by Candui.

"What are you doing?" She'd been tasked with weaving together wood splinters I'd gathered after dinner last night to form baskets so we could collect food easier.

"I'm going to let out my clothes. Everything is too tight."

She gave me a sympathetic glance. "We should have done so sooner. Even with the loose style of clothing you have been wearing, I've noticed your growing belly. Do you need help?"

I didn't want to think about my belly. I didn't want to be huge, but I wanted a good, healthy baby. "I've got this, but thank you."

It was almost second nature to unpick the seams of the black dress and sew on extra material. Candui gave suggestions as I went, and we fell into a steady rhythm that reminded me of when we used to wash laundry together, though this was much nicer.

As we did our tasks, the men took turns bringing in logs and cutting them. It wasn't long before they had a good pile going. I didn't know anything about putting a cabin together, but based on Scerta's home, Richart would make a nice little place for us to live. And Candui would have the knowledge to make a roof that would keep us dry.

Despite knowing that, it was difficult to think of all the tasks we had before us, to make this area livable. We needed to accomplish it before my little one came.

At some point, the men switched from working on the shelter to finding food. They would take turns coming back, with little bits at a time. When they were finished, there was more food than I'd seen since we were at my parents' house. My mouth watered, as I looked at the stacks of berries, tubers, and roots in Candui's woven bowls, along with some greenery we'd have to eat today or tomorrow before it wilted.

"How did you find so much in these cool spring temperatures?" Candui asked.

Aphier gave a sly grin. "You have to know where to look. Besides, this isn't that much, for how long we were out there looking. It's going to be a lot easier come summer."

"What should we have for dinner?" I tried not to look at the ingredients too eagerly.

The others laughed, and I blushed.

Richart said, "We might as well get something cooking. It's almost dinner time anyway. Candui, what would you suggest we do with this?"

While they discussed food, Richart brought me a basket of berries. I put down the last dress I'd been working on and dove into the basket with more enthusiasm than was warranted. For the first time in weeks, things were looking up.

THINGS WERE DEFINITELY NOT LOOKING up. I lay in our tent, being sprinkled with water from the rainstorm that'd been going since the middle of last night. I was drenched.

Finally giving up, I crawled toward the opening and grunted. Everywhere hurt. Richart had trained me hard last night, teaching me more fighting skills. I'd never been this sore before. Once I pulled myself up and out, I had to avoid puddles, but couldn't avoid the mud.

Aphier was working through the rain, and Richart had to be out, getting food or materials for the house. The fire sputtered but didn't go out under the light patter. Candui was nowhere near the fire. I glanced around and found her trying to take refuge under a tree.

When we made eye contact, she said, "There's some breakfast for you here." She held up one of the baskets she made yesterday.

I sloshed over to her and grabbed some berries. "Did you get any sleep last night?"

"Nope. You?"

"Not really. Everything's wet, wet, wet. And dirty. Feels like I'll never be warm and clean again."

"I hear you." She grimaced.

I couldn't just be negative. It wasn't helpful, and she had enough to deal with as it was. "At least spring is continuing to warm up, and summer is coming."

"True. We'll have to find seeds to plant, if we want to make a garden. It needs to be planted now."

"Good point." Should have thought of that sooner and brought some with me, but now we'd have to make do with what we could find.

Richart came in the clearing, pulling a tree trunk after him. His muscles strained, his tunic wet and plastered to him. He had to be as miserable as we were under this tree, if not more. Despite that, he came over to us with a smile when he was done.

Candui brought up the need for seeds, and he said, "I got some from my aunt's house. One thing she has a lot of."

"That's great." We could eat something new in a few months' time when they grew.

"We'll start on them tomorrow," he said.

I met his gaze, and my stomach did a flip. Was it the baby moving, or something else?

The rain pattered out, and I joined Richart in his foray into the woods, looking for food while he searched for wood that would make a better cabin. We worked through the day, stopping only for lunch. After dinner, we trained together, sometimes with Aphier's help.

I fell into bed at night exhausted and woke up groggy but managed to get up and get to work.

The days became a routine. Working all day and training at night. As my skills improved, my stomach grew. My little one was getting bigger, insisting on showing himself to the world.

Candui slowly healed, helped tend the garden, and put together thatch for the house that was almost finished. It was small, but would hold us all and perhaps a table and chairs one day, but before we could get to that, we switched to working on a smoke house to preserve meat for the winter.

As the days passed and my body changed, everything else seemed to stay the same. My relationship with Richart was different than before I became pregnant, but I wanted more.

The summer was plentiful in food, and we had too many run-ins with creatures of the forest. It wasn't a perfect life, but it was life, and I was happy.

We worked harder than I ever did in my entire life, but it left me feeling like I accomplished something. I worked on making baby clothes, blankets, and nappies out of whatever scraps I found, and I also assisted the others in finding and growing food.

Candui was the perfect friend. Doing laundry was my least favorite chore, but it was made easier with her at my side. We grew closer than when we were in Bola.

In contrast, Aphier was solicitous, but we kept things light between us. I wanted to know more about who he was, but it never felt like the right time to ask.

As summer waned, my stomach grew uncomfortably large, and sleeping more than an hour or two at a time became almost impossible. The men grew scruffier, only taking the rare occasion to shave off their beards. Other than my belly, we all became leaner but tougher. Our food might be plentiful, but with all the work we did, it was difficult to keep up with our dietary needs.

Training concentrated on me throwing knives or daggers, now that my body was more cumbersome. It wasn't ideal, but then, I would be able to better protect my baby soon enough. Candui and Richart thought the baby would come any time now.

Aphier and Candui were off gathering water for supper while I had a moment to sit and relax on a sturdy chair Richart had made. He'd finished putting dinner together and let it simmer by the fire when the baby gave me a good kick in the stomach. I let out a gasp and a giggle.

"What is it?" Richart asked.

"Your son is doing some training of his own in my belly."

He chuckled before coming to sit beside me. He was quiet, pressing his lips together over his beard and relaxing them.

"What is it?" I asked.

He clamped his hands together, and stared off into the distance. "I was wondering if you'd mind if I felt the baby while he's active."

A thrill chased through me. We'd only touched to train and kept to ourselves other than that. The thought of his hand on my belly, feeling our child, brought me a surge of unexpected joy. "I should have thought of letting you do so sooner. Please go ahead."

"Really?" A goofy grin spread across his face.

"Of course."

He turned toward me and rested a hand on my belly. Warmth spread across me, starting where he touched and blooming through every part of me. The baby responded swiftly with a kick.

The look of joy on Richart's face was unlike anything I'd seen before. "That was our baby."

I grinned at him, trying not to let my emotions get the better of me. "He's strong, like his daddy."

We were silent for a few moments as the baby continued to kick and squirm. After my little one settled down, Richart's expression became more serious, and he slid his hand from the front of my belly to my waist as he drew nearer.

"Adriella, there something I have to tell you." His face was only inches from mine.

I wanted to close the distance between us, but more than that, I wanted to hear what he had to say. "What is it?"

"I'm s—"

The sound of a branch snapping reached my ears. I whipped around to find another person in our midst.

CHAPTER TWENTY-SIX

"Nopli? What are you doing here?" More than that— "How did you find us?" I hadn't seen the elf since we left her gypsy encampment.

She was thinner than when I last saw her, her eyes sunken in. "I need to speak with you." She took several steps forward, but Richart jumped up and put himself between us.

"Say what you must from over there." He put a hand on the hilt of his sword.

"It has to be said only to her." She slouched as if she didn't think he'd listen.

I stood and nudged Richart aside. "It's all right. I'll be fine. You can stay within sight at all times. Will you please get her something to eat?"

"Do you trust her with our child's life?" he asked.

I searched her gaze. "I do." And if not, I had my handy dagger.

"If you're sure." He hesitated.

I gave him what I hoped was a reassuring smile. I wanted to know why and how she had found us. It could be important to keeping others away. What was more, her expression was earnest. I approached her.

She glanced at Richart, who'd moved to the fire but hadn't taken his hand from the hilt of his sword, and whispered, "I don't tell many people, but I have visions. A gift, if you will. That is how I found you."

I wanted to be surprised, but I wasn't. If I could do magic, what was stopping her from having visions? "You didn't lead anyone else here, did you?"

She shook her head. "No. My visions lately have been about you. They consumed all my thoughts, until I had to let them lead me to you or go crazy. I left my people to find you. That's how important this is."

I didn't want to admit how much this scared me. What could be so important? "And?"

"Someone is going to betray you."

I gave a small gasp as she stared at Richart. I turned to glance at him, only to find him watching us. Slowly, I turned my attention back to her. "My husband?"

"No. Yes. Maybe." She sighed. "The truth is, I don't know who it will be, but you have to believe me that it will happen."

The scary thing was I did. If her visions could lead her here, what was to stop them from telling her something like that? "Why is it so important to tell me?"

"I don't know. Visions are rare, but they always have a purpose. This drove me almost mad. Whatever the reason, it's vital."

Now that I looked closer, she seemed to have a weight lifted from her. Her eyes weren't as sunken, and color was returning to her cheeks.

"What am I supposed to do with this?" I asked.

"That is for you to decide. I can't help you any further. I must get back to my people." She took a step away.

"Wait. At least get something to eat and stay the night with us." Though I wasn't sure I wanted her around with the words she had told me. I didn't want a reminder. Who would betray me? There were only three people I lived with currently. The rest of the world had faded away—until she came along.

She hesitated. "I will eat, but then I must go."

"I insist you stay the night."

She glanced over the clearing, the small home we'd made for ourselves. "I would like to, but my people need me."

"I understand." And I did. Sometimes there were things bigger than you.

I led her over to Richart, who handed her a bowl of vegetables and rabbit. He stepped closer to me, hand on his sword's hilt, and asked her, "What do you want from us?"

"Nothing." She hurried and finished her bowl, and before I could do or say anything, she turned and ran back the way she'd come.

I wanted to call after her, to thank her for the warning, but fear held my tongue. What if she was right? What if someone did betray me? And who would it be?

CHAPTER TWENTY-SEVEN

Days passed, and nothing happened. Aphier, Candui, and Richart were as true as ever, though I was warier toward them. They couldn't have anything against me and the baby. It didn't make sense. I had to be safe.

Nopli's vision had to be wrong.

But then, why would it drive her here?

I wasn't certain I wanted the answer. Richart tried to get what she said out of me, but I kept quiet. I didn't want him to worry any more than he already did.

Despite my not telling him, there was a closeness growing between us. Something that I had longed for but still didn't understand.

"I'm going to fetch some berries," Candui announced, her leg having healed.

Aphier was off, hunting for meat.

"Are you sure you want to go alone?" I asked. She'd done so before, but it made me nervous, especially since Nopli had found us.

"I'll be fine." She waved away my concern, scooped up a basket, and headed toward the forest.

It wouldn't stop me from worrying over her even though her leg was completely healed. I headed toward the garden, to see how I could tend it. Heat crept up my face as I passed Richart. He turned from what he was doing and followed me.

"You look prettier every day," he said.

I stopped walking, my cheeks growing hotter. "Bigger every day. Maybe this is where the myth about dragons came from. Giant pregnant women, breathing fire because of how huge they are."

"I'd pay to see you breathe fire."

"Pay what? Food? If that's the case, I'll get right on it."

He laughed. "What sounds good?"

"A buttery, flaky pie." We had no way to make the crust, though, which was what I craved most.

"Ah. Well, I suppose there will be no fire-breathing today."

"That's unfortunate. I was looking forward to it." The baby gave a hard kick. "Oh. He's moving. Feisty little thing. Would you like to feel?"

His eyes brightened. "Where should I put my hand?"

He reached out toward me, and I took his hand in mine. The calluses scratched against my palm but I didn't want to let go. His touch shot tingles up my arm. I placed his hand on my stomach where the baby kicked and enjoyed the feel of his hand pressed against my giant belly.

He stayed there a moment, not doing anything. "I don't feel any— Whoa. That was my baby. What a kick. He's going to come out a tough tyke."

The grin on Richart's face made me want to lean in closer, but not only did my belly get in the way, there was also his hand between us. The baby threw a few more punches, and I laughed. "He's going to be a handful. That's certain."

Richart's face grew serious. He slipped his hand to the front of my stomach, across my side, and around my back, pulling me so close to him my belly pushed against him. My breathing turned shallow as I looked up at him. I licked my lips, trying to ignore the pounding in my chest.

We were back to where we were before Nopli had interrupted. Would he finish saying what he wanted to? Or would something more happen?

Just because we made a baby together didn't mean we'd ever kissed out of love before. Was that what was going to happen now? Was this warm fluttering in my chest what it felt like to be in love? I wanted more of it. Lots and lots more. I wanted to be held by him. Touched by him. Kissed by him. If only my growing belly wasn't getting in the way.

He leaned down, and I found myself tilting my head toward him while holding onto his arms, both around me now. We were going to do what I'd dreamed about for months. His lips were going to touch mine. The thrill that went through me couldn't contain itself. It sent me on my tiptoes, aching to reach him.

His breath was warm across my lips. I strained toward him.

A growl reverberated through the air, and we snapped apart. I asked, "What was that?"

A quick glance around showed Aphier running back into camp. Candui followed him with an empty basket, and they both looked around the clearing.

"Do you have your dagger?" Richart asked, voice tight.

"Yes."

"Get it out." He pulled out his sword while Aphier did the same.

My dagger was in my hand before I realized it. The growl came again, the sound of it sending a chill through my body. Whatever the creature was, it sounded big. Very big. And hungry.

Richart snaked his arm around me. He whispered, "Stay close to me. Don't get separated."

Candui and Aphier silently made their way over to us slower, crossing the clearing a footstep at a time. The moment they reached us, an enormous animal bounded into the little area that had been our area for months, its huge fangs dripping with saliva. It had a long, thin body of gray with darker spots on its hind end. It was low to the ground, but agile.

Aphier swore. This creature wasn't something I'd seen before, and it looked hungry. If Aphier was this upset, it couldn't be a good thing.

Another roar sounded, the black hairs on the back of the creature's body standing on end, as a second and third animal joined the first.

Richart stuck his arm out in front of me, sword in the other hand, and slowly started backing up. The others did the same. At least we were getting some space from the beasts, but the way they eyed us, it wouldn't be that way for long.

Without warning, the first of them leaped across the distance between us in a single bound.

Richart slashed at it, making it dart away. To us, he yelled, "Run!"

I didn't dare turn my back to the monsters coming at us, but I did hurry backward as fast as I could. Unfortunately, that meant going away from the cabin as the creatures surrounded it.

Candui grabbed my wrist, dragging me along with her. I stumbled and fell, and the other two creatures dived for me. Richart's and Aphier's swords swished through the air so fast, it was difficult to follow, but they kept the animals off me.

The pain in my bottom barely registered as Candui helped me to my feet. Richart and Aphier moved with grace in a singular purpose. Candui turned me around and forced me away from the fight.

I moved my legs, trying to keep up with her. Despite training all along, the movements were hard with my large belly, and she slowed to stay with me.

The growls behind us were loud. I glanced back to find Aphier and Richart losing ground. "We have to help," I told Candui.

She stopped tugging me, looked behind us, and widened her eyes. She turned and pulled a dagger from her boot that I didn't know she kept there.

I kept my dagger ready, not wishing to have to use it, but knowing I needed to protect myself and my baby. A rustle to my right had me turning in time to find a smaller, but still well-fanged and well-clawed creature coming at me.

I grunted as I swung my dagger toward it like Richart taught me. It met its mark, and the creature howled and moved away with a hiss. I didn't want to have to keep fighting this thing, and hoped it would leave me be since blood dripped from its shoulder, but it came at me again.

Diving toward the ground, I wished on all the stars that I could save my baby. I rolled and landed on my side, instead of my stomach, the wind rushing past as the creature jumped by me. The pain wasn't bad, but it would be if I couldn't do something about it.

I twisted onto my back as the creature returned, snarling in my face. With a quick slash, I swung upward. The creature fell on me, heavy on my bulging stomach. I shoved it off, ignoring the smear of blood it left across my tunic, and stood.

A hand gripped my shoulder. I whirled, only to find Richart turning away from me to fend off another attack.

"Are you all right?" he yelled.

"Fine." In a manner of speaking.

"We have to go. These things aren't giving up." He took a couple steps, exposing the dying creature I had stabbed.

The bigger creatures stalked toward us until they reached the downed littler one. They stopped and howled. Aphier and Candui reached us. Richart tugged me toward him, and I followed, not daring to take my eyes off our attackers. Walking backward wasn't easy, but it was better than getting jumped from behind.

I felt my way with my feet, making every step precise and avoiding things poking up from the ground. I thought I was doing well until a stick cracked under my foot.

The creatures lifted their heads, their teeth barred as they growled at us. I had unwittingly drawn their attention. This wasn't good.

"Turn around and run," Richart whispered. "I'll hold them off."

"I'm not going without you," I replied.

"Stubborn woman."

We continued to back up while I expected to be pounced on by the angry creatures. Instead of coming at us, they bent their heads back down, sniffing at the downed animal. I wasn't happy I had to hurt it, but if it kept us safer for longer, I was grateful I did so.

We dodged trees, Richart stepping in front of me each time we came to one.

We were far enough to barely make out the creatures through the trees when Aphier said, "We should get out of here faster, before that gruta dies. If it does, those things are going to be after us in no time at all, harder than they were before."

I glanced at him, only to find blood running down his left arm. Beside him, Candui looked rumpled, but with no wounds I could see. She nodded at me, holding out her hand. I took it, and together, we turned and ran.

The soft thud of footsteps followed us, letting me know Aphier and Richart were close by, coming with us. I don't know what I would have done if they hadn't stuck by our side. I needed them both in my life, as well as that of my baby's. We wouldn't have survived as long as we had without them.

We'd been running only a few minutes when a chilling howl reverberated through the air.

Aphier swore again. "Faster. We have to find a safe place."

Where would we possibly find shelter now our cabin was no longer an option? I pushed myself as quick as I could, dodging trees and rocks while keeping a hold of Candui with one hand and my dagger with the other. I grunted out, "Can't we climb a tree?"

"In your condition?" Richart sounded as if he wasn't even out of breath.

He was right. There was no way I could get up a tree without considerable effort and help. I tried not to think about the blood trail the dagger was dripping as we went, but it was hard to ignore. It might help lead them to us. After wiping it on my pants, I shoved it in its sheath, hoping I wouldn't need it again.

The howls continued, pressing me on. If only I knew where we were running to, but I hadn't a clue. We passed the farthest area from camp I'd been since we arrived here. The others might have gone farther without me. Candui seemed sure as her steps pounded next to mine, our breathing coming in gasps.

The howling stopped, the forest going still except for our somewhat rapid escape. I was aching in ways I hadn't ached before, slowing us down.

Determined not to let my pain get in the way of escaping the creatures, I pushed myself harder. We ran and ran until I had to slow to a speed-walk. It wasn't enough, but it was better than standing still. Richart and Aphier were at our backs, and whenever I glanced back, one of them was doing the same, looking at the trail we came through.

No new howls or growls sounded. Instead, the life of the forest slowly picked up. Birds chirped and sang.

"Are we safe?" I asked.

Aphier's eyes were tight. "Mayb—"

A growl tore through the air as one of those things landed on Richart and fell with him to the ground. I whipped out my dagger at the same time as Aphier stabbed at it. The creature turned about, baring its teeth at us. I brandished my weapon at it, growling back.

Richart, who still lay on the ground, whipped up his sword and pierced its side. The animal snarled before running off.

"Now we may be safe," Aphier said.

"May?" Candui asked.

I focused my attention on Richart, my voice coming out frantic. "Richart? Are you all right?"

He grunted. "I've been better. That thing was heavy."

"Tell me about it."

"It got on you?" After I nodded, he asked with concern in his voice, "Are you well? Is the baby?"

I shrugged, hoping we both were.

He groaned and rolled onto his side before pulling himself to his feet and coming to me.

"We don't have time to check," Aphier said. "No one seems in critical condition. We need to get as far from here as we can." He walked toward the opposite direction than the one the creature had left in.

Richart took me by the hand, and we followed him and Candui.

I hated to ask, but the words slipped out before I could stop them. "Does this mean our home is gone?"

"To us, probably. I wouldn't dare go back there for at least a week, if ever. The gruta are highly territorial, and with two or more of them wounded, I wouldn't be surprised to see them take up our site."

I sniffed but didn't let out any more of my emotions. Now was not the time for that—not while we were still running for our lives. But—sunblasted—we worked so hard. Why didn't we foresee something like this happening and make plans for it?

Months and months of hard work gone in moments. What were we going to do? How were we going to feed ourselves now? Where would we find shelter in this nightmare of a forest? We should have never gotten so comfortable in a place that could be taken over at any moment. We needed something better than what we previously had, especially with the baby coming soon, though I didn't know how much longer I had.

Where would we find such a place?

CHAPTER TWENTY-EIGHT

W e spent the next couple of nights sleeping wherever we could and always keeping watch, which was normal but felt more necessary than ever. The days were spent with us wandering from place to place, looking for anywhere we could make our new home. We'd left everything behind, except the clothes we wore and weapons we had on us. Food was scarce. I felt it but tried not to show it, though the others gave me most of it.

I was slower than ever, trudging my feet through the squishy ground and wishing for my bed back at camp, not to mention all of the supplies we lost.

I groaned softly.

"Are you doing all right?" Richart asked.

I glanced up ahead at Aphier, who led the way, Candui close behind him. Richart and I had fallen back a ways but were close enough that they should be able to hear my reply. "Just tired."

"We could stop for a break."

Aphier turned to look at us. "Do you need one?"

"On this swampy ground? There would be nowhere to have a

break." Though I ached for one. "Let's keep going until we find hard ground again."

"We do seem to have hit swamp land," Aphier said. "I'm not familiar with any swamp in the Umpi Forest. Maybe we should turn around."

I gritted my teeth. Backtracking wasn't something I wanted to do when we hadn't found anything good behind us. Though there was nothing good where we were at either, and it seemed to be getting worse.

"That would be for the best," Richart said.

"Why don't you lead us for a while? Candui and I will hold up the rear," Aphier replied.

I turned, hiding a yawn from them, and followed Richart. The ground stayed squishy, until at some point, my feet were sinking into it. This couldn't be good. "Is this the way out?"

"I thought so, but now I'm beginning to wonder. Aphier?" Richart said.

Aphier shook his head. "I thought it was the way out too."

"But it's not, is it?" Candui put a hand on her hip. "We're lost in a swamp, with a pregnant lady who needs to find dry land to rest on. What are we going to do?"

Quiet descended on our little group until Aphier said. "Let me climb a tree and see if there's any hint as to where we are at and how to get out."

He took to the nearest tree, grabbed a hold of the limbs, and pulled himself up. The smell had at some point gone from fresh, clean air to a stench rather like rotten eggs. My stomach churned. At least I wasn't hungry anymore. A mosquito took a bite off my arm. I swatted at it without taking my gaze from Aphier, who climbed to the top as I smacked several more mosquitoes.

Once he was up there, I could barely see him through all the foliage. His voice carried down. "The mountains are back that way, but I don't spot another way out."

Another mosquito bit my neck, and I slapped at it. "That's wonderful. We're going to be stuck in this swamp forever." Or until we died from swamp sickness. One of the two. If I could climb a tree, I could get out of this muck for a while, but I was stuck down here.

Candui gave my hand a squeeze. "We'll figure something out."

"Sorry." I sighed. "I don't know what's come over me. I want to be done with this place." And find a safe spot to call *home* before the baby was born.

"Don't worry about it. We're all under a lot of stress." She slapped at her arm. "Darned mosquitoes."

"They're getting you too?" Richart scanned the area.

"And me," I said. "They're bad here."

Aphier was almost down from the tree when something tickled my left arm. I slammed my hand over it, not even glancing at it. As soon as I hit it, I knew something was wrong. Very wrong.

It was big. Much larger and sturdier than a mosquito. Slowly, I moved my hand away from my arm, cupping whatever was in it. "Oh no."

Richart and Candui looked at me.

Candui asked, "What is that?"

"That's a dead fairy," Richart said.

I didn't know they existed, though I shouldn't be surprised. And I had no way to magic it back. What had I done?

It was about as long as my fingers and looked like a human with gossamer wings that were bent because of my actions.

Aphier jumped down and landed next to me. "We are in so much trouble." He took the limp form from me and held it. "This isn't good."

I put a hand to my mouth, holding back the bile. I had just

killed a fairy. He lay motionless on Aphier's palm, barely fitting on it. "I—I didn't mean to. I thought it was a mosquito."

"We need to get out of here before something worse happens." Richart put an arm around me.

Despite his trying to offer comfort, all I could feel was horror at having killed an innocent. I meant no harm, except to a mosquito.

Aphier moved toward the tree, holding the dead fairy extended out toward a limb, when a buzzing sounded. It started off soft and gradually grew.

Aphier winced, and Richart said, "Don't put your hands on your weapons. We couldn't beat them if we tried."

"That's right. You couldn't," a little voice chirped.

I glanced around as the buzzing subsided to a low hum. We were surrounded by fairies of all colors, their wings glistening despite the overcast. Their variations were as many as—or even more than—the humans and elves I knew, only they were small and had wings.

Aphier turned to them and said, "I'm sor—"

"You will take this up with the queen," the little male speaker said, flying right to Aphier's face before turning to the rest of us. "All of you. She will decide your fate. If it were up to me—and the queen usually goes along with what I say—it would be death for you all, for killing one of our fellow fairies."

"But—"

Before I could finish, he flew in front of my face, sticking his sword to my nose until it gave a little pinch. "You will not talk until asked to do so."

He flew away, and I rubbed my nose. My hand came away with blood on it. What did I get us into this time? It didn't sound like something we'd be able to get out of, with how sharp that sword was. Sure, we could handle one tiny person poking at us, but a whole pack surrounding us? I doubted we'd last long against them, despite their size.

"Forward. Fly," called the little fairy, moving forward faster than I expected.

The swarm around us moved, forcing us to do so as well or be punctured by a thousand little swords.

Three fairies came and took the body of the dead fairy from Aphier, then zipped away with it. Richart took my hand, and we set off, following as fast as we could. My legs moved swiftly, but it wasn't fast enough. It seemed like the fairies behind us were getting closer by the second, and they weren't afraid to use their weapons.

"Move it," a female fairy chirped from behind me. The back of my neck stung. I went to swat it but stopped myself in time. Was it a fairy or a mosquito? I wasn't about to risk our lives even more by killing it. I could handle itchy bites; I couldn't handle being put to death by a fairy.

We hurried forward, sloshing through the wet that grew deeper, up to mid-calf and then to my knees. Did the fairies live here because they could fly and no one else could stand the stinky wetness? Whatever the reason, I wanted out. I wanted to hope that we could make it, but I wasn't feeling as confident as I liked.

The clouds grew thicker overhead until a downpour splashed out. It didn't take long before I was soaking wet, exhausted, and famished. All I wanted was to be dry, warm, and satiated, but it didn't matter. I'd do whatever needed done.

The trees became so thick it was hard to walk two-by-two. Richart moved behind me, and I let my arm trail behind, so I could keep hold of him—my palm the only thing left warm. The branches were so impenetrable overhead that the rain stopped, though I could still hear a far-off pattering. Up ahead, light grew, until I was blinking to let my eyes adjust.

"Stop," a female voice called.

I stood still, not wishing to make them angrier than they were. My gaze came to terms with the light. There was something—no, someone—in the middle of the light. She was a fairy, the smallest of the bunch, and it radiated. Or perhaps that was the light behind her.

She—for she definitely had a female's body shape—was divine. Perfect, tiny features, shiny, long, blond hair, and a pair of delicate gossamer wings.

At some point during my perusal of her, the light dimmed and it was easier to see. The worst part was the little fairy's face was drenched with tears, and a scowl marred her perfect features.

"You killed my fairy guard." Her voice tinkled through the air.

"I did, but—"

She raised a hand, stopping my words.

Silence permeated the area, except for the sound of water falling from the sky. Not even the buzz of wings could be heard. The other fairies had all found places to perch and were bowing to the perfect fairy. She must be their queen.

She made a motion with her hand, and the fairies stood on the limbs of the trees they were on. Not many were at our backs. I was tempted to run, but what good would it do? I needed to stay calm and collected about this. They'd come upon us so fast, I had no doubt they'd catch us.

"We must mourn," the queen said. "While we mourn, you will stay here, with guards. They may not look like many to you but know that, if you try to escape, you will be killed without question. Do you understand?"

"Yes," Richart said.

"I need to hear it from you all."

We all gave our affirmation, and they left, except for a few who stayed behind, staring at us.

I bit my lip. What should I do? "Richart?"

"Mmm?" He didn't look up at me.

"I'm sorry. I apologize to you too, Candui and Aphier. I didn't mean for this to happen."

Candui placed a hand on my shoulder. "I know. Everything will be all right."

"Even if we're..." I couldn't bring myself to say *killed*. It would all be my fault. If only I'd looked before I swatted, we wouldn't be in this mess.

Richart tightened his arm around me, pulling me in closer. The wet mess we stood in was miserable. Even if we somehow survived this, I'd catch my death from this freezing swamp water. It wasn't something I wanted to experience, but maybe there was something I could do with magic to fix the situation.

Then again, maybe not. I didn't know much about healing. Mother had taught me other spells, some that had to do with things like minor weather helps, but we spent little time on healing. And certainly nothing on bringing a fairy back to life.

Could magic get me out of this situation in another way? Help us escape somehow? I hadn't been paying attention to the stars, like I should have. I needed to see how they were aligned and if any had faded or new ones appeared to have a better idea what I could or couldn't do. Unfortunately, it was day, overcast, and a thick covering of tree branches prevented me from seeing the sky.

There was nothing I could do.

As the time wore on, I found myself leaning into Richart and resting my head on his chest. I closed my eyes, wishing this would all go away and give me a chance to have a happy little family. I missed my boring life from before I discovered I was pregnant and the high king was doing away with babies.

In the distance, voices were singing. The sound was beautiful but melancholy. A tear in the last of daylight.

The air grew colder as the sound vanished. The light around us faded, except for where the fairy queen had stood. I'd thought it was her who glowed, but now I realized it was a fire behind her. How did they get it so bright? It made my eyes hurt to look at. Or perhaps it seemed that way because of the growing dimness around us.

I shivered, wishing we had our packs with all the things we'd made in the wilderness. And food. Lots and lots of food. Granted, my stomach was so small I couldn't eat much at a time, but I'd get to it, eventually—if I had any food.

It wasn't long before I was dreaming of food just out of reach, in a cold, wet room. I chased the food down a long hall that didn't end, but I never reached it.

Something shook me. I stirred. I'd been sleeping. I started to say something, but Richart shushed me, putting a finger to my lips. I blinked rapidly, and the world came into focus, showing me the fairies returning.

They surrounded us again, on the branches around us. The fairy queen came last, floating more than flying, and took her place in front of the fire.

I yawned. How did I fall asleep standing up, even if I was leaning on Richart? Not how I planned on spending my last few hours. What I did plan, I wasn't sure, but this wasn't it.

I straightened and moved away from Richart.

He pulled me back to him before I could get too far. The strength of his body next to mine gave me courage, if not hope.

The queen glared at me as if I personally insulted her. I couldn't blame her. I was the one who killed the fairy, though unwittingly.

"Leave us, all of you. Take everyone but the killer with you." The queen whisked her hand to the side.

The fairies flew around us, pushing space between Richart and me.

"Adriella," he called, anguish coating his words.

"Richart." My heart felt as if it was collapsing in on itself. What if I never saw him again?

He grasped my hand and held on tight but not tight enough. Tiny hands pried our fingers apart until we no longer held on to each other. I cried out for him again, and he strained to get to me.

"Go, before I order my guards to injure you." The queen's voice was firm.

I had no doubt she'd go through with her word. Taking a deep, calming breath to ease myself, I said, "I'll be fine, Richart. Go." Though who knew if I'd really be. My insides felt as if they were tearing apart. But I had to make the goodbye easier for him.

The fairies pushed him on, but he hesitated to follow them. "I love you," he said.

I swallowed, wishing I could have heard those words months ago. Wishing I could have said them months ago. But a peace settled in me, knowing I felt the same way. That we could share the knowledge with each other before we were parted. "I love you too."

He gave a sad smile before turning away from me. I watched my husband and our friends leave until I could no longer see them before turning toward the fairy queen. "What do you want from me?"

I should have asked more nicely, but the words came out brisk, full of the emotion I tried so hard to hold back.

"Silence. You have no right to speak until I ask you a question." Her voice was stern.

I pressed my lips together, willing myself not to say anything.

"That's better." Despite her grief and anger, her tone was melodic. "Now, why did you kill my soldier?"

He was a soldier? "I didn't know there were fairies in the forest. There was a pinch on my arm, and I thought it was a mosquito."

"So you killed him?"

"Well... yes, but it wasn't intentional. I've never met a fairy before and didn't expect to meet one today. If he had announced himself, I wouldn't have swatted him."

She put a finger to her lips. "You may mean that, but it doesn't take away from the fact that you killed one of my loyal guards. I sent him there to find out what was causing such noise in my land. He and a team of my best men and women were on the job. They saw what you did to him."

"I'm so sorry." More than words could say.

"Did you know no one is allowed in this swamp without my permission?"

"We didn't. We've only been in the Umpi Forest for a few months and didn't realize this swamp existed."

After a moment of silence, she said, "I believe you are telling the truth, but I cannot let this crime go unpunished."

I forced myself to keep eye contact. "I understand."

She perused my person. "Why is there blood on your tunic and pants?"

"From a gruta."

She raised her eyebrows. "How did you have a run-in with them?"

"They attacked our camp."

"I didn't know any humans lived in the Umpi Forest."

"We have, though only through one season and part of another."

She was quiet so long that I thought she wasn't going to respond. "Your belly is round like you are with child," she said.

Not where I expected her to go. "I am with child, one I think will be coming sometime in the near future." If she allowed us to live. Which didn't sound all too likely.

"The prophecy isn't entirely clear, but the high king has taken definite action against it."

She knew of the prophecy and high king way over in here? "What do you mean it's not clear?"

Not answering, she said, "Tell me how you wound up here?

Her curiosity seemed better than death threats, so I went with it. I started with my story, from realizing I was pregnant when the high king was killing babies to now. "We've had a rough time of things. All we want is for this baby to be safe."

She replied, "Babies are very dear to me and my people. I think you mean well, even if you did what you shouldn't. I will pardon you."

Hope sparked bright inside me. "And my companions? They are helping keep me and the baby alive and well."

"They will be spared, on the condition that you are exiled from my domain, never to return, on pain of death."

If I hadn't been standing in water, I would have gotten on my knees to thank her. "I'm so grateful you are granting us mercy."

She waved her finger at me. "It is the child I'm concerned with."

"Nevertheless, you have my gratitude, and I'm certain you will also have the gratitude of my companions."

"Just leave and never return."

"Yes, my lady. Only, we're lost. We don't know how to get out."

She snapped her fingers, and three fairies flew out of the forest. She told them, "You will escort this woman and her group away from the swamp and make certain they do not return. Go fetch the rest of her company."

They flew off. I twisted my hands together, wishing I knew what to say to her. She spared my life and theirs and didn't seem to want my *thanks*. "What is your name?" I asked.

"Xataywa. Why do you ask this?"

"I believe I will have a son, but if I'm wrong and I have a daughter, I will name her after you."

She tilted her head to the side. "Why would you do such a thing?"

"Because you pardoned us."

She pursed her lips. "I would be honored, then. And whether you have a boy or girl, I send my blessing that it will be a healthy, intelligent child." She spurred into action, flying to me and pressing a tiny hand to my belly. There was a soft glow and then a flash before she flew away several paces. "It is done."

I didn't feel any different, but if that was truly what she blessed my child with, I was beyond fortunate. "Thank you."

"Think nothing of it."

The three fairies returned, my friends trailing behind them, looking grim. I gave them a genuine smile, hoping to reassure them.

Richart reached me first and pulled me into a hug. "I thought I would never see you again."

"We're together now. It will be well," I said. "She's banishing us from this place, but not killing us."

"Thank the moons." He squeezed me more tightly.

Candui joined in, hugging us both, with Aphier standing off to the side, smiling.

"I can't believe you did it," Candui said. "How did you convince her?"

"Come now," the middle of the trio of fairies said, voice stern.

"We'll talk about it later." I disentangled myself from them and faced the fairies. "We're ready."

They turned and flew off. I hurried after them. "We're not that fast." Especially in the muck.

One of them zipped back, got behind me, and pushed on my shoulder with surprising strength.

I hurried forward. "I'm going. I'm going."

Aphier stepped ahead of me and quickened his pace, Candui following. Richart took me by the elbow, and we went forward.

We weaved back and forth, like we were walking in circles through the swamp. It took hours and hours, or it felt that way. The muck stayed at knee-level for some time before slowly receding.

The sky cleared, and the air smelled faintly of flowers. The sun was gone behind the mountains, but its rays shone above them. Night was almost upon us, but we were alive and free.

The fairies stopped and faced us.

The middle one said, "Do not return."

"We will do our best," Aphier said.

"Do better than your best, because should you return, you will die." All three zipped away, leaving no trace of them behind within moments.

"That was encouraging." The words were out before I could stop them.

"We'll stay away from anything that gets the least bit soggy," Aphier said. "Besides, I have a better idea where the swamp is, and we can better watch out for it in the future."

"What now?" Candui asked. She stood closer to Aphier than she usually would.

What was that about? Her seeking his comfort? She couldn't be falling for him. Humans and elves never coupled, that I knew of. Maybe she needed something concrete to hold on to. Something to ground her. And she happened to choose Aphier.

"You say you know where we are?" Richart asked Aphier.

"I do."

"Is there anywhere safe nearby we could stay for the night? Maybe find something to eat?"

The last part of that comment felt directed at me, not that Richart would say it. I was starving. The baby wiggled like he was hungry too.

"There isn't a lot around here. Maybe we should get going and walk through the night." Aphier's expression was tight.

"There's something you're not saying." Worry over what it could be crept up on me. I'd rather have answers than the unknown.

When Aphier didn't reply, Richart lifted his eyebrows. "Is that true?"

With a huff, Aphier said, "It is."

"What aren't you telling us?" Richart's words were firm.

Aphier glanced around the forest, and I couldn't help but look too. There was nothing out of the ordinary. Despite that, I was tense, ready for something to happen. For a creature to jump out at us and finish us off.

"We're in orc territory." Aphier's words made a chill slice through me.

Those fairies must have been trying to get their revenge to drop us off here.

Candui went pale. "Orcs?"

"I'm afraid so. So you can see why I'm eager to be on our way and not wanting to stop for the night."

"How do you know about orc territory but not the fairies?" I asked.

"I've seen this area before. Never saw the swamp, though. I'm not sure how I missed it, unless it's growing or moving, which would take magic."

"Don't say such things," Richart said. "The dangers of the forbidden ought not to be mentioned when things are already dark."

My throat tightened.

"Sorry. Just a fact." Aphier scowled.

Richart's hand was on the hilt of his sword as he turned his attention on me. "Can you keep going, or do you need to rest?"

A rest would be wonderful, but I wasn't about to take it with orcs around. "I might be slow, but I'd rather be moving."

"Let's go, then. Aphier, lead the way." Richart motioned for me to go ahead of him as Aphier took the lead.

I moved behind him, Candui taking a walk up next to me, with Richart behind. As we walked, Candui was still pale. Very much so. I couldn't blame her; the thought of orcs made my skin feel like it was peeled from my body, and she had it worse. The orcs might not like humans, but there was great enmity between them and elves. Wars had been fought over the slightest infraction. I'd hate to be the cause of a new one, for the first time in a hundred years.

I struggled to keep up. Aphier slowed down his pace, but we had to get out of there if we were going to survive. Candui put a hand on my back, supporting me. Behind us, Richart was so silent, I kept peeking back to see if he was still there. He always was, but fear that an orc snatched him wouldn't leave me.

The trees were as dark as ever, the underbrush we tramped through thicker than I was accustomed to, slowing us down even more. It wasn't the most ideal of conditions for getting away quickly. The lower sides of my belly ached. The baby's punching didn't help either. I kept going though, determined to keep him safe.

Aphier came to a stop and turned toward us. "Maybe we should stop for the night."

We were going pretty slow, but it was better than not moving at all.

"Is it safe?" Richart asked from behind me.

"No, but we're on the edge of their land. It will take hours to reach relative safety from here, and we all need a break."

All, as in me. My stomach ached, pain shooting through both of my sides. It couldn't be good for the baby, but neither would being caught by orcs. "We should keep going," I said.

Aphier stared me down. "Are you up for it? We've slowed

down to a crawl this past hour. We'd make much better time if we stopped for a few hours."

I didn't want to admit defeat, but stopping sounded so wonderful. "Fine. A few hours, though. We shouldn't stay long."

"The sun will be up soon, and we'll have light helping us out again," Aphier said.

"Both of us should keep watch," Richart said.

"Is that wise?" Candui asked. "Don't you need some sleep?"

"I won't be able to sleep until we're out of their territory," Richart replied. "And I'd feel much better if we had more eyes on the situation."

"I can help watch. I probably won't be able to sleep, either." Despite my drooping eyelids, fear raced through my veins, leaving me feeling like I'd never slumber again.

Richart and Aphier exchanged a look I barely caught in the dim light of two moons.

Richart said, "That's fine, but why don't you do it from a resting position?"

I glanced around the forest. There were lots of rocks and trees, but little else.

Candui must have sensed my problem. "Why don't I lean against a tree, and you can lay your head in my lap?"

"I don't want you to be miserable to make me comfortable."

"I promise it will be fine. I don't mind at all." Not waiting for my response, she picked a tree, sat down, and inclined against it. "The baby will be warmer and more comfortable this way."

I couldn't argue with that, not when she brought the baby into it. I slipped down next to her, resting my back on her. Richart and Aphier turned outward, scanning the dark forest around us. I too watched for those dark orc eyes to glisten back at me.

Having never seen an orc, I wasn't sure what I was looking for, but I'd heard tales. They were bigger than humans but smaller than elves and made by demons. They were pure evil brought upon the land. I didn't know much about their twisted ways, other than that I should be frightened of them. Very, very frightened.

But we would be fine. We were on the outskirts of their territory. We would rest for a few hours, and then we'd be back on our way, never to return.

The forest was full of noises normal for this time of night. The hooting of an owl. The rustling of bushes, as something small passed. Nothing that would say orcs were near as I stared into the dark forest.

I jolted awake. When did I fall asleep? And why was I leaning against Candui?

It came rushing back to me—where we were and what we needed to do.

Get out of this forsaken place.

I couldn't believe I slept. How did I manage that?

The forest was lighter, the sun's rays coming from somewhere in the distance, though I couldn't see the sun. My stomach growled, loud and long. I would put a hand over it, try to silence it, but it was so enormous now, it wouldn't do any good.

Richart's hand popped in front of my face, full of berries. "Found a treat for you."

"Thank you." I took the handful and ate. I wanted there to be more but didn't dare ask since the others either ate while I was asleep or didn't eat at all. I wanted to talk about our declarations of love, but it didn't feel like the right time with others so close.

I turned to Candui. "Thank you, too. Apparently, you make for a good pillow."

"No problem. I'm glad you were able to get some sleep."

Aphier was restless, leaning from side to side. "We should get going."

Richart held his hand out to me. I put mine in his, enjoying the feel of his calluses as he pulled me to my feet. My unwieldy belly bumped into him, and I held back a snicker. Now didn't seem like the best of times to burst out laughing with how tense Aphier was. But Richart smiled at me, rubbing his thumb across the back of my hand before letting go to help Candui up.

As she got up, I brushed myself off as best I could. My clothes were filthy, tattered, and still somewhat bloody. I needed a good long bath and new tunic and pants. These needed to be burned, they were stained so bad. My companions were in the same state, nothing but dirt and tears covering them.

Aphier didn't wait for acknowledgment before heading out. He turned and headed toward where the sunlight was coming from. Candui followed him, and I came behind, letting Richart bring up the rear again.

The day wore on as I waddled through the forest, wishing I could go faster. I had a strong inkling that, if it wasn't for me, they would have been out of orc territory by now.

It was chilly, making me wish I had something to warm myself with. Walking was good, warming me up, but my limbs and skin were still chilled. I combed my fingers through my hair, hoping to tame it some. Perhaps I needed to hack it all off, but I was loathe to do so after growing it out for years. If only we hadn't lost our campsite, we'd be in such a better place.

I continued to hike as fast as I could, letting my hand stray to the hilt of my dagger at my side every so often. Eventually, the trees thinned and the sun shone on us stronger. It was still on the cold side, but much better with the sun out.

Winter was coming. What would we do, without our food stores and blankets?

With the trees thinning, Aphier's pace slowed. Was that for me or if we were out of orc territory? I wasn't about to ask with how quiet everyone was being. I wouldn't be the one to set the orcs off to our presence.

We continued until the sun was almost straight overhead. Aphier stopped in a small clearing. "We should rest here for a while."

"Are we out of orc territory?" Richart asked what I wanted to know.

"We are, but still close enough to it we should be cautious."

The tension sagged out of my shoulders. Orc territory, I couldn't do. *Cautious,* I could.

I didn't wait for anyone to coddle me; I picked the softest looking spot on the ground, packed some leaves on it, and lay down.

Richart was beside me in an instant. He told Aphier, "Wake me when you're ready to switch." And then he turned on his side and rested his hand on my belly.

Warmth flooded from the spot he touched and throughout my body. It was the most at peace I'd felt since we'd been kicked from our forest home.

The baby kicked at Richart's hand, making him smile, though his eyes were closed. I stared at him as time passed, my eyelids growing heavy. At some point, I went to sleep with that warmth taking care of me.

I woke to cold. Richart was standing up. It must have been his turn for watch. I yawned and stretched. Aphier was tense, his hands balled up at his sides when Richart reached him. Though I couldn't hear his words, the sound was strained.

Richart straightened his back, reaching for the hilt of his sword. Something was wrong.

It was difficult to ignore the tingles of fear tickling my skin. I struggled to get to my feet and noticed Candui, awake and watching, not far away. Once I got to my feet, my belly trying to hamper me at every turn, I made my way over to the men. Their whispers stopped as I approached. "What's going on?"

Aphier looked to Richart. "You might as well tell her. She has a right to know."

I turned my full attention to Richart. "What is it?"

"I believe we're being watched. I'm not sure by what or who, but Aphier has felt uneasy for a while. We should get a move on."

Candui was on her feet in an instant. Aphier took the lead, and without another word, we fell into line. I did my best to keep my footsteps quiet, but tension filled the air with its terror.

As we trudged on, I searched the area around us for signs of life. It was strangely quiet. I wanted to be free of this place, but that wasn't happening any time soon. What could I do, to help us out of this situation? There had to be something. Then a thought hit me.

I could use magic.

It wasn't something I'd want to show them because of how magic was viewed. Mother always taught me to keep it secret. Keep it away from the prying eyes of others, lest something bad happen to me because of it. But now, it may be life or death for me, my baby, and my friends. I needed to keep us safe, and if exposing my magic was the only way to do that, I should.

Besides, we'd been with each other for long enough that I knew they would accept me, even if they were a little hesitant about it. I just needed to wait for the stars to appear in the sky, to make sure I would be able to cast a spell that would help. They weren't visible now, and I hadn't seen them last night to know what would work or not. There had to be something to assist us, though.

We walked until the sun dipped behind the mountains, the final rays dying. The moons weren't out yet; it was growing dark. Perfect for star gazing or finding out what type of magic I could do.

Aphier came to a stop.

Candui asked, "Did we lose them?"

He shook his head. "They're playing with us."

That didn't sound good. Richart put his arm around me, resting his hand on my shoulder. It was the comfort I needed to move on.

I looked up at the stars, searching for the different alignments that were needed to create spells. Then I found one that was perfect. There were three stars in a row, with a forth making a sort of triangle. "I may have something that would help," I said.

"What is it?" Richart gave me a squeeze.

I licked my lips. It was now or never. "I can harness the power of my star stone to make us invisible to others but still be able to be seen by each other."

They all looked at me until Candui said, "You mean, like magic?"

"Yes."

Richart recoiled while the other two staring at me with wide eyes. Aphier put his fingers up, crossing one another forming an x and thrusting them in my direction. Not the reaction I was hoping for. "I know it sounds scary and you've heard how bad magic is your entire lives, but I promise it's not. It can help in this situation."

"No." Richart's voice was firm. "The only reason I'm not leaving you in the forest alone, to face whatever it is out there, is because you are carrying my child."

"That's a little harsh, don't you think?" Candui asked.

My sentiments exactly. My heart was reeling, trying to fix itself from the pain inflicted from the man I'd grown to love. He said he loved me. Was that a lie? Or was his hate of magic stronger than his love for me?

"Not harsh when she's carried this secret from us that could destroy us all." Richart pulled out his sword and did something I never thought I'd see. He pointed it at me. "You will not take us in with your wicked ways."

"I already used it once, to heal you after the fight with the ankock." I held my head high.

He sucked in a quick breath. "No." The word came out aghast.

"It's true. You wouldn't be here without my using magic to save your life."

He shook his arms as if that would get rid of the taint he thought was there. "You will not use the forbidden on us."

"But it's no—"

He cut me off before I could protest further. "Not something we will speak of further. Be glad I'm sparing your life."

Aphier's lips were pinched, his eyes saying he agreed with Richart's assessment. Of course he would. I couldn't imagine the two ever disagreeing on something as important as this.

My eyes grew misty as Richart forced me to follow Aphier, Candui keeping a wide berth between us. I wasn't going to have a single friend after this. I should have known to keep my mouth shut, but I had to do something. Using magic had to be better than being taken by orcs or whatever it was out there playing games with us.

A horrid thought hit me. Nopli said I would be betrayed. My friends and husband had turned their back on me because I could do magic. They betrayed me just like she said, yet here I was wanting to help them out of this mess. Why should I when they had treated me such?

I steeled myself to not let my emotions get control of me until I had a chance to fix this. They might not like it, but I had to do something. If we were being followed by orcs or another creature, there was little chance for us to get away unless I used magic. No matter if it was considered evil, I knew better, even if they didn't. Even if they forsook me.

With my star stone touching my skin, my breastbone, I

glanced at the stars and harnessed their power to make myself invisible to anyone who wasn't part of this group.

It was over in an instant. I knew the power had taken hold, but the others kept walking like nothing had happened, ignorant of the fact I'd used magic. When they looked my way, they'd know I'd either done magic or hid from them, but it didn't matter if they couldn't see me.

If only there was a way to cast the spell on them without them realizing it. Since I needed the star stone to touch them, to cast the spell, I wouldn't be able to do it unless they were asleep. Not something likely to happen any time soon.

A call went through the air, vibrating the very trees around us. "What was that?" I asked.

"Quiet," Richart said, not looking my way. He turned to the others. "Was that what I think it was?"

Aphier came back to us, nodding.

"What?" Candui asked.

I was grateful for her question. They would answer her even if they were ignoring me.

"Orcs."

CHAPTER TWENTY-NINE

I wanted to move into action, to grab my star stone and touch each of them with it. To protect them. They were out of reach, though.

My dagger was at my side. I could help protect myself and maybe them when the fighting came. I reached down for it, when a second call sounded, closer than the last one, and a dark shape jumped from a tree.

Richart whirled around, letting his sword face the opponent. Before I could think, we were surrounded by more black, crouching figures.

"You will come with us, humans." The voice was gravelly, thick with phlegm.

"Try to make us." Richart stood firm.

Something snapped, and Richart's sword flew through the air. It was gone before he had a chance to do anything about it.

"Now, now. No fighting us," the voice said. "Come with us, and we'll consider making this a fast death."

I didn't think they could see me, but I wasn't certain. I

slipped to the side, careful to stay far from any of the dark shapes. No one said anything. Maybe it was working.

"We'll go willingly, if you promise not to hurt us," Aphier called out.

"Not likely. Come on."

The sound of fingers snapping filled the air, and before I knew what was going on, the others were tied up. I contemplated trying to stop the orcs, but I only had a little dagger to help me out. That wouldn't be much help now, though it might in the long run. My best bet would be to follow after them, making sure not to bump into any of the orcs.

Richart glanced around and met my eyes. He opened his mouth, and I shook my head. He snapped it back closed, gaze unreadable.

Was he confused or hating me? Neither sounded good.

"Forward," the gravelly voice called out.

An orc took each of my companions by the arm and shoved them forward, while the rest of the thirteen moved. I glanced around, waiting until they were all ahead of me before following so I didn't risk touching one of them. This spell might protect me from being seen, but I was still here and would likely end up getting captured despite being invisible.

An orc was coming right for me. It was going to collide with me. My pulse quickened. I shifted to the side, a branch breaking beneath my foot.

"What was that?" the orc grumbled, turning his head my direction.

I wished I could see it better, but then again, maybe it was for the best I didn't know what it looked like. Didn't have its image burned into my brain to give me nightmares.

It took a step toward me. I held my breath, certain it would be able to hear my heart pounding.

"Snogwolp, get moving," the gravelly voice called out.

The dark shape in front of me turned forward and marched on. I let out the tiniest sigh of relief, unable to believe it didn't catch me.

I took several more steps back, careful of where I walked so as to not make any more noise. The orcs continued to go by. There were so many of them. Was this one of the reasons horror stories were told about them? They had great numbers roaming the Umpi Forest, looking for victims? I didn't want to be caught in their clutches.

I waited for the last one to go by, before taking up the march behind them. I hurried after, determined to keep up, but it became apparent I wasn't going to be able to. The orcs' pace was too fast, and my waddle too slow. I had to, though. I was my friends' only hope, even if they'd turned their backs on me. I held each of them close to my heart. They were loved dearly, and I wouldn't let them be taken away by orcs, to have who-knows-what happen to them.

Soon I was panting, and they were out of sight. Though I'd done a little tracking, it was dark, and I couldn't see well enough to go on. What was I going to do?

I wanted to sit down and cry. To give up. But I wouldn't allow myself one moment of self-pity.

Taking care to not stray too far from the area, I searched around for something to eat. I had to take care of my little one throughout all this, and the best thing I could do for him was to get some food and rest. It would be the only way to help my loved ones too—if they lived long enough for me to put a plan into motion.

Despite feeling helpless, I pushed on.

CHAPTER THIRTY

Morning came brighter than I expected. I strained to roll over, my belly letting me go to my side. I didn't want to get up, but I had to. My friends needed me.

I struggled to my feet, wishing I'd found something to eat last night before going to sleep. I'd checked the stars and had a couple days of the spell lasting. After that, the orcs would be able to see me, and all would be lost. Not that I knew what I would do to save my friends if I found them, but now I had hope. In two days, I wouldn't have even that.

I followed the path the orcs tread last night, crushing all sorts of vegetation on their way, determined to get as far as possible before the day was over.

The path was much the same as what we'd dealt with before, only this time there was nothing to protect me except my dagger and my magic. It had to be enough.

I walked and walked, slowing to a crawl when my belly started tightening. I put a hand on it, and found it hard and not soft. This couldn't be a good thing. It didn't hurt. I knew having a baby hurt a lot. This was just uncomfortable.

As I forced myself to go on, many more times did my belly tighten and then soften again. The baby was active in between these times, so I held out hope that everything was going to be fine.

The progress I was making was so little that despair told me my friends would be dead long before I got to them. I pressed on anyway, ignoring that disheartening voice. Pretending it didn't exist.

I stopped to rest every so often. The sound of a stream trickling by reached me. My mouth ached for a drink. While my belly tightened again, I held still, listening for where the sound was coming from. When my belly relaxed, I headed to my left and found a little stream.

I sank down and scooped up water in my hand to drink. Once I had my fill, I sat back on my feet, readying myself to go again.

A *crack* sounded behind me.

I slowly stood and turned around so as not to make any noise. Whoever or whatever it was shouldn't be able to see me.

A man in a brown cloak was walking past in the forest. A man whose gait was familiar. He looked away from me, then toward me, though his gaze wasn't focused on me.

"Edpol?" My word seemed loud in the forest despite trying to keep it quiet.

"Adriella?" He glanced around the area, looking for me.

Right. The spell would prevent him from seeing me. I called on the star stone, drawing on the powers of the unseen stars to let him see me while still keeping me invisible to the orcs.

He jumped back. "Where did you come from?"

"It doesn't matter." I didn't want yet another person upset with me because I could do magic. "Why are you here? How are you here?"

"Ho—How are you here? There was nothing, and then you were there." He looked rather pale.

I might as well tell him. I wouldn't get any answers from him until I did. Ready to lose another friend, I said, "Magic."

He gave several heavy blinks. "Magic?"

"Yes. I cast a spell, hiding me from orcs. I should do the same to you, if you don't want to be caught."

"You can do magic?"

Trying not to get annoyed, I said, "It's something I've always been able to do. I promise it's not as dangerous or scary, like everyone makes it out to be. It's like cooking food, only I cast spells."

He cleared his throat. "All right. Magic. I can understand that."

"You can?" It was hard to process his words.

"It's not easy to accept, but if there are orcs in the area, which would make sense from the tracks I've been following, then there's not much time to contemplate it. I believe you."

"And you're not frightened?"

"Of you?" He smiled. "Never."

"Oh." I wasn't certain how to process that. But like he said, there wasn't time.

"You are looking, uh, rather rounder than last I saw you. When is your baby coming? Is this why you ran?"

Miffed at him calling me rather round, I huffed. "Yes, this is why we left home. And my child should be coming soon. We don't have time to talk about it, though. Would you let me make you invisible to the orcs and other enemies as well?"

"Will it hurt?"

It was my turn to grin. "Not at all. But it will only last for a little while. Another two days or so."

"Not permanent, then?"

"Unfortunately not, or I could have saved myself a lot of trouble." I moved a step closer to him. "Are you ready?"

"What do I need to do?"

"Nothing." I pulled my star stone out from beneath my filthy tunic. Being near his relative cleanliness made me realize how dirty, torn, and bloody I was. Ignoring that, I held the stone in my hands. "I need to touch this against your skin."

He approached, and I took his hand, pulled it up, and touched the stone to his skin. I called on the magic, aware of the connection between me and the stars. I basked in it, letting the feeling soar within me. There was nothing quite like it.

I channeled that energy, perceiving the alignment of the stars I needed. Then I looked at him. "There."

"That's it?"

"That's it." I tucked my star stone in my tunic, letting it hang low against my skin so it would be there if I needed it again. There and hidden.

"I would never have guessed you were capable of something so amazing." There was a note of awe in his voice.

Heat rose to my cheeks. "It's nothing, really. Just what my mother taught me. Aren't you scared of it?"

"The high king has lied to us about so much. Why would this be any different?"

"Because the fear doesn't come from what he says, but also from other citizens of Erta. You have to know that."

He took a step closer and almost brushed against my stomach. "Yes, but where do the citizens get their ideas? From the high king. What he wants everyone to think, he plants or manipulates others to feel that way."

"I never thought about it like that." And it was a little scary. If the high king manipulated the people that much, what else was he doing that we didn't know about?

"And it seems you've been keeping something else from me."

"What's that?"

He pressed a hand against my belly. "You're going to have a baby."

I stepped away, putting some space between us. We'd been friends almost as long as I could remember, but we never touched one another. "I didn't want to risk your life by letting you know."

"Or risk my telling the guard?"

I looked at the ground. "That too."

His lifted my chin with his finger so my eyes were on his. "I would never turn you in."

I searched my feelings, trying to decide what was going on inside me. "Thank you."

He looked so serious. I didn't want to know what he was thinking.

"What are you doing here?" I motioned to the trodden down path I'd been following and began walking.

He came to my side. "Something was wrong when you visited, but I didn't know what. After you departed so suddenly, I was even more positive. When I asked your brother if he knew anything, he went crazy, telling me to mind my own business and shutting me out. I hope he didn't react the same way when a couple weeks later the guard showed up, looking for you and your husband."

The fact that the zasin hadn't discovered us yet was good, but Edpol found me, which meant others could as well.

"Now I know it's because of your pregnancy and the high king's edict, but then I didn't know why. It crossed my mind that perhaps you both ran away or did something else illegal. I had to find you, no matter what it took. And believe me, darling, it took some doing. I learned from your family where your husband was from and traveled there."

"What about your job? Your duty to the high king?"

He shrugged. "If you ran, it had to be for a good reason. Coming after you made sense. Once I discovered Richart's aunt, who—whoa—is something else, I deduced you were in the Umpi Forest. I couldn't figure what drove you in here, but I was determined to find out. I know you're married, but I hoped if I found you, if we talked perhaps...

"I crossed the border, spent a month looking for you, and eventually came upon a camp that gruta had taken over. I followed the path away from it until it reached the swamp, where I couldn't follow your tracks anymore. I thought you were dead." He brushed a thumb across my cheek.

I backed away, not sure what to think. His touch hadn't done anything to me like it used to. How was I supposed to feel? He came all this way just for me. He hadn't shied away from my magic. He hadn't betrayed me like the others. My mind said to lean into him, to trust him.

"I circled the swamp anyway, and found a trail leading out. Followed it and found you. Or rather, you popped out of nowhere and found me."

"That doesn't explain how you were able to survive in the forest all this time." We barely had, and I was with someone who knew what he was doing.

"I've got weapons from work." He patted the sword at his side. As he moved his cloak, there were many more weapons all along his person hiding under his cloak. "I practiced with them, to know how to use what I was making. My father not only taught me his trade, but also how to live off the land. I've kept the skills up, learning more when I could. They might come in handy, to provide extra support to my family when one came, but one never did."

His father was a healer so that part made sense, but the rest? Why didn't the combinare set him up with a wife? I started to ask but stopped myself. "It's been four, probably almost five years now. There's so little I didn't know about you. I can't believe this. It's like you're a whole different person."

He stepped forward and grabbed a hold of my hand. "I'm the same person I always was. Your best friend."

But after being away from him for so long, I wasn't sure that was true anymore. Besides, I had Richart. Or did I? He'd rejected me and what I could do—something that could have saved his life.

"Now tell me," Edpol said. "What are you doing out in the forest, wandering alone? I know you're following a multitude of tracks, but I can't figure out why."

I pulled my hand away from him and settled it on my belly. What did I tell him? That I was risking my baby to save the life of my friends, though they betrayed me? I didn't know what else to tell him, but maybe I didn't have to tell. "We're in orc territory."

"I gathered that from the few I've... uh... run into."

"How did you survive that?"

"I hid in the trees. Plus, I have my weapons."

I didn't want the particulars of that. "They captured my friends, Candui, Aphier, and Richart. I'm going to save them."

"By yourself? And pregnant? Is that a good idea?" Though his words were skeptical, his tone remained neutral.

Not at all. "I won't leave them to die by the hands of orcs."

He studied me closely, before saying. "All right."

"That's it? You're not going to fight me?"

"Not on this. I can tell you're determined, and if your friends are in danger, I'm willing to help."

Thankful he didn't mention the baby, I said, "Do you know where they're taking them?"

"Haven't a clue, but we can follow the tracks. Now that I'm invisible to orcs as well, it should be much easier."

"I don't know if the invisibility will last long enough to get the job done." Or if the others would still be alive by the time we find them.

"We'll deal with things as they come," he said. "How are you doing? Do you need anything before we start? Hungry?"

"Famished."

He gave a wicked grin, pulled his pack in front of him, and brought out some tubers.

"Thank the stars." I took a few bites while he chuckled. "We should walk while I eat," I said.

"If you insist." He pulled out some more vegetables before putting his pack away. He carried some of it but didn't eat any.

"We're going to have to be quiet. They can still hear us, just not see us," I said between bites.

"I understand."

We went much more slowly than I'd like, but I had water and food in my system. According to the sun dipping in the sky, we'd walked for some hours when something huge came into view.

"What is that?" I whispered.

"Let's get a closer look." Edpol lead the way.

By the time we could see it through the trees, sunlight was barely visible behind the mountain, but the building was lit up by thousands of torches.

"I think we've found the orcs' fortress."

CHAPTER THIRTY-ONE

"We can't go in there," Edpol whispered. I felt like whispering too, with that thing so close. "That's where my friends are, that's where I'm going. You to stay right here, and I'll find you when I've rescued them."

I started forward. He grabbed me by the upper arm and pulled me back. "You can't think I'm going to let you go in there by yourself."

"It's easier to do magic if I'm alone than if it's two of us. I can work faster."

"But you need a sword at your back."

"I have a dagger. Besides, if I do need a sword, it'll already be too late." I tried to move forward, but he stopped me again.

"You may be right, but I don't like it."

"You don't have to like it, but I'm invisible, and I have magic. I'll be fine." I gently moved his hand off my arm. "I'll see you soon."

I hurried away, hoping he didn't follow me. I couldn't risk more people I cared about. It was bad enough he was here and so close to the orcs. We might be invisible for now, but it wouldn't last much more. It depended on how long it took for the stars to finish moving out of alignment. I needed it to be a while yet.

The forest cleared the closer I got to the fortress. If I had to guess, I would say the orcs cleared the trees out, making way for their hive of activity. The closer I got to the building, the more orcs I saw. It was dark enough that it was difficult to make them out. Plus they were cloaked, which made them harder to discern. What was it with them hiding their appearance? Did they not like it? Or was there another reason?

Whatever the reason, if my invisibility wore off now, I was dead.

As I neared the fortress, I decided going in the front door was a bad idea. There were so many orcs coming and going from the entrance, I would have a difficult time getting in without bumping into them, which would be disastrous.

I circled the building, my attention split between watching out for orcs and staring at the building itself. It was by far the biggest structure I had ever seen. Countless towers reached up into the sky, looking like they were trying to poke at it with their pointed tips. There must have been at least five stories throughout different parts of the building. The whole thing was coal black. What was it made out of?

I dreaded entering it.

But I was determined. I would do whatever I could to save my friends. They'd risked so much for me and my baby. I only wished I could have left the baby with Edpol.

I was beginning to think the only way in this monstrosity was through the front door, when a flash of light caught my eye. Glancing to the left, I found an entrance barely closing, letting out light from the inside. Perfect.

I got closer to it and watched everything happening. It was probably the servants' entrance—if they had any. I didn't know how they worked, but that seemed to be the case. There were no guards outside it, but with so many orcs about in the middle of the Umpi Forest, they didn't need them.

Keeping my feet as quiet as could be, I waited by the side of the door. When someone opened it going out, I rushed in after they left. I hurried to the side, just avoiding being bumped into by another set of orcs leaving, the hoods of their cloaks up. They were too close for me to breathe.

When they were gone, I let out a relieved sigh. But I still had to find my companions. How would I ever do so in such a large place? Maybe they'd be in the dungeon? Those typically were in the basement, so I headed down the hall looking for stairs that might lead down.

After passing a number of doors leading off to the side, but no staircases, I finally found one. They were narrow and went up and not down, but this was end of the hall. It was either go up those stairs or backtrack.

With how enormous my stomach was, it would get in the way of squeezing past anyone on the stairs, so heading back the way I came and taking another passage seemed like the best option. I turned to do that when I saw a set of orcs coming my way. They moved fast, and there was only one destination at the end of the hallway. I was standing right in their way.

The orcs spoke, but I didn't process the words as I hurried up the curving stairs, trying to be as quiet as possible and hoping no one was coming down the steps.

Though I was moving as fast as I could without making a noise, the orcs were gaining on me. I pushed on, hoping their voices covered any noise I made. My heart hammered in my ears, like when I used to go to my father's shop while he worked. The *thud, thud, thud* was loud, making it so I could hear nothing else.

They were almost upon me. I continued up, turning to follow the stairs, when a doorway appeared. Only a couple more steps, and I'd make it. Something brushed against my back.

"What is that?" a gravelly, female voice asked.

I dashed through the doorway, and down a corridor.

"What was what?" a second voice asked.

"I thought I felt something. No matter."

They continued up the stairs, and I leaned against the wall in relief. That was too close. Any closer, and I'd have found my companions in a manner that wouldn't help anyone.

I caught my breath and started forward, wishing my knees weren't shaking. It wasn't helping anything, but there was nothing I could do. My fear of this place was palpable.

I'd press on.

I wandered for a good long time, upstairs and downstairs, through hallways and rooms. No sign of my friends. I plastered myself against a wall, sinking to the ground while rubbing my forehead.

If only Richart was here... He would have a plan of action. I'd jumped into this too fast without thought for how I would manage it. Perhaps I should have let Edpol come with me. Then again, he might be as lost and hopeless as I was. He might be even now, out in the forest. Who knew?

"Hello."

It sounded like a young girl, though with rocks in her throat. I glanced around to find a creature staring at me. It sounded like a young girl, though with rocks in her throat. She was taller than me while I was sitting on the floor. If she were human, I'd guess she was eight or nine. Clearly, she wasn't human, though.

Her skin was as black as the building we were in, wrinkled, and dry. Her nose was long and hooked down at the end. Her eyes were dark and glassy, and focused on me.

"You can see me?" Why was I talking to this orc girl?

"Yes. You look funny, like the raiders that came, but fat in the stomach."

I pursed my lips together to keep from laughing. No one had

called me fat, but I definitely felt it. What was bad was that I was no longer invisible. *Sunblasted.* The alignment of the stars must have moved far enough to get rid of my spell. How was I going to find my companions and get out of here without it? "What raiders?" I asked.

"Are you mean, like them? Have you come to take me away?" Her gaze was so focused on me, I found myself telling the truth whether or not I wanted to.

"No. I'm looking for my friends. An elf woman and two human men. Have you seen them?"

"The intruders." Her voice grew solemn.

"Do you know where I can find them? We didn't mean to intrude. We wanted to find someplace safe to stay."

She cocked her head to the side, staring at me a good long while. "Come with me."

"Are you taking me to them?" I didn't want to trust this orc child, but what other choice did I have? She wasn't calling an alarm, though whoever she took me to could do that.

"Come." She turned and skipped away.

I glanced back the other direction. I wasn't getting out of here without help. Not now that everyone would be able to see me.

Despite being tired deep in my bones, I hurried after her, hoping I would get to see my friends before we were all killed by the orcs.

Thankfully, we didn't meet anyone along the way. We twisted through many corridors, winding our way up through the great fortress. The girl stopped at a room, opened the door, and skipped right in. I hung back just inside the door so she could close it.

"There you are, you little imp," an older-sounding female said. "I thought you'd never return."

"I met a friend." She turned to look at me, drawing the older orc's gaze to me.

She gripped the child by the shoulders and pulled her back, holding her close. "What have you done?"

Not knowing what else to do, I said, "I mean you no harm. I'm looking for someone."

"Lots of someones is more like it. And you're trying to start with darling Ugfha. I won't have it. You'll have to kill me before you take her."

"Who's Ugfha?" Or what. It sounded strange to be a name.

The little orc laughed. "Me, of course."

"Oh." I pulled myself together. Whoever this orc was to Ugfha, she might be my only hope of staying alive. "I'm not here for her. I just want my friends, and then we'll leave and never return." There were a lot of places we were never to return to lately.

She tightened her wrinkled, gray lips. "You will come with me and won't put up a fight?"

"I promise." My stomach tightened uncomfortably, and I put a hand on it.

She eyed my belly. What did she think about it? It needed to be something that would help. More likely, she was thinking I was bringing another dratted human into the world.

She made a sort of growling sound. "You will walk ahead and only go where I say."

I didn't want to turn my back to her, but I saw no other choice. "All right."

"Good. Out the door. Ugfha, you follow."

My stomach relaxed as I turned and went out. Ugfha's keeper gave me instructions I followed. I hadn't a clue if she was taking me to my companions or somewhere more sinister, but she hadn't hurt me or taken my dagger away.

We climbed down a few sets of stairs before coming to an opulent room. The sun's rays barely shone in with the light of morning. The black floor glistened where the rays touched, brightening the room. Besides the sun, there were torches all around, helping me see where the floor and walls ended and the orcs began. It was difficult to tell, since they were the same color, but there was a bumpiness to the orcs' skin.

In the front of the room, there were four large chairs. Though I hadn't seen a throne before, they were about what I imagined one to be like—tall and spiking out in all different directions. One was larger than the others, and it was one of the two occupied.

Ugfha ran past me and jumped into the arms of the orc in the smaller chair. None of the others in the room took their eyes off me. I made certain to keep my hand far from the hilt of my dagger, where it might set them off.

Ugfha's keeper—Aunt? Caretaker?—came forward, apparently no longer worried about keeping me within sight. There were enough orcs here. I didn't blame her. Most of them had wicked-looking blades strapped to their sides.

"Ugfha found this woman wandering the palace. She says she wants her friends."

The orc in the bigger throne turned his attention on me. Something nudged me forward. I glanced back to find a spear pointed at me. I hurried forward, until I was no longer being poked, which left me in front of who I suspected was the orc king.

He took me in from my worn shoes to my mess of hair, his gaze lingering on my bulging stomach. "You are coming for the group we captured?"

My vocal cords wanted to shut down, but I forced out words. "I am. My husband is among them, and the others are my friends. We didn't mean to intrude on your land. I want to take them and leave your territory."

"You are with child." It was a statement more than a question.

I answered anyway. "I am."

He looked at the orc woman holding Ugfha. Something passed between them. I hoped it was something good for me. Instead of the orc king speaking, she asked, "Why are you in Umpi Forest?"

Did it matter? Either way, they were going to kill me. I couldn't see the reason making a difference but was honest anyway. "Because of the high king's edict to kill young children and unborn babies. My companions and I were trying to prevent him from harming my unborn babe."

"How can we be certain you are not deceiving us?" the king asked.

I put a hand on my belly. "Would you carry this around a forest if you didn't have to?"

"If you were trying to deceive my people, yes."

"What purpose would I have for doing that? I just want my friends back."

"I believe her," the orc woman said.

"If that is the case, you are free to leave."

They were going to let me go? Why? "With my companions?"

"They fought when we brought them in. There is little that can save them now."

"I won't survive the Umpi Forest without them. I've barely survived with them." And I so desperately needed them.

"You have to understand my concern for my people. I can't have humans around that will hurt them."

How to counter that? "They were only defending themselves and trying to protect me."

"You weren't there. I have no reports of your presence."

That was because I used magic, but I couldn't tell him that. "I was hidden." Which was true, in a sense. "That's why they fought so hard. They didn't want you to find me."

"And yet you came here?" the orc woman asked. Ugfha sat quietly, taking everything in.

I swallowed past the knot in my throat. "I had to try to help them."

"Your values seem sound," the orc king said, "but after the high king sent his men to raid our fortress for our young and our females with child, you can understand my concern with letting them go."

"The high king raided here?" Hard to believe with the sheer number of orcs I'd seen around the place. Although I hadn't seen any pregnant women or toddlers.

"You did not know?" the orc woman asked.

I shook my head. "I didn't think the high king would dare send men into the Umpi Forest, let alone here, where you have so many armed orcs."

The orc men around the room stood taller, their cloaks flowing around them.

"That may be what you think, but the high king is scared of the prophecy, as I'm sure you're well aware of, having run to the Umpi Forest yourself."

"The prophecy includes orcs as well?" That was news to me. I never thought of it before.

"We don't know," the orc woman said. "But the high king must think so and be scared enough to send men in the Umpi Forest to die."

Which means he must not have found the chosen one yet. I put a hand to my belly. Could it be my child? No. The odds of that were slim. So many others had been taken. One of them was surely it.

"All they left us was Ugfha, who was hidden, and a few orcs with child who don't show yet. The rest of our pregnant women and children were lost."

"But Ugfha has to be at least eight years old." I thought they weren't taking older children?

"They must be getting desperate, because they took them all."

I put a hand to my mouth, trying not to be sick. How could the high king do this? How could the Sunsit help him?

"So you see our dilemma in letting your friends go."

"Not if I need them to protect me. If you don't let them out, you'll be responsible for another woman losing her child. Whether it's through my death out in the forest or the zasin finding me, you'll be culpable." I silently begged and pleaded the orcs would see I needed my people, but it was hard to hold out hope they'd do what I so desperately needed them to.

"I don't think it wise to let them go." The orc king leaned back in his chair.

I slumped my shoulders. How could I break Richart, Candui, and Aphier out of this place when I didn't know where they were? What spells could I use? I wanted a good look at the night sky, but morning was here. The alignment of stars didn't have to be perfect to cast a spell, but it needed to be close enough. I should have paid better attention to the stars before venturing in here. I'd become too complacent about my magic since living with Richart. It didn't matter. I was inside, surrounded by orcs, and without a plan. At least they were letting me go?

The orc woman whispered something to the king. He pursed his lips as if contemplating it before nodding.

The orc woman opened her mouth at me, showing a set of fangs. Despite her monstrous look, I was comforted by her attempt to smile. That or she was going to eat me.

I went forward when she beckoned to me.

She said, "I am Queen Plofgog. I'm sorry for how you've been treated. I would like you to join me for dinner, along with Ugfha, if you would."

Not like I had much choice. I wanted to not be on the menu and that Edpol wouldn't come rushing in to save me. "It would be my pleasure. Thank you."

Queen Plofgog slid from her chair with more grace than I expected from an orc. There might be a lot of things I thought wrong about them. She was taller than me by quite a few inches, her cloak a brilliant purple, the only color in the room besides me.

Four guards surrounded her, and I followed them. I kept expecting someone else to join us, but no one did.

We wound through the palace, and though I wanted to take time to see where we were going, they went so fast and took so many turns. It was difficult to keep track of it all. Finally, we turned into a room with a table, two chairs, and a spread of food.

Apparently, I wasn't to be dinner.

The queen settled in one chair, and I sat across from her. She waved her guards away before turning to me. "I want to trust you, but we've been used by humans before. Know that I have a stiletto on me and know how to use it with deadly accuracy."

"I believe you. And I promise not to do anything to harm you." Unless she started it. It was hard not to be uneasy about the whole situation, but the food smelled good, a scrumptious feast the likes of which I hadn't seen—well—ever. It looked especially delicious because I'd been eating what we could scrounge from the forest for months. "This looks wonderful."

She put a piece of flaky pastry on her plate. "Please eat whatever you would like. I'm afraid they always prepare more food than I can consume."

"Thank you." I tried to hold back, but I couldn't. I piled my plate high and began eating, thankful that orc food was human friendly.

"How long have you been in the forest?"

"Longer than I know," I said between bites. "Since before I showed. I could still get away with being in public, but only just, and even then someone who knew me well would be able to tell I was thickening."

"How have you survived?"

We went back and forth, her asking questions about our time in the woods and me answering them.

She asked, "You survived the fairies?"

"Barely."

"Hmm."

I finished eating long before I wanted to. My eyes were bigger than my stomach. If I could save the food, I would, but I had nothing to carry it in, and unfortunately, the baby was pressing on my stomach, making it more difficult to keep it full.

"You have a remarkable gift of getting people to believe you and be on your side," the queen said.

I stared. What was I supposed to say to that? It wasn't something I heard every day. "Thank you."

She smiled, showing her fangs but looking less fearsome than before. "It's probably that you glow with motherhood. Or perhaps that we all come together in times like these to protect our children."

"I think the latter is true. I can't believe how many are going along with the high king's orders, though, or that he can reach you here."

Her eyes misted. "It is a sad day indeed when his reach is so far. I want nothing more than to have the women and children back in our midst. They are dear to me, even those I don't know well. We are a close community. So, you see why it's hard to let humans go after what they've done to us."

I didn't want to, but I did. "I wish there was something I could do to show you my companions mean no harm. Not all humans are alike."

"And not all orcs are either. Tell me, before you came here

today, would you have hesitated to kill one of us had we shown up in your house?"

Tricky. "I'd like to think I would have spared you long enough to hear your story, but I admit it'd be hard. The high king has spread such rumors among our people to make us fear you, it's difficult to see past them."

She studied me closely. "I believe you would have listened to our story, but you're right. The high king has perpetuated disturbing lies. He needs to be stopped, and we need to find the child who can do that."

"I would like to help. Do you know where the children are taken?"

"You cannot help in your condition." She waved away my concern, her long, pointed nails flying through the air. "They are going to Inta keep, where the Sunsire doles out his duty as the high king's first in command. Any child who goes near him will not survive."

"How do you know this?"

Her eyes narrowed. "That I cannot tell you. It would be breaking everything I believe in to tell a human my secrets."

"I understand." Though curiosity still ate at me.

"You are most unusual."

"I'm simply me."

Once again, she studied me. I worked hard not to fidget with my napkin and fork. She said, "My husband agreed that you and your companions will be set free, on the condition that you all wear the robes of our people, hiding yourselves from the orcs. We don't want to raise further alarm within the orcdom when we can prevent it."

Joy so strong coursed through me, I wanted to bounce to my feet. I barely contained myself. "Thank you, Your Majesty. I promise we will get away from your orcs and not harm them on our way out. Or ever again, if I can help it."

"I wouldn't go that far. We are like humans—some good, some bad—but I appreciate the sentiment."

"What can I do to show my gratitude?"

"Keep your child safe, in case he or she is the one who will save us all."

That I could do. "I'll do everything in my power to keep him safe, though I don't know that he will be the one."

"Neither do I, but I can hope it is the chosen child who survives the high king's purge."

So did I.

CHAPTER THIRTY-TWO

A fter a servant provided me with packs full of food, clothes, and things for the baby, along with dark cloaks, I changed into clean pants and a tunic. I still wasn't clean, but I was in a better outfit, the tunic stretching across my giant belly.

I waited in the room alone for my companions to be brought to me. I couldn't help but feel a sort of anxious joy at being reunited with them. Of seeing *him* again.

Granted, I wanted to see them all, but I was most nervous about meeting with Richart. Something in me both sang in delight and cowered in fear at the thought of seeing him again. Mostly, my blood ran hot.

I wanted to be with him again. To feel his hand on my belly. To have his arm wrapped around me. Of course, that would never be now that he knew I wielded magic.

I held my shoulders straight, not wanting to give into the discouragement dancing inside me. I had to focus on keeping the baby alive. That meant freeing my companions and getting away from the orcs, as nice as they'd been to me.

The door opened, and instead of my friends, an orc came in

that looked much like the others. Fangs, barely any hair, dark glassy eyes, and pruning dark skin. From its shape, I could tell it was a woman. She had better not be here to tell me they'd changed their minds.

When she said nothing, I spoke up. "Can I help you?" Maybe she lost her way.

"I am coming with you." She tilted her head up, daring me to refuse her.

Why would the king and queen wish for this? Perhaps they wanted to spy on us? But that didn't seem like what they planned previously. "All right. May I ask why?"

"Doesn't matter why. I have Their Highnesses' permission." She jutted out her jaw.

Exactly what we didn't need—an ornery orc joining us. I held in a sigh. "I'm Adriella."

"Togafui."

I nodded an acknowledgment. I wasn't about to say it was a pleasure to meet her when it clearly wasn't.

She stayed in one corner of the room with her pack on her shoulders beneath her cloak. That, or she had a rather large hump on her back. I remained in my corner by the packs left for us.

The next time the door opened, my companions entered the room. I wanted to run to them, but didn't know if I'd be welcome. I hovered there, waiting to see what they'd do.

Richart was the first to spot me. His eyes grew wide. "They captured you too? I thought you managed to get away. I wanted the baby to have a chance."

I couldn't help the smile that blossomed on my face. "I came here of my own free will and negotiated with them." I motioned to the cloaks and packs at my feet. The orcs had surpassed what I expected of kindness, even from my own people. "We are free to go, but we must do so disguised as orcs so as not to drum up the fear of humans roaming free among them."

"How did you manage that?" Candui's eyes were wider than Richart's.

I shrugged. "It was because I was pregnant. I'll tell you more about it on our way out. It's dark now, so we can go, and I want to make the most of it before they change their minds." And hurry to get back to Edpol before he did something stupid like attack the fortress on his own.

"By all means." Aphier came over to the pile and grabbed a cloak. "Let's get to it." To me, he said, "Thank you. You didn't have to come for us, but I'm grateful that you did. We likely wouldn't have lived much longer if it wasn't for you."

I shrugged, ignoring the heat rising to my face.

Candui grabbed a cloak of her own and a pack. She put them on before wrapping me in a hug. "Thank you."

When she pulled away, Richart was ready to go, though he wasn't meeting my gaze.

Still angry about the magic. It wasn't his fault there were such prejudices against it, any more than it was his fault orcs and humans didn't get along.

That didn't stop the sting in my heart.

"Who's this?" Aphier nodded toward Togafui.

I introduced her. "She will be journeying with us."

Candui scowled and muttered something under her breath. The other two didn't appear much happier. I might feel the same way, but I tried to hide it. No wonder they weren't offered freedom like I was. What had happened to them?

We gathered up the rest of everything, put on our hoods, and headed out the door. I almost expected the guards at the door to stop us, to say it had all been a joke, but they let us go without a word.

Somehow, someday, I'd find a way to thank the orc queen. It was because of her this was happening.

One of the guards pulled away from the others and took the

lead. We climbed down stairs and through corridors until we reached another side entrance, different than the one I'd used before. As I passed by him on the way out, he whispered, "Good luck."

"Thank you." The door was shut as soon as the words were out of my mouth.

We were on our own, unless you counted Togafui.

Aphier started to lead, but I stopped him. "There's something we need to grab first. This way."

He tilted his head at me but didn't stop me from going forward. I was grateful two of the moons were out tonight, brightening up the sky enough to light the path. We wove through the orcs outside. They could spot us at any moment, and we'd be done for.

I licked my lips, wishing I could go faster. It was just as well; if we ran, it would look suspicious. I wanted out of here, though, and soon.

Togafui had her hood on, but kept it back farther than ours so her face was clearly seen. As much as I didn't want her along, it did help to have someone with us who could show their face and give validity to our being here.

The hike away from the palace was quicker than I expected, with all the stress of leaving. I turned around once to look at the building and send silent good wishes to the king and queen. Would we meet again someday? Hopefully, it would be under better circumstances.

When we got away from the others roaming around in their cloaks, Aphier asked, "Where are we going?"

"I told you, we have to pick something up. What happened to you in the orcs' fortress?"

"We were locked in a prison." Candui gave Togafui a dirty look. "I didn't think we'd ever get out—not until we were to be killed."

"Glad I could be of service before that happened." The forest looked familiar, on the edge of the wooded line with tight trees and bushes. "It should be around here somewhere." Edpol should be nearby. I almost called out his name, but I didn't want to attract unwanted attention. Besides, I was a little concerned with how Richart would act when he found out Edpol was the thing we were searching for.

A shadow stepped out from behind a tree. The *clink* of weapons being drawn filled the forest air, and metal flashed, pointed at the shadow.

"Adriella?"

I pushed Richart's sword down, and Aphier lowered his own.

"I thought you had been taken when I couldn't find you," I told Edpol.

"And I thought you were dead. You left so long ago, I thought the orcs had gotten to you."

"Then why are you still here?" Why didn't he come after me?

"I was holding out hope."

Togafui was oddly silent. Was she trying to make us forget she was there?

"What's he doing here?" Richart turned to Edpol. "And why did you let Adriella go where the orcs might have killed her?"

Edpol and I started talking at the same time. He motioned for me to go first.

"Edpol found me in the forest." I gave them a quick rundown of the story. "And I demanded that he let me go alone. I have the means to take care of myself. I did come out alive and with all of you."

Richart's lips thinned.

Edpol sauntered closer. "You should give her magic more credit."

Though his sword was lowered, Richart's grip on it was so tight, I wasn't certain it would stay lowered.

I said, "It's not something we have to discuss. We should get out of orc territory."

"She's right," Aphier said. "Let's go. Can I lead the way now?"

"Be my guest." I would only end up getting us lost at this point. Togafui had to know her way around here much better, but I wasn't about to suggest such a thing.

Aphier took the lead while Edpol and Richart glared at each other. Togafui went after Aphier. Candui took my arm and guided me to walk behind Aphier. "How are you doing?" she asked.

Trying to ignore the men behind me and the orc in front of me, I said, "Been better. My stomach keeps tightening."

"Is it painful?"

"Just uncomfortable."

"Those are contractions. Your body is getting ready for the baby to come. I'm not sure how much longer we have before your delivery."

Aphier increased his speed, and I held back a groan. We needed to get out of this area as soon as possible, especially if I was going to have the baby soon, but I didn't want to speed-walk anywhere. I just wanted to lie down and take a nap.

When I glanced back, Richart was taking up the rear. Edpol, right behind me, gave me a half grin. Richart's face was marred by a scowl. I couldn't blame him for being upset by this turn of events. It was difficult to know I still loved him, despite the fact that he hated my magic and would never accept it.

I tried to keep my mind on other things as we walked. My pack was heavy on my shoulders, which I was grateful for since it meant food and comfort, but the straps made my skin ache.

We journeyed on through the night and well into the day, taking a few short breaks during which no one talked. I was well aware there could be orcs around, and we could be recaptured, though our cloaks might keep that from happening. Togafui kept her face out, which would also help, but I was nervous.

The sun was low in the sky when Richart said, "We should stop."

Aphier turned back toward him. "We're still in orc territory. We've got a ways to go yet."

"I know, but we should stop." Richart leaned his head in my direction.

I wanted to protest that they didn't have to stop for me, but the truth was I was flagging. Exhaustion was overbearing, and the contractions were more frequent and a little painful.

Aphier took one look at me and circled around the clearing we'd made it to. "This is a great place to stop for the moment. Who's hungry?"

I didn't respond, just dropped to the ground and sat like a lump.

Candui crouched down beside me. "You doing good?"

"I'll be fine in a minute. I simply need a break."

"How are your contractions?"

"Still there."

She knit her eyebrows together. "You may be entering labor, but it could also be the strain of everything you've gone through. We'll know more in an hour or two."

"An hour or two?" I didn't want to deal with this that long.

She gave me a funny look. "You know, labor for the first baby can last a long time, sometimes even a day or two."

"Two days?" She had to be kidding.

"It'll be fine. I'll be there with you the entire time." With a tentative smile, she stood to talk to Aphier.

The smile made me think maybe, just maybe, she'd forgiven me for doing magic. Or maybe she was overlooking it. It felt good to have a connection to her again. To all of them.

Something brushed against my back. "Here," Richart said. "Lean against me."

I wanted to protest, but even pride wasn't enough to keep me from resting against him. He wrapped his arms around me, holding me tight. He held me up as he rested a hand on my belly. The baby kicked in response, and I couldn't help but grin. Someone knew his father.

Warmth surrounded me. I closed my eyes and relaxed, wishing there was more I could do to convince him I wasn't evil because I was a Starda, holding the power of the stars. I was so exhausted I couldn't think straight. I wanted to sleep for a week.

Before I could drift off, Richart whispered in my ear, "I had a lot of time to think. We all did, once we were captured as well as today, while we were walking. What I thought about—well— doesn't matter. I want you to know I'm sorry for the way I treated you just because you can do magic. It scared me to think you could do it after all I've heard, but you're a kind woman with a pure heart. You would do anything to help people and especially to take care of us. I know that now."

His words brushed peace through me. I wished he'd understood that from the start, but then I wouldn't have realized how much like humans orcs could be, though they looked so very different. "You're forgiven," I said.

"Thank you." His breath was warm against my ear.

I settled back into him and closed my eyes. It felt like only a minute before Edpol called my name. I opened my eyes to find him holding an unidentified tuber.

"Thank you." I snatched it and ate it as he laughed.

Behind me, Richart tensed. I knew why he had hard feelings toward Edpol, who I'd expected to marry, but it would be nice if they got along. This was going to be hard enough without them fighting.

"Where are we going to go now?" I asked, trying to diffuse the situation. "Any ideas?"

Aphier came and sat beside us. He said, "I found a map in Candui's pack that must have been put there by the orcs. It shows a circled spot, not too far outside orc territory. Given how kind they were to us once they figured out Adriella was pregnant, we should at least look into the location."

"It is an area not claimed by others, with few beasts," Togafui interjected.

When no one replied, I said, "Thank you."

Richart's chest rumbled behind me, as he spoke. "How long will it take to get there?"

"A few days."

"Do we have that long?" he asked.

"Have that long for what?" Edpol leaned in closer.

"Before the baby comes." Candui sighed. "I'm not certain. She's been having contractions, so we need to take it easy whatever we do, but if she doesn't go into full labor tonight, we may have the time we need. I'd feel better if we were a little more settled before the baby came."

"As would I." I didn't want my child to be born in the wilderness at all, but since that wasn't a choice, I could give him some semblance of a home. At least he wouldn't have any memories of his early years.

"What do we do in the meantime?" Edpol asked. "Can she walk to where we need to go?"

"I can walk fine." Sort of.

"We'll take it nice and easy," Richart said. "But the sooner we get out of orc territory, the better."

"Agreed." Aphier stood. "I'm going to get wood for a fire. It may attract orcs, but it's cold enough we're going to need it."

And Togafui should help if there were any issues.

"I'll help," Candui said.

I glanced at Edpol, expecting him to do the same, but he sat watching me. "I can help as well," I said.

Togafui was gone. Would she be back? Why was she sticking with us? What did she want? At that point, I didn't care.

When I tried to get to my feet, Richart gently pulled me back against him. "I know you can, and you'd do a good job of it, but let's give the baby some rest. The longer he stays where he needs to be, the better."

I sighed, wanting to refuse, but he was right. The baby needed me, and I was going to give him all the rest I could. All the care. He needed to remain inside me long enough for us to do what we had to.

CHAPTER THIRTY-THREE

The day dawned bright and early. The others woke me earlier than I was ready to get up, but at least I was with them.

The real question was why was Edpol still here. He'd found us, and now I was safe with my husband and friends. Why didn't he leave? Was he a fugitive too? Or was it something more? It was the last part that had me hesitating to ask.

"Are you still having contractions?" Candui asked.

"I don't think so."

"Good. We may be in the clear. We'll take it slow today, just in case."

We ate breakfast, packed up, and walked. And walked some more. It wasn't my favorite pastime, but now that my stomach wasn't tightening every twenty minutes or so, things were easier.

The day passed much the way yesterday did. Lots of little breaks for my benefit and lots of hiking. It was well into dark when Aphier came to a stop.

"Are we camping here for the night?" Richart asked. "It would be a good idea."

Aphier raised a hand, stopping him from saying anything further. I listened, wondering what it was Aphier heard or saw that had him being cautious.

Nothing.

That didn't stop me from grabbing my dagger. I wanted to be ready when trouble came.

Richart did the same, his hand on the hilt of his sword.

Finally, Aphier put his hand down. "We can stop here for the night."

"You're certain?" Richart asked.

"If he said we can stop here, it's fine," Edpol said, pulling his pack off.

Richart ignored him, his full focus on Aphier. "What did you hear that had you hesitating?"

"I'm sure it's nothing. Just a disquiet in the air."

Richart scowled. I didn't like it either. Aphier wasn't perfect, but he did a good job knowing when predators were about.

Togafui looked from side to side while Candui glared at her. It had to be the hatred between the two races because I saw no other reason for the dirty look. It wasn't like Togafui caused Aphier's discomfort.

"We should keep going," I said.

Aphier looked at me like he was trying to decide how much I meant that. "No. We'll stay here for the night, but I don't want a fire. It's not needed," he said.

"Not needed?" Edpol approached Aphier. "I'm freezing."

"We all are, but that's not a reason to risk our lives." Aphier stood his ground.

Thankfully, Candui moved between them. I didn't want to come between my childhood friend and one of the people who'd kept me safe for so long, but Aphier was right and Edpol needed to back off.

But why? Usually, it was to our advantage to keep a fire going.

"We'll sleep close together and use the blankets and cloaks the orcs gave us," Candui said. "We'll be all right."

Edpol snorted. "Whatever."

I rolled my eyes. You'd think he was the one having a baby.

Richart helped me settle with him on one side and Candui on the other. Edpol glared down at us. "It would be better if Adriella were by me. I can keep her warm."

"I'm her husband. If anyone's going to keep her warm, it'll be me."

"But you do better at keeping watch."

"Boys." I'd had enough Edpol's reactions. "No more. Richart will be at my side. I want to get some rest. Can we stop fighting about this?"

"Fine," Edpol said, "but don't come crawling to me if you get cold in the night."

What had gotten into him? If anything, he must have regretted coming after me and having to live in conditions he wasn't accustomed to. Or was it something else? I felt like he was hiding something from me, but what? And why? We never hid anything from each other in the past, but now there was so much.

Whatever it was, I'd deal with it later.

Candui handed me something to eat and I gobbled it down without tasting it. "You doing well?" she asked.

"Well enough. I feel like a yipra—giant and grouchy."

She gave a small chuckle. "I remember feeling the same way during the last month of my pregnancy. I wanted nothing more than to have my baby." Her voice grew sad.

If only there was a way to help her—a way to find out who her husband gave their son to—but I didn't even know where to begin. It wasn't right that he could do such a thing to her.

She gave my shoulder a squeeze, voice sounding more cheerful. "Soon your little one will be here, and we can all coo at him."

I grinned. "I can't wait."

She settled down, and so did I, feeling warm despite the chill touching my skin. Richart scooted close. Everything was silent without the crackle of a fire. I missed the noise, but it was worth it, to feel safer. I yawned and soon fell asleep.

Pangs woke me. I needed to use the necessary. I groaned. Everything was dark. Richart was still by my side as was Candui, so it couldn't have been long since I fell asleep. The moons were all high in the sky, though. Where was Aphier?

I sat up, and Richart immediately did so as well. "Can I help with something?" he asked.

"No. I just need to go to the bathroom."

He gave a low laugh. It had become the most common reason for me to get up in the middle of the night. He stood and reached down to help me up. Edpol lay on the other side of Candui, though not touching her. Both were sound asleep. Togafui was curled up on the opposite side of camp. I couldn't help but feel a touch of guilt. She had to be freezing.

Richart was walking me away from them when Aphier appeared. Richart explained the situation while I found a tree to go behind. When I came back, they were quietly arguing.

"You can't stay up all night and all day," Richart said. "Let me help you keep watch. You need some sleep."

"I'd feel more comfortable if I did all the watching. There's something in the woods that's making me uneasy."

"I understand that, but you have to get some rest. Without it, you're no good to us. Besides, I'd rather have you at Adriella's side than Edpol."

Aphier sighed. "Maybe you're right."

I wasn't sure if he was. Edpol might be acting a little strangely, but he was a lifelong friend. There was no way he would do anything to hurt me, and I hoped the sentiment carried over to my friends. Despite that, something held me back from saying anything.

Richart glanced up and met my gaze. "There you are. I was beginning to wonder if you'd gotten lost."

"It would be easy to do, but no. Not yet." I smiled.

"Let's get you back to bed."

"If I can relax. I'm exhausted but so uncomfortable. It's going to be hard to sleep."

"That's not what your snoring said earlier."

I gave him a playful shove. He grinned and wrapped an arm around me. "I'm going to take over watch for Aphier, so he's going to sleep beside you and keep you safe and warm for me. Is that all right?"

"It's fine."

"Good. I'll be awake the rest of the night so let me know if you need anything."

A midnight snack would be nice, but knowing from past experience how quickly supplies dwindled, I didn't ask. "Thank you."

Richart helped me settle in next to Candui before Aphier lay down at my other side. I'd much rather it was Richart, but I did feel safer with Aphier there than no one. He would take care of me and the baby if things got bad.

Richart slipped into the shadows as I tried to drift off. I tossed and turned, sometimes dozing but never really falling back asleep like I wanted. I felt like a fire, hot and wiggly. Despite that, my fingers and toes were chilled. I rubbed my hands together, trying to warm them up.

After what felt like a long while of not being able to sleep, morning came. I wanted nothing more than to curl up next to Richart and sleep the day away. Preferably in a bed as opposed to the hard ground. I sat up, using my arms to push myself up.

Everyone else was still asleep, but nature was calling me. Again. It was maddening being up so often. I took care of business and headed back to camp.

A shape jumped out at me.

I shrieked, grabbing for my dagger.

"Whoa. It's me." Richart put his hand on mine to prevent me from pulling out my weapon. "Sorry. I didn't mean to startle you. I thought you knew I was there."

"I must not have been paying attention." Still too groggy. Or was before the scare.

He pulled me into his arms, my stomach getting in the way. I leaned as close as I could anyway, tilting myself toward him. Did he really forgive me for using magic? Or was he looking past it? It was a big leap to take. Aphier and Candui appeared to have gotten past it, but they were still a little cautious around me. Richart didn't seem cautious at all as his lips found my forehead.

I sighed into his gentle touch before pulling away. As much as I wanted to receive more of his attentions, I had to know. "Richart?"

"What is it?"

I licked my lips. "Do you really understand about me using magic? You seemed so against it before, it's hard to imagine you got over it."

He sighed but didn't let me go. "If you must know, I still find it a little... disconcerting. There are so many stories of how evil magic is. How it ruins lives. But I've come to realize that we all have secrets, and we all have aspects of ourselves that may seem different to others when they are the way things are."

I leaned farther away. "What secrets do you have?"

He pressed his lips together.

"You can tell me, you know," I said. "There's nothing you don't know about me now. I've trusted you with everything. It's time you did the same with me."

"You're right. It's just hard. I don't know how you're going to react." He sighed. "The thing is, I—"

"Want some breakfast?" Edpol held a leaf of food in front of my face, between me and Richart.

He was getting really annoying.

"Not now, Edpol," I said, trying to be kind. "Richart and I were having a private conversation. I'd be happy to eat breakfast in a little while."

"I think you need to eat now."

I rolled my eyes. "Really, I'm fine."

"It's for the baby." He held the leaf out to me again.

Talk about frustrating. I took the proffered leaf and stuck a piece of food in my mouth. "Mmm. Thank you. I'll finish this and be over in a minute."

"We don't have a minute," Aphier said. "Something is in these woods. We need to find a place to hide."

Great.

Richart took the leaf from me, grabbed a root he handed to me, and flung the rest back at Edpol. I munched while we quickly gathered our things.

"What's in the forest?" Richart whispered to Aphier.

"I don't know, but it's not good."

That was the only talking we did. No one else spoke as we put on our cloaks and packs. Aphier lead us out of the clearing, Togafui hurrying after him.

We walked more quietly than we had the day before. I took care where I stepped, though it took more energy out of me. My legs and stomach hurt. I wanted to come to a halt before we got very far. My lower back was the worst, a growing ache diving through me. It grew and grew, making me want to groan in pain and stop for a break. But I wouldn't.

I would keep this baby safe, even if it meant continuing to walk when pain ratcheted through me.

A hand warmed my back. I glanced over to find Richart at my side. I gave him a forced smile.

"Are you all right?" he whispered.

I nodded, though I feared it wasn't convincing.

His hand slipped down my arm until he twined his fingers with mine. We walked like that for some time. Despite the pain, I felt better than before, knowing he was at my side.

Late in the afternoon, we stopped.

Aphier turned to us. "I haven't sensed anything for a while."

"That's good, right?" Candui asked.

He shrugged. "I'm not positive. If what I sensed before is out there still, it could be a problem, but if it's gone, we're all right."

It would be nice if he was more sure than that. It didn't make a difference. I was exhausted, hurting, and ready to die if I had to keep going. I found a tree to lean against and put my back to it, not bothering to pull my pack off.

Richart crouched down beside me, Edpol's gaze on us. "Do you need anything?" Richart asked.

I shook my head.

"Let me know if that changes."

I nodded. It was too much work to speak.

He brushed a kiss on my forehead before standing and going to speak to Aphier. I couldn't hear what was said. Edpol watched from a distance. What was going through his mind? I wanted my childhood friend back, the person I could trust, not this man who acted so weird. No matter how hard I wished, some things had to change.

Togafui scouted out the area, not making eye contact with anyone. It was hard to know what to think of her when she kept so quiet all the time.

Candui knelt beside me. "Hi, there. You doing all right?"

I nodded.

Instead of looking less concerned, she wrinkled her forehead. "What's going on?"

"Tired. Pain. The usual."

"Where are you having pain?"

"Lower back."

She scowled.

"I'm fine. Just need rest." I thought.

"How long has it been hurting?"

"Don't know. Started sometime early this morning."

"Let's get you more comfortable." She pulled off her pack, grabbed a blanket, and put it behind me folded up.

I leaned against it, grateful for the cushioning. "Better. Thanks."

"I'm going to gather a few things. I'll be right back."

I nodded.

She studied me another moment before moving to Aphier. Where did Richart go? Not far. I needed him should the worst happen. Or the best, for that matter. Plus, I wanted to know what secret he was carrying. What was going on in his mind? I ached to find out—just not as much as my back and lower stomach hurt.

I couldn't bring myself to pull the energy it would take to go find him, though. I'd rest a little longer before searching for him.

Aphier started roaming the perimeter of the camp, staying mostly within sight but sometimes ducking behind trees. Togafui did the same. But where was Edpol?

I caught a flash of a cloak off in the distance. Was that Candui, Edpol, or Richart? A feeling pulled at me. I rolled to the side and hauled myself to my feet. Whatever the reason, the pain had ebbed and the need to follow that cloak was great. Maybe it was to help Candui gather what she needed.

I had a dark feeling it was something more.

Hurrying as fast as I could waddle, I crossed the clearing and headed into the woods, where I saw the flash of color. I walked a little ways before glancing back. The clearing was no longer in sight. What was I doing? This was stupid. I couldn't go wandering off by myself on an inkling. Not in this forest, when I was about to have a baby.

"What are you doing?" Richart's voice sounded far away.

At first, I thought he was talking to me, but he wasn't in sight. Knowing he was ahead pushed me on. I would be safe with him. Still, I didn't want to attract any more attention in this place than necessary.

I crept forward. When I moved past a tree, I stopped, trying not to gape. Edpol was there, his sword digging into Richart's side.

"What are you doing?" The words tumbled from me.

Edpol started but didn't take his eyes from Richart. "You shouldn't be here, Adriella."

"Clearly, I should. What are you doing to my husband?" I took a silent step forward, putting my hand on my dagger.

"You know he's no good for you." Edpol's voice came out as a shout. "It should have been me you married and had a child with, not him."

Richart shook his head, shifting his weight away from Edpol.

As of that moment, I was beyond grateful Edpol hadn't been chosen as my husband. I wasn't about to tell him that, though. A contraction came, shooting pain across my stomach. My voice came out more strained than I would have liked, though I forced it to be soothing. "I know, but killing him isn't the way to fix it. You don't have to do this. You know me. Know I don't like death."

"Which is why you shouldn't be here." His voice was hard.

I took a step forward, grateful the pain in my stomach eased. "But I am here, and I'm pleading with you not to do this."

I was almost to him now. A few more steps.

"Sorry, Adriella, but this is for the best." He shoved his hand forward as Richart moved, cutting into Richart's arm.

I called out, "Aphier, help!"

At the same time, I leapt forward, bringing my dagger to Edpol's neck. "Drop your sword."

Something happened inside me, like a pop or the baby kicking real hard, and then a gush of liquid came out of me. "That can't be good."

"What?" Richart and Edpol said at the same time.

I used the distraction to shove my dagger harder against Edpol's neck. "Let him go."

"You'll thank me later." He brought his arm back, the sword dripping blood.

I yelled and moved my hand, wishing I didn't have to, when a blade came whistling through the air to land in Edpol's hand. Richart swiped his hand back and forward, punching Edpol in the face. Edpol swooshed backward, bumping into me, and I stumbled, lost my footing, and tumbled to the ground. Edpol cried out as another blade hit him in the thigh.

"Don't kill him." The words escaped me before I could stop them.

Aphier was at Edpol's side in a moment. Leaving the dagger in his leg, he pulled out the one in his hand. He twisted Edpol's arms behind his back, holding him vulnerable to Richart. "Stop moving this instant, or you're dead no matter what Adriella says."

Togafui stood nearby, her fangs showing in a way that made me want to hide from her. Luckily, her glare was directed at Edpol.

Richart stepped forward as Candui came to my side. "Is she all right?"

"Are you?" Candui said, looking me over.

"Something happened. Is the baby hurt?"

"No. It looks like your water broke."

Aphier swore. "We've got to move. There are soldiers in the forest, and they're sure to be coming after all this noise."

"What?" Panic overwhelmed me. It was difficult to do anything at the moment.

Richart was by my side, bleeding out his arm. "Let's get you on your feet."

"They're going to find our baby." The words tumbled from me.

"No, they won't. I'll keep you both safe." His hands were on me, helping me up.

"But the baby—he's coming."

"Not yet, he's not," Candui said. "We have time. If you feel contractions, let us know, otherwise we've got to run."

"Can I leave him behind?" Aphier shoved Edpol forward.

"No. He'll give us away—at least that we're in the area, if they haven't figured that out already," Richart said.

Candui grabbed my arm and helped me walk. Richart stuck by me even as Aphier went forward. Togafui took up the rear. I was oddly reassured with her back there.

I wanted to ask so much—how Aphier knew soldiers were in the forest, when the baby was going to come, if we were going to be safe—but I knew enough to be silent. If nothing else, I needed to not lead the zasin straight to us.

We walked—well, I waddled along while Richart and Candui helped me. The time felt short. My breath came in labored gasps.

Aphier turned to look at me and whispered, "We're almost there."

Where? I wanted to ask but stayed silent. I made myself go forward until a wracking pain hit my stomach. I curled toward my stomach, grimacing but keeping my mouth shut tight so as not to make a sound.

Candui rubbed my back in small circles while Richart held on tight. This wasn't the way I planned on having my child. I wanted some control over the situation and the ability to scream when I needed to. Grunts escaped me, despite my trying to keep quiet.

Richart's arm dripped blood on me, and fear spiked through me.

I whispered, "We have to get that wrapped."

He shook his head and pulled me forward. If I was well enough to talk, I was good enough to continue forward.

We'd walked a ways farther when another pain wracked through me. I hunched over, grunting in pain and grinding my teeth. This amount of agony couldn't be normal. I internally screamed, waiting for the pain to end. It went on and on, my stomach tight, the ache in my back not as bad as the anguish in my belly.

Finally, it subsided. I straightened the best I could and glanced around. Aphier and Edpol had disappeared. I was about to ask where they were when Aphier appeared behind a bush. "Over here. There's a cave I've hidden in a couple times."

Candui went first, getting on her hands and knees to enter the cave behind the foliage. I didn't want to go through there—didn't want my child's life to start in a cold, dark cave—but then, it was better than being born among the zasin.

I forced myself to my knees and crawled forward.

"Keep coming." Candui's voice was soft, prompting me on.

My hands and knees came across pebbles that dug into my skin, but it felt like nothing compared to the torment in my midsection. I halted.

"Come on," she said.

I gritted out, "Contraction."

"They're coming," Richart said from behind me.

I silently cursed all that was unholy and wished for this to be over. I forced myself forward, hand and knee at a time until Candui helped me roll over onto my back.

Richart and Togafui were in by the time I looked, and Aphier was covering up the entrance with the bush he'd crawled around.

It was dark, except for a faint light coming from between the leaves of the bush. I should be grateful it still had some leaves this time of year, but I was too busy catching my breath.

I needed something, anything, to help.

Candui reached over and put something to my lips. Trusting she knew what she was doing, I tasted bitterness. It was quickly followed by a water skin at my lips. I swallowed a few gulps before she took it away.

Richart moved behind me, propping me up. I sank into him, loving the feel of him next to me and needing his strength. I relaxed into him, waiting and dreading the moment of the next contraction.

Something else touched my mouth. A stick. I bit down on it softly and hoped I wouldn't need to bite harder as I heard someone talking outside the cave.

"Any sign of them?" a gruff male voice asked.

"Not yet," a second answered.

"I want them found, and now. If that is the chosen one, and it gets away, you will be brought before the high king, to face his punishment."

"Yes, sir."

Richart was tense beneath me. I grabbed his hand was resting on my stomach and gave it a gentle nudge. He needed to be bandaged up before he bled out. Oddly enough, I didn't much care if Edpol bled out. It was his fault we were in this situation. If it wasn't for him, my husband wouldn't be hurt, and we would have had more time to get away. Plus, I wouldn't have called for help or screamed, alerting the zasin to our presence.

Maybe I should have let my companions kill Edpol.

It might have been for the best.

He was still my childhood friend, though, and to think of his death, me saying it was all right, was more than I could bear. My stomach tightened with misery. I grimaced, clenching down on my stick and willing myself not to make a sound.

I had to do this now. I had to keep myself together, if not for everyone else here, then for the baby. I wanted him to come into the world safe. It didn't matter if he was the chosen one or not. I wasn't risking his life. Sure, I wanted him to have a normal life, but if he was destined to kill the high king, I wasn't going to stop that.

I focused on Richart's breathing behind me. Slow and steady. I realized I was holding my breath, and I let it out. A whimper sounded from me, and I cringed. I hadn't meant to let out a sound.

The contraction ended, but not soon enough. The damage was done.

"Did you hear that?" Gruff-Voice asked.

"No, sir."

"There was something. Find it."

The sound of people shuffling through leaves and rocks and things being moved, reached our little cave. I glared at Edpol now that my eyes had adjusted to the dark. I wanted to throw my dagger at him for putting us in this situation.

His face was turned toward mine, but with the shadows, it was impossible to tell his expression. He better have regretted what he had done. No one here would be held liable for their actions if we lost this baby because of him.

Aphier was closer to the entrance of the cave, sword out, hunched over to fit inside. I didn't know how he did it—the position looked so uncomfortable—but I was grateful to him for risking himself. For being willing to help my baby.

Just as legs blocked the light trickling in through the bush, another contraction hit. I was careful to breathe through it this time, trying to be as silent as possible. Richart stroked my arm as I hunched over to ease the pain pummeling across me.

I was going to die.

There was nothing else to it. This torment was so great. I wouldn't live much longer. No one could feel like this and live. No one. It wasn't possible.

The pain kept on and on, like there was nothing else. Richart rubbed my belly, and I held onto that feeling, as a reminder for me to be silent. If I was going to die, it would be for the baby. No better cause.

"I'm not finding sign of anyone," the second voice said, just outside our cave.

"Keep a close eye. They're in the area somewhere. We have to find them," Gruff-Voice replied.

I let out a slow, steady breath, determined to keep control of myself as I bit down on that sun forsaken stick. The pain eased, and I fell back into Richart. The man in front of the cave moved on.

Richart brushed a hand against my arm. I ripped a piece of cloth from the bottom of my tunic and handed it to Candui. I motioned to Richart's bad arm and lifted myself up off them. I didn't know how long I could hold myself like this, but I tried as she worked behind me.

Several too-long moments later, she put a hand on me and guided me back. I let myself fall back into Richart, who pressed his lips to my hair. I took a long, deep breath, wishing I was anywhere but here. My baby deserved better.

After three more sets of contractions, Candui leaned over to my ear and whispered, "You need to take your pants off."

I held back a groan. I did not want to go there, but how else was the baby going to come out? I nodded, and between me, Candui, and Richart, we managed it. Candui checked me while we waited in the darkness. She came back over and whispered, "Still a while yet."

Was that good or bad? I wanted to cry, but that would make too much noise. The zasin may or not be out of the area. I hadn't heard them in a while, but that didn't mean they weren't there. They should have been gone for the sake of my sanity.

The time rolled by more slowly with each contraction that grew stronger and closer together. Every moment I felt closer to death, but managed to keep silent. Somehow.

Candui checked me again. She came over and whispered, "You're doing great. Almost there."

Almost there was an eternity. I couldn't believe the end was almost here. Now I didn't feel like death was coming, I wanted to die. I *needed* to die, to leave this agony. Pain ripped through me, tearing me to shreds.

"Push," Candui said.

I pushed. And pushed. And pushed. All with little breaks in between. Still, there was nothing happening.

"You can do this," Richart whispered in my ear. "I've got you. You're strong. You can bring our little one into the world."

Tears rolled down my cheeks as Candui told me to push again. I did, and all at once, the baby came out—a relief like nothing I ever felt before.

His cry sounded. Candui did something I couldn't see then shoved the baby at me. "Feed the baby, to keep him quiet."

I wasn't sure what to do, but I remembered my mother breast-feeding my sisters. I lifted my shirt and put the baby up to me. He quieted and nuzzled against me for a moment. A bit later, with some coaxing, he began sucking.

Did the zasin hear the cry? Did they now know with certainty there was a baby in the forest? I didn't want to find out, but I couldn't leave either. Candui was still doing things to me, and I didn't feel up for walking yet after all that torture.

Richart reached around and stroked the baby's head. I did the best I could to clean him off with my tunic, wishing I had more. I needed to change clothes again after this and burn these. Thank the stars the orcs had sent us off with changes of clothes. They would be a life-saver at this point.

I waited for the zasin to come back as the baby suckled. Waited for any sound that might be them, coming to get my baby.

I didn't know what to call my baby. I couldn't think of a name when my thoughts were tied up in whether or not he'd survive long enough for me to call him anything. I wanted to—so desperately, I wanted to—but it wasn't something I could just make happen.

I wanted to check him, to make sure he wasn't the chosen one, but it was too dark to see anything. And what would I do if he was? I hadn't a clue other than knowing I would never give him to the Sunsire and High King.

Eventually, the baby stopped feeding, and I tucked my tunic back down. Candui handed me a blanket, and I did my best to wrap it around my baby in the dark. It was impossible to do a good job, but it was better than nothing. And he was being quiet. That was most important.

We waited in the silence as the night grew colder. Or perhaps it was cold all along and I was just now noticing because I was no longer wracked with pain.

Aphier finally came back beside us. "We need to leave and find another place. Are you ready?"

"I am." Frankly, I was drained, but we couldn't stay here. I'd find the energy needed to keep my child safe.

I handed Richart the baby, grateful the child was silent. I went over to Edpol, ready to punch him in the face but restraining myself. "You will not attack anyone here again. Do you understand me?"

"I can only promise I won't do anything while you're in danger."

I wanted to rip into him, but there wasn't time or energy to do so. I tore a few more strips from my tunic. "Bandage yourself up, and be grateful I'm not leaving you behind or killing you." Maybe infection would do it for me.

Richart helped me find clean clothes in my pack, and I changed into them, grateful it was dark and no one could see. The clothes weren't as loose as I wanted. Didn't most of the weight come out with the baby?

We gathered what we could and left the rest. I crawled out of the cave after Aphier, Togafui, Edpol, and Candui, and then turned around. Richart held out the baby, swaddled tight in a blanket. I took the baby, and Richart crawled out and motioned for me to give it back.

I whispered, "Let me hold him. I want you to be ready to fight, if needed." I could do it, but he was much better and more likely to do what needed to be done. Besides, I felt an aching need to be close to my little one. To not let him go. There was love in my heart for him already, bursting stronger than anything I ever felt before.

Richart nodded, bent down, pressed a kiss to the baby's forehead, and then pressed a kiss to my lips. I kissed him back, wishing it could be longer.

Aphier headed out, having tied Edpol's hands together behind him with material we'd scourged around from my old tunic. Edpol could break out if he wanted to, but it felt better than letting him loose.

Togafui kept close to them.

We headed away from the cave as fast as possible. I was stronger than I thought I was going to be, but it was still hard.

We walked until well past sunrise, and I finally got a good look at my baby. He wasn't as cute as I expected from seeing other babies. He was red and wrinkled and still a little slimy. I wiped him up the best I could and kissed his little cheek. He was perfect.

As soon as Aphier brought us to a stopping place, I sat down and pulled the blanket away to look at his hands. I uncovered first the right and checked both sides and then the left, again turning it both ways to make certain I didn't miss anything.

"There's nothing there." Relief coated my words. "He's not the chosen one."

"And he," Richart said with a smile, "has soaked through his blanket. Let me get you another one."

He pulled a blanket out of his pack, and together we went to unwrap the baby.

We both gasped.

"What is it?" Candui asked, running over.

She looked and gave a small, quiet chuckle.

He was a *she*. "Oh my darling, girl, I'm so sorry I ever thought you were a boy."

I pressed a kiss to her head.

"I'm sure she'll forgive you." Richart grabbed a nappy out of the pack the orcs had given us. Once she was wrapped up, we bundled her in the new blanket, and I fed her again while Richart sat close.

I had eyes only for her, and a little for him. He beamed at both of us, never having looked happier in the years I knew him.

Once the baby was fed, I handed her to him in his good arm and pointed to the arm Edpol had shoved a dagger through. "How is it?"

"Just a scratch. I'll be good before you know it." His focus was on our daughter.

"What should we name her?" I asked.

"I don't know. I wasn't expecting a girl and haven't thought of any girl names."

I said, "I did promise the fairy queen we would name the baby after her if it was a girl."

"What was the fairy queen's name?"

"Xataywa."

"Hmm." It was a pleasant sound.

"Are you ready to go?" Aphier asked, coming to us.

"We are." Richart handed me our daughter.

Our daughter. Those words sounded so good. Rich with things to come. And best of all, she wouldn't be heavy with the burden of being the chosen one. She would be special where she needed to be, and not a bit more.

A cloud passed over the sun, leaving as quickly as it came.

I glanced up and held back a scream. A dragon was circling our clearing.

CHAPTER THIRTY-FOUR

R ichart placed a hand on my arm. "It's all right."
"It's not all right. We've got to run." I tried to move, yet he held me firm.

The dragon, silver and bright, landed before us.

A scream threatened to come out as smoke flared from its nose, but I bit it back. I couldn't attract the attention of the soldiers. Though we wouldn't live long enough for it to matter with a dragon standing right before us, waiting to gobble us up.

I yanked my arm from Richart, but he wrapped his arms around me from behind, holding me in place. "You wanted to know my secret. This is it."

"What? That you're sacrificing me and the baby to a dragon?"

"I'm not here to eat you." The dragon's voice rumbled, though it sounded feminine. "I'm here to bestow a gift."

Candui raced out from behind the dragon to plaster herself in front of me. "You can't have them unless you get through me."

"That would be easy, child, but that is not my purpose." The dragon pinched her claws together over Candui's shirt, lifted her up, and placed her on the ground, not far off. "I have a much bigger purpose."

Togafui stood nearby, sword out, but didn't come any closer.

The dragon moved her head to one side, so her eye was focused right on me and the baby. "Uncover the child."

Richart shoved me behind him, keeping a hand on me. "What do you want with our baby?"

"Why are you talking to it and not killing it?" I tried not to let hysteria enter my words. Dragons were the thing of nightmares—this one came true.

"It seems you've been keeping secrets from your wife, Richart." The dragon laid its head on its front paws, curling up on itself. It still took up the entire clearing and some.

How did the dragon know Richart's name? What was going on?

While the dragon watched on, Richart turned his back to it and faced me. "My secret is that I'm a dragon tamer."

"A what?" The words didn't make sense.

"It means I am a friend to dragons and they are friends to me. We work together. Unlike most people believe, some dragons are good. Izla is one of them." He motioned to the dragon behind him.

"She has a name?"

Did the dragon really just roll its eyes? It seemed such a human gesture. I expected it to breathe fire, roasting us all alive before eating us. But it didn't. Could Richart be right? Was there such thing as a good dragon?

"It's like your magic," Richart said. "People have said bad things about it for longer than anyone can remember, but those things are wrong. This is what made me realize your magic might be good—the fact that I'm a dragon tamer and know they are not what we've been told. The high king doesn't want us to know these things for some reason, but I'm determined to show people you can do magic, and I can be a dragon tamer, and nothing is wrong with that. If anything, it's right."

I bit my lip. Was he right? Was this dragon a friend? "Why is it huffing smoke at us, then?"

"Dragons have a hard time turning their inner fire off, so they usually blow at least a low-grade level of smoke." He put one hand on each of my upper arms. "I promise it's going to be all right."

It was hard to believe that when something as giant and rumored to be deadly as a dragon sat here watching us, wanting something with my baby. "I can try to believe what you say, but you have to understand how hard it is and that I will do whatever is in my power to protect our child."

"No one can blame you for that." He leaned his forehead against mine. "Whatever Izla wants with our daughter, we'll figure this out together. I promise you that."

I closed my eyes, taking a moment to breathe him in. There was nothing I could do about our situation but make the best of it.

Once he let me go and moved aside, I said to the dragon, "What do you want with our baby?"

Izla lifted her head, longer than a human was tall, and gave a wicked smile. Or it looked wicked to me. She said, "I'm not certain if I want anything with your baby yet. I need to see the child."

I clenched my teeth. This went against everything in me saying I needed to protect my child.

Richart put an arm around me. "It's all right."

I could do this. The dragon wouldn't harm my baby without harming me. My fear was thick in my throat, but I shoved it down. I gave my child a kiss on her little forehead and opened her blanket to the cool air.

The dragon's head neared, and it took all my strength not to draw my baby away. The air warmed, but thankfully, the smoke stopped steaming from Izla's nose. I expected the dragon to turn her eyes to us, but instead, she sniffed us out.

Though worry still ate at me, the longer the dragon went without doing anything, the safer I felt. Maybe it was going to be all right.

Izla took a deep breath, drawing in the air around us. Time seemed to stop, yet go on into the depths of nothingness. I was perfectly warm and felt safe. My child was lucky to have a dragon paying attention to it. The dragon wasn't gobbling her up but deigned to take the time to see my baby. Everything was going to be fine. I felt that deep in my soul.

"Ah," Izla said, her words warm on my body. "Finally."

She reached a claw forward and before I could stop her, she took my baby's arm and delicately flipped her hand so the palm was up. Izla then bent down and gave a single, small huff of air. The air glittered in the sunlight, fell down perfectly onto my baby's palm, and blackened into a star.

It took only a few short seconds to realize the dragon had marked my child as the chosen one.

CHAPTER THIRTY-FIVE

"What have you done?" Horror filled my words.

"What I must," Izla responded.

Richart glanced down. He took our baby's hand and tried to wipe away the mark. "You can't do this." He sounded more frantic than I felt.

"I already did," Izla said. "She will have a hard life, one not guaranteed to fulfill her destiny."

"Then why did you do this to her?" My voice was shrill, but I didn't care. "Why would you destroy her life like this?"

"Because she is the only one who can save us all."

"You just said she's not guaranteed to fulfill her destiny."

Izla leveled her eye with me. "There are no guarantees in life, Richart's mate. You would do well to remember that."

I sputtered, not knowing how to reply.

"I must be going," she said. "And you must too, if you don't want the zasin to find you."

"Can't you take us with you?" Richart asked.

"It is not within my power."

She backed away before I could say anything, and with a great sweep of her wings, took flight and disappeared into the distance.

I turned on Richart. "How could you let this happen? You said it was all right. Clearly, it's anything but."

"I didn't know this would happen, or I would have never let Izla near our daughter." His words were so mournful, I wanted to be angry with him but couldn't blame him any more than I blamed myself.

Our daughter. The chosen one.

How would we ever help her through this task? How would we ever break it to her that she was the one to destroy the high king?

"I hate to break up the moment," Candui said, "but Izla was right. We need to get going before the zasin arrive."

I'd forgotten the others were here. I wrapped the child back up and held her close. Nothing would harm her if I could help it. She'd be safe with me.

We gathered together, Aphier leading the way from the clearing. We needed to get away fast and far from where the dragon had made an appearance. Her landing and takeoff were certain to have drawn the zasins' attention. I hoped we could get away fast enough.

We half-walked, half-ran through the woods. I tried to be quiet. Richart was by my side the entire time, helping move branches out of the way and making certain we were all right.

Candui was graceful, ahead of us. Aphier kept a hold of Edpol, though I wouldn't be sad if Edpol fell. It was rude of me to think that of another person, but after what he tried to do to Richart, it was difficult to think anything but rude thoughts about him. Togafui was bringing up the rear again, sword still out.

I hurried along for a good while, trying to keep the baby from jostling around. Aphier slowed. He turned and put his finger to his lips. Zasin must be close. I gritted my teeth. There was nothing I could do but hope they didn't find us.

Richart led me to a tree with a bush next to it. We crouched down behind it while the others climbed trees. I wanted to do the same, but I couldn't with a baby in my arms.

We waited, not moving or doing anything except hovering and listening. The forest was oddly quiet—more so than I was accustomed to. I wanted the birds to come back. Maybe some grunting boars. Anything to make the silence seem less ominous.

But there was nothing.

The baby woke from her nap and looked at me, her sweet blue eyes wide and soulful. I wanted to keep her safe more than anything else. Her hand worked loose of the blanket, and I turned it over with my finger and brushed against her mark.

What did Izla see in her that made my child the chosen one? It wasn't the life I wanted for her, but maybe if I could help her grow old enough to do something about it, she could help with the injustices of the world. I didn't want her in danger, but if it helped other people from being carted off and killed, it might be worth it.

A king who did things like kill babies and pregnant women should not be on the throne. I wasn't the person to overthrow him, but perhaps she was. I would do whatever it took to help her get there, even if it cost my own life.

I tucked her hand back in her blanket and listened for any sound.

Something rumbled in the distance. Thunder. Great. Rain—just what we didn't need. There had to be someplace safe we could take the baby out of the rain. Someplace dry and hopefully warm. Plus, I needed to eat something. If I was to feed her, I needed to keep up my own strength.

The thudding of feet marching through the forest drew near. I crouched lower, willing them not to spot us. To go the other way and leave us be.

"Any sign of them?" the same gruff voice asked.

Was this the man in charge? How did he know we were in the area? What led him back to us? So many questions, but the only thing that mattered was them leaving without spotting us.

"No, sir. We'll keep searching."

"With a dragon nearby, they may have been eaten," a third voice said.

"Incompetent fools. They are in the forest. I know it." Gruff Voice grew closer.

"But, sir—"

"Find them," he shouted.

"Yes, sir."

The feet thudded away from us, but through the bushes, I saw a man's pants as he stood a short distance from us. If he looked hard enough, he'd see us, and we'd be done for. My baby would be done for.

I wouldn't allow it.

I held my breath. Richart was so still and silent next to me, he could have been dead. That was an ominous thought that should never have entered my mind. I had to think better if I was going to deal with such things. I needed to be strong for my child.

The man continued to stand in front of us. I had to take a breath. I did so as slowly and quietly as I could, hoping the rain would hide the sound. He didn't seem to notice the faint noise, though it felt loud to me. He just stood here. What kept him?

If only there was a spell I could use to help with this situation. I needed to have a great knowledge of magic than I did. I knew so little, and none of it came to mind as a way to help.

A rustle sounded in the direction opposite from us. Gruff Voice strode away, heading toward it. We were going to make it.

Somehow, we would pass by the zasin and find a safe place for my daughter.

Just then, my baby cried out—a short but loud squawk. I put a hand to her mouth, but it was too late. Gruff-Voice was heading our direction and calling out, "Over here, boys."

Richart drew his sword. I got out my dagger while holding the baby in my left arm. Now she was silent.

Before the man reached us, Aphier sailed out of the tree and landed on Gruff-Voice's back. Gruff-Voice bucked him off, swiveled around, and had his own sword out as zasin flooded the area.

Togafui was out, slashing her sword toward Gruff-Voice.

"Stay by me." Richart stood, sword drawn.

I remained crouched low, hoping the cover would help. What I needed to do was run. I turned to look behind me, only to find more zasin coming up behind us. "Richart."

He whirled around, and moments later, swords were clashing together. The sound filled the forest with its violence. The baby started to cry, but I couldn't take the time to hush her. A zasin got past Richart's defenses and came at me.

He said, "Come with us, and we'll let the others live."

I held out my dagger in front of me while I considered it. My baby's life and my own would be forfeit, should I give us up. Not only that, there was no guarantee they'd let my friends live. Besides, he wasn't the one in charge.

"Leave me alone." I dashed forward and slashed at his thigh.

He hollered, grabbing at his thigh and falling back.

More men took his place as the others fought valiantly to keep my daughter safe. There was no telling what the zasin would do if they captured us. I could only hope they would keep her alive until they took her to the Sunsire, like they were supposed to, but if they saw the mark, perhaps they'd just kill her.

I tightened my hold on her and did what I could to fend off

the swords with my dagger. The blades came at me fast, and I was used to training with a big belly, not with a baby in my arms. It threw off my balance, making me clumsier than usual.

This couldn't be the end.

My dagger flew at the swords aimed at me, clashing against them. I fought, sweat dripping from my brow, as the men tried to get at me.

"Over here," Candui called.

I didn't look at her, but the zasin did, long enough for me to slam my blade into the closest one. I pulled it out and turned to run, but smacked straight into Gruff Voice.

He wrapped an arm around me and put a sword to my neck. "Stop fighting, or I'll slit her throat." His voice rang out, stopping the fighting.

My companions looked at me mournfully. Richart took a step forward, and the sword bit into my skin. I hissed.

"By order of the High King, she and the baby are to come with us. Anyone who tries to stop us will die."

"Please, let me go," I said. "You can't hurt a baby and her mother."

Gruff Voice laughed. "I can do whatever I want."

He made a motion, and each zasin held off the one of my companions closest to them while Gruff Voice dragged me off.

I fought against him, brought my dagger back into his gut, and twisted. I tumbled out of his arms and raced toward Richart.

How were we going to make it out of this? At least I was no longer in the hands of that man.

Richart was fighting his way to me, despite a bleeding gash on his left arm above where Edpol had cut him.

I pushed myself forward only to be grabbed at the waist. The zasin who grabbed me shoved me backward, making me stumble and fall. I twisted so the baby wouldn't get hurt, trying my best to protect her as I slammed into the ground.

Before I had any time to recover, someone yanked me by the hair. I hurried to my feet, wishing I could fight my way out. I reacted without thinking about it, taking a swing at my captor's hand. He caught my wrist, forced me to drop my dagger, and dragged me away from my friends.

I turned back to look at my friends, my hair and the wind tearing at my face. Candui was surrounded. Aphier lay on the ground still as could be. Edpol was kneeling next to him, a zasin holding a sword above him. Togafui battled with a couple zasin. And Richart—my sweet husband was running toward me when a blade pierced him through.

Trees blocked me from seeing much else.

"Richart!" I screamed as loud as I could. I tried to hurry to him, but I was still pulled along.

The trees got thicker, making it impossible to see anything of the attack scene. My daughter howled, her cries filling the air, as I was yanked forward. I turned the direction we were going so as not to fall again.

No matter what happened from here on out, I had to protect my daughter. That would be my first and foremost concern.

The farther we went, the more zasin surrounded me, hemming me in. Fighting them felt more impossible with every second—not that I had a weapon or any strength left.

We came to a clearing where a group of women and children were chained together, faces and clothes dirty. Many of the women were orcs and held babies or small children. The rest had toddlers at their side. There were about a dozen or so mothers, and I was about to join them.

I yanked against my captor and slipped from his grip, only to be caught by another zasin.

He said, "You're not getting away from us this time." He grabbed me by the wrist and pulled me forward until we reached the chained women. He picked a manacle off the ground and locked it around my wrist before chaining up my ankles, leaving free only the hand holding the baby.

"I heard fighting," a gravelly, feminine voice said.

I turned to see Scerta, her old weathered body leaning against a cane. "You. What are you doing here?" I asked.

She ignored me as a zasin approached her. "We couldn't help that they fought us," he said.

"You promised my nephew wouldn't be harmed if I helped you find his wife."

I gasped as her meaning became clear. Nopli's words came back to haunt me again. "You betrayed us." Nopli should have warned me how many betrayals there would be. My heart couldn't take any more of them.

She still wouldn't look at me, but the zasin talking to her laughed. "Certainly, she did. All we had to do was ask for you, and she promised to help us find you as long as we didn't hurt her nephew. It wasn't like we cared whether we did or not, though."

Scerta snapped up her cane, whacking him across the chest.

The man rounded on her. "For that, you can find your own way home."

She pursed her wrinkled lips. "You promised."

"I lied." He shoved her to the ground and left her there.

As much as I hated that she betrayed us, that she turned in her own great niece, I didn't want to see her pushed around. I called out to her, "Richart isn't far from here."

I felt sick as I watched her stare at the ground she lay on. She looked up at me, her eyes full of regret.

Too late.

The group started forward, surrounded by more zasin than I ever saw in one place before. I had to move, or I would fall. The chain chaffed my skin, reminding me how much of a prisoner I was. At least they hadn't checked my daughter's hand for the mark she carried. I would hide it from them as long as possible.

Not that it mattered.

We were going to the Sunsire to be killed.

AFTERWORD

If you enjoyed reading this book, please consider helping the author by leaving a review where you purchased the book and/or on Goodreads. Even a simple one line review helps.

You can sign up for Janeal Falor's Newsletter and receive a free book at www.janealfalor.com with the newsletter sign up on the contact page. Or talk to the author directly at janealfalor@gmail.com

ACKNOWLEDGMENTS

This book has been dear to my heart for a long time. To finally bring it to fruition is amazing. I'm so grateful to have it here and to be able to share it with you. Without numerous people helping with it, it would still be an idea in my head. Which is super sad to think about. I'm beyond grateful for everyone who has encouraged me, asked about my books, and let me know they're reading and loving my books. That means the world to me.

I need to thank my first readers. They do an awesome job of giving me feedback and helping me improve even when I'm not getting the message across that I'm trying to, they do an amazing job of assisting me in making it better. Grace for giving me encouragement when I needed it and spotting inconsistencies. Tala and Jessie Wolf for helping me fix up grammar and story items. Jordan from The Anxious Princess blog, for lots of great catches, brilliant comments, and even making me laugh out loud.

I'm a part of two critique groups that helped me polish a few chapters. My Wednesday Fantasy Critique Group for assisting me with the first several chapters and giving me great feedback I could use to make it better. And Monthly Cache Valley Critique

Group, especially Brandon and Elizabeth for reading over the first chapter and giving me suggestions.

If it wasn't for my copy editor, I would never be able to express what I mean to. Sotia Lazu is beyond amazingly fantastic. She rocks my editing world and helps me make my books so much the better.

Yesenia Vargas does such a great job proofreading and helping me polish my words. Roxanne is my last line of defense, assisting me with finding those hard to spot typos. I'm grateful for the help from both of you, making me have fewer mistakes in my book.

Also, my reviewers. Not only do they take the time to read and review my books which means the world to me, the often send me the typos they find so I can fix things up. Thank you all!

My biggest thanks has to go to my family. My mom for being a great example to me, and my dad for reading me stories from when I was a little girl. I can still hear your voice reading to me. I love you both! All of my siblings have been great at supporting me and asking me how things are going. I appreciate each and every one of them so much.

Almost everyday, I write. My kids are so patient with me while I write, understanding when I need a minute to finish before I can help you with something. You're all so sweet and my biggest supporters, telling everyone we come in contact with that your mom is an author. It never fails to make me smile that you all are so excited about what your mother does for a living.

The biggest thanks has to go to my husband, Erik. You are the love of my forever! Through everything, you're always supporting me, and prodding me to continue, even when I'm ready to give up. You listen to me talk about my books, even when I probably don't make much sense, and help me develop ideas. I couldn't do this without you. I love you!

ABOUT THE AUTHOR

Janeal Falor lives in Utah with her husband and three children. In her non-writing time she teaches her kids to make silly faces, cooks whatever strikes her fancy, and attempts to cultivate a garden even when half the things she plants die. When it's time for a break she can be found taking a scenic drive with her family or drinking hot chocolate.

www.janealfalor.com
janealfalor@gmail.com

www.ingramcontent.com/pod-product-compliance
Lightning Source LLC
Chambersburg PA
CBHW051242260626
47162CB00002B/556